The Chronicles of
Vladimir Tod

ELEVENTH GRADE BURNS

Books by Heather Brewer

The Chronicles of Vladimir Tod series:
EIGHTH GRADE BITES
NINTH GRADE SLAYS
TENTH GRADE BLEEDS
ELEVENTH GRADE BURNS

Heather Brewer

The Chronicles of Vladimir Tod

ELEVENTH GRADE BURNS

razorbill

PENGUIN

▼ ▼ ▼

To Jackie Kessler, the best friend and
critique partner in the world

RAZORBILL

Published by the Penguin Group
Penguin Books Ltd, 80 Strand, London WC2R 0RL, England
Penguin Group (USA) Inc., 375 Hudson Street, New York, New York 10014, USA
Penguin Group (Canada), 90 Eglinton Avenue East, Suite 700, Toronto, Ontario, Canada M4P 2Y3
(a division of Pearson Penguin Canada Inc.)
Penguin Ireland, 25 St Stephen's Green, Dublin 2, Ireland (a division of Penguin Books Ltd)
Penguin Group (Australia), 250 Camberwell Road, Camberwell, Victoria 3124, Australia
(a division of Pearson Australia Group Pty Ltd)
Penguin Books India Pvt Ltd, 11 Community Centre, Panchsheel Park, New Delhi – 110 017, India
Penguin Group (NZ), 67 Apollo Drive, Rosedale, Auckland 0632, New Zealand
(a division of Pearson New Zealand Ltd)
Penguin Books (South Africa) (Pty) Ltd, 24 Sturdee Avenue, Rosebank, Johannesburg 2196, South Africa

Penguin Books Ltd, Registered Offices: 80 Strand, London WC2R 0RL, England

penguin.com

First published in the USA by Dutton Children's Books, a division of Penguin Young Readers Group, 2010
Published in Great Britain in Razorbill, an imprint of Penguin Books Ltd, 2011
001 – 10 9 8 7 6 5 4 3 2 1

Text copyright © Heather Brewer, 2010
Designed by Jason Henry
All rights reserved

The moral right of the author and designer has been asserted

Set in Parkinson
Printed in Great Britain by Clays Ltd, St Ives plc

British Library Cataloguing in Publication Data
A CIP catalogue record for this book is available from the British Library

ISBN: 978-0-141-33409-7

www.greenpenguin.co.uk

Penguin Books is committed to a sustainable
future for our business, our readers and our
planet. This book is made from paper certified
by the Forest Stewardship Council.

Contents

1

A SLAYER'S RESOLVE

THE VAMPIRE SPUN AROUND, a wild, unhinged look in his eye. He lunged forward but the slayer skillfully dodged his blow, delivering a hard roundhouse kick to the creature's throat. The vampire fell to the ground, coughing, choking on its own blood. The slayer could have killed the beast a half hour ago. But this wasn't just about ridding the world of another abomination (though that was definitely the end goal). It was about a slayer needing to release some pent-up hostility and cleanse himself of all of his clouded thoughts.

Thoughts that were now perfectly clear.

These bloodsucking *things* could not be trusted. Not even when they donned the mask of a relatively normal teenager. Not even when they claimed to be your friend. Especially when they used their insidious powers to gain your trust and get you to reveal secrets that even those closest to you didn't know. Especially when their name was Vladimir Tod.

Joss was done playing games. With Vlad's face planted firmly in the forefront of his imagination, he slipped the silver-tipped wooden stake from his backpack and approached the vampire on the ground with an eager step. He whispered, "For you, Cecile," and thrust the stake forward, before the beast could draw a single breath. Blood—hot, slick, so deep red that it seemed black in the light of the moon—poured out over his hands. The nameless vampire fell still.

Joss straightened his shoulders, triumphant.

From his backpack, he withdrew a cell phone and hit number two on speed dial. When the voice at the other end answered, he said, "This is Joss. I need a cleanup on the ocean side of Russian Gulch State Park. The target is secure. Am I cleared to move on to my next objective?"

When the voice on the other end answered in the affirmative, Joss hung up the phone. There was no need to continue the conversation. Small talk didn't matter.

All that mattered was that he was going back to Bathory.

And this time, he would walk away with no regrets.

2
ABSENT FRIENDS

VLAD TWISTED HIS WRIST, pinching his fingers together, spinning the bronze coin on the table. When it fell, he picked it up and did it again, counting. Thirty-six times it had fallen Slayer Society up. Twenty-two times it was down. He spun the coin again, but before it had a chance to fall a hand came down on it from across the table. Henry looked at his best friend, his eyebrows drawn together in concern. Vlad sat back, a dark cloud hanging over him. "When?"

Henry plucked the coin up in his hand and turned it over, frowning. "Next week."

Vlad watched the coin, rereading the inscription on one side: FOR THE GOOD OF MANKIND. "How long have you known?"

"As soon as my mom told me I came straight over to tell you." Henry dropped the coin and ran a hand through his hair, groaning. "What are we going to do?"

The coin rolled across the table and off the edge. Vlad's hand moved so quickly that Henry couldn't even see it. He returned the coin to the table and once again spun it on the table's surface, returning to his former silence.

"We have to do something, Vlad. You can't just sit here spinning that stupid coin and waiting for Joss to come finish the job. Now that your invincibility is gone . . ."

Vlad spun the coin again, harder this time. Henry was right. They had to do something. Henry's cousin Joss was moving back to Bathory, this time with his family, and Vlad bet that it wasn't due to coincidence or the fact that Henry's family lived here. Joss was coming to kill him. And ever since D'Ablo's stupid ritual last year, he was very much in danger of dying.

But Vlad couldn't think about a solution. All he'd been able to think about since the Freedom Fest was Meredith, and how much he wished they could be together. But they couldn't. He was too much of a danger to her. So he'd broken her heart and, in turn, shattered his own to pieces. He was empty. He was alone.

And now he was in danger of dying at the hand of a slayer, his former friend.

He spun the coin again. Henry picked it up and threw it across the room. It clattered on the floor behind Vlad. "Do something!"

Vlad looked at him somberly. "Like what?"

"Anything. You act like Joss coming back to town is no big deal. I know you're still all torn up about Meredith . . ." Vlad shot him a warning glance, but Henry wasn't about to back down. "What? You've been like this all summer, but you did what you had to do. Now you act like you don't care if Joss comes back here and sticks another stake through your heart." Henry's eyes shined in frustration. "But I do."

His words hung in the air between them, weakening Vlad's resolve.

Henry turned and walked to the other side of the kitchen, reaching up to wipe his eyes on his sleeve, trying to keep it hidden from his friend. "Look, man, I don't want to get all chick-flick on you or anything, but you're my best friend and I almost lost you last time. I can't go through that again. I won't."

Vlad sighed, saying everything with his eyes that he couldn't bear to with his voice. He couldn't do anything. Short of killing Joss—Henry's cousin, Vlad's former friend—he couldn't do anything at all. "You're right. I just don't see how I can stop him without . . ." He didn't have to say it, and neither of them wanted him to. He couldn't kill Joss. That just wasn't an option.

"What about mind control?"

Vlad frowned. "I can't control him for the rest of his life, Henry. Besides, sooner or later, my concentration would break."

"There has to be something . . ." Henry returned to his seat, a look of desperation washing over his features. "What about Otis? He's like a million years old."

"Three hundred and two."

"Whatever, he's old. He's dealt with slayers his whole life, I bet. You should ask him what to do."

After a moment, Vlad nodded thoughtfully. If anyone would know what to do, his uncle would.

Henry nodded too, looking somewhat relieved that Vlad was actually going to take action. "Anyway, I'd better get back. My mom is on a cleaning rampage because of our extended family moving to town. If I'm not there, who knows what she'll throw out! The woman has no respect for the treasures of an adolescent male."

Henry stood and glanced at Vlad, a worrisome expression on his face. "You sure you're okay?"

"Yeah. I'm fine." Vlad forced a smile, and Henry walked out the front door, closing it behind him.

As soon as the latch clicked, Vlad reached down and retrieved the coin. A deep line creased his forehead as he read the inscription over again. He focused on Otis and spoke with his thoughts. *"Otis? I need to talk to you. I could use some advice."*

"Just let me finish up my meeting with Principal Snelgrove and I'll be home shortly, Vladimir." A pause, then Otis's voice once again in his mind. *"Is everything all right?"*

Vlad turned the coin over in his hand. An image flashed in his mind. A small point of silver at the center of his chest.

And blood. Lots of blood. Vlad shook his head, willing the memory away. *"No. But it can wait until you get home. Just . . . hurry, okay?"*

Otis grew quiet for a moment, then said, *"I'll be there shortly."*

Vlad gripped the coin in his hand and leaned forward, pressing his forehead to the tabletop. He fought, but the memories burst through his dam of resistance. Joss's eyes narrowing at the sight of Vlad's glowing mark. The bitter accusations of betrayal. A whisper: *"For you, Cecile."* The feeling of being punched in the back. Looking down and seeing the silver tip of the wooden stake. He'd coughed, and the pain had dragged him under.

Afterward, when Joss had visited him in the hospital, Vlad had been almost certain he'd apologize. But he didn't. Instead, he told Vlad that he was leaving. Their friendship, it seemed, was over. No longer friends, they were more than enemies. They were natural foes—vampire and slayer.

And Vlad still wasn't sure how he felt about it.

The staking incident had been horrific to endure. And recovering from it had been no picnic. But the worst part of it was that he missed Joss, missed his company, his insight, his impossibly dorky way of looking at the world. When Joss had slammed that hunk of wood through Vlad's chest, Vlad had survived . . . but their friendship had not. And he was still mourning it, still grieving over the loss of a very good friend.

Not to mention the reason Joss was returning.

He didn't need to hear it from Joss's lips. The note he'd left on Vlad's locker before he skipped town freshman year had said it all: *Friendship over*.

And if it really was over, then Vlad was going to have to formulate a plan pretty quickly on how to face Joss the slayer, rather than Joss the friend.

He sat up, gripping the coin tightly, and watched the door for Otis's return. After many minutes, the door swung open, and his uncle entered.

Otis immediately met his eyes. "What's wrong?"

Vlad sat the coin on the table in plain view. "How'd the interview go?"

Otis furrowed his brow with a questioning in his eyes. "It went well. I'll be teaching mythology full time at the high school." He paused for a moment and wet his lips. "Is everything all right?"

"Congrats on the job. A lot of students have missed you since eighth grade—they'll be happy to have you back. Me too." Vlad dropped his attention to the slayer coin and released a tense sigh. "I have a problem, Otis. Joss is moving back to Bathory."

Otis closed his eyes for a moment and sighed, visibly relaxing. He took a seat opposite Vlad with a small smile affixed to his lips. "You had me worried for a second."

Vlad's eyebrows drew together in confusion. Clearly Otis had lost his mind. "You're not worried anymore?"

Otis shook his head. The bemused expression on his face

irritated Vlad, though he wasn't sure why. "Vladimir, there are far worse things than a slayer who's out for blood. Besides, if he steps out of line and threatens you at all, he'll be easily dispatched. Especially with two, soon to be three, vampires living here in Bathory."

"Dispatched?" Vlad blinked, dropping his gaze momentarily to the coin on the table between them. "I don't want to kill him."

Otis seemed perplexed by this. He grew quiet, obviously mulling over something in his mind. Finally, he nodded and said, "If you're more comfortable with it, I'd be happy to—"

"You're missing the point." Vlad's jaw tightened defensively. "I don't want anything to happen to Joss. I don't want you to touch him or hurt him in any way. He's . . . my friend."

For a long time Otis didn't speak. Neither did Vlad. He was too busy trying to figure out how the conversation had gone so quickly from asking for advice to killing his friend.

After a while, Otis leaned forward, tension and disbelief ebbing from him. "We are speaking of the same boy who drove a stake through your chest from behind, in the most cowardly way possible, yes? And you want to, what, give him an opportunity to finish the job?"

"No."

"Then the matter must be dealt with."

"But he's my friend, or at least he was. I don't think he'll try anything like that again." It surprised Vlad how easily the lie slipped from his lips. Maybe it shouldn't have. He'd been doing a lot of it lately. Pushing the image of Snow from his mind, he met Otis's gaze.

Otis furrowed his brow. "Fine. If Joss keeps his distance, I'll leave him be. But so help him if he threatens or harms you again."

Vlad shook his head. "Then I'll deal with him. I don't want him hurt."

The corner of Otis's mouth twitched slightly. "You've made that abundantly clear. So what *do* you want?"

The thing was that he had no real idea of what he wanted. The only thing he could think of was for time to spin backward, for Joss to have never become a slayer in the first place. And that wasn't exactly an option.

Vlad sighed. "Your advice. I want to know how to make a slayer back off without killing him."

Otis sat back, shaking his head. "To tell you the truth, I don't know if anyone's ever tried. As far as I've seen, you can't. Once a slayer has his mark, he will stop at nothing until the task has been completed. It's always just been easier to take them out of the picture altogether."

His voice took on a disgusted tone and rose as he continued. "They call it that—a task. Did your *friend* mention that? I suppose it must make taking the life of a person easier to refer to the act as a *task* instead of *murder*."

He threw his arms up, disgusted and angry and acting very much like Vlad wasn't on his side. "Just as referring to vampires as *things* and *monsters* must make it easier to stomach the idea of killing *people* who happen to have fangs."

Vlad watched him, wide-eyed, slumping back in his seat. "Why do you sound so angry?"

Otis stood suddenly, and slapped his palms on the table, his eyes fierce. "Because I am! How can you defend him, Vladimir? How can you spare his life when he nearly took yours? He's nothing, just a slayer, a foolish assassin armed with a wooden stake. They are the ones who declared war on us, and we have every right to defend ourselves when we know an attack is about to happen. That's all Joss is, Vlad, another casualty of war. He just doesn't know it yet."

Otis sat down in the chair opposite Vlad, his eyes seething. "If you ask me, the world would be a better place without him and his kind walking around, free to do as they please."

Vlad shook his head wordlessly. When he spoke, it was in near-whispers. "Listen to yourself, Otis. You're grouping them all together and plotting their extinction. You sound just like they do. Maybe you're not all that different."

Otis clenched his jaw and pointed a stern finger at his nephew. He stood abruptly, pushing the chair sharply back from the table. Vlad instantly knew that he had gone too far, but he didn't care. He braced himself for the words that were soon to come flying out of his uncle's mouth. Hateful words. Words filled with venom and justification.

But the words didn't come. Otis turned and walked out of the kitchen. When the front door slammed, Vlad winced, but only slightly.

The coin lay on the tabletop where he'd left it. Plucking it up in his hand, he spun it once more, and wondered if Joss had noticed its absence, or if he had any idea where it might be now. It had to be his, after all. There were no other slayers in Bathory. It had to be Joss's coin. Maybe that's why Vlad had kept it. Maybe that's why he couldn't stop looking at it.

3
UNTOLD TRUTHS

"THIS ISN'T HEALTHY."

Vlad blinked up at Nelly from his seat at the kitchen table. He hadn't been listening but assumed she was referring to whatever it was she was stirring in the saucepan on the stove.

Nelly frowned and sat the wooden spoon on the counter. Yellow goo pooled around the end of it. "You've been moping around the house ever since Freedom Fest, Vladimir. It's not good for you to stay indoors and sulk for so long."

Vlad dropped his attention to the tabletop. There was little sense explaining how he felt. It seemed that each day was worse than the one before it. First, the situation with Meredith, then he learns that Joss is moving back to town, presumably to finish what he started over a year ago. And to top it all off he and Otis hadn't been on speaking terms for almost a week, not since Vlad had turned to his uncle for his counsel and compared him to what Otis considered to be the enemy.

Nelly sighed and pulled a couple of twenties out of her purse, dropping them on the table in front of him. "Why don't you call Henry and go see a movie or something? One last huzzah before school starts tomorrow?"

Tomorrow. Vlad had almost forgotten he'd be starting his junior year in less than sixteen hours. Meredith would be there. He hadn't seen her all summer. Joss would probably be there too. As if it wasn't bad enough having to face one of them alone.

Deciding that maybe Nelly was right, maybe he should go out with Henry, Vlad decided to give his drudge a call after dinner. Plus, it couldn't hurt to ask if his cousin had finished moving in, or maybe changed his mind and decided to move to Alaska instead. He could simply go for a walk to see for himself, but there were two things wrong with that idea: One, he simply couldn't risk running into Meredith, and two, he didn't exactly want to be alone out in the open, where a vengeful slayer might be waiting.

He closed his hand over the money and met Nelly's concerned gaze. "Nelly, do you think I did the right thing by breaking up with Meredith?"

Nelly wiped her hands on a towel and sighed. "I think that's a question that only you can answer, Vladimir. Do you think it was the right thing to do?"

Vlad thought back to the Freedom Fest. Meredith's face flitted through his mind, shocked, then saddened. He'd hurt her with his words, and then he'd shoved her. She'd fallen to the ground, sobbing, and all he could do was walk away. He wet his lips and looked at Nelly. "It was the only way I could protect her."

Nelly sighed, then gave his shoulder a squeeze. "Does your father's journal say anything at all about how he resisted feeding from your mother?"

Vlad shook his head. Tomas had always told his son that he only fed from blood bags, but lately Vlad was finding that enormously difficult to believe. Personal experience in the form of monthly feeding sessions with Snow had taught him that once a vampire has fed from the source, blood bags were like trading in that brand-new Harley-Davidson for an old scooter. So the question remained, where had Tomas been getting his blood from? The idea that he'd fed from Mellina, Vlad's mom, sickened Vlad to no end. It had to have sickened his dad too, so it had to be someone else. But who?

Vlad flicked his eyes to Nelly.

No. Nelly would have said something.

She patted his hand. "Well, I'm sure everything will be okay. You just need some time to get over the breakup."

Groaning, he said, "Yeah, and there's plenty of fish in the sea too, right?"

Nelly offered a reassuring smile. "Believe it or not, heartache doesn't last forever."

Maybe not. But it certainly sucked for as long as it decided to hang around.

Vlad's thoughts turned to Otis. He had looked rather haggard lately, so Vlad had no doubts that he was sticking to their agreement that Otis wouldn't feed from humans while he was staying in Bathory. But how was he managing it? How was he nuzzling Nelly's neck without taking a bite? His resolve must have been made of steel. Vlad rightfully felt like such a hypocrite, keeping Otis bound to an act that he himself couldn't keep to.

Nelly said, "Why don't you give Henry a call? I'm sure Melissa wouldn't mind giving him up for one night while you two have some fun."

Vlad opened his mouth to say he thought that was probably a good idea—even though he didn't, not really—but then Otis walked in the front door and Vlad snapped his mouth shut again.

He wasn't mad at Otis; he never had been. But Otis was very upset with him, and Vlad knew why. Otis despised the slayers. Vlad was sure he had his reasons for it, but Joss wasn't like the rest of them. At least Vlad hoped he wasn't. Really, Joss was the only slayer that he knew, so he had no real basis for comparison. He only knew that he had hurt his uncle by what he had said, and he felt bad for saying it. But he and Otis both knew that he was right, and that felt worse.

Having his uncle reside in the same town had turned out

to be a learning experience in many ways. Initially, they'd been inseparable. Otis had recounted stories about him and Tomas and their adventures together. But ever since the construction on Vlad's old house had been completed, when Otis moved out of Nelly's home to stay there, things had been different. And Vlad wasn't exactly sure why. They were at odds over the littlest things, and Otis seemed troubled by something that he would not give voice to.

Otis brushed his lips against Nelly's cheek, whispering his hello in her ear. Nelly blushed and smiled and eventually went back to cooking.

Vlad stood, money in one hand, Joss's coin in the other, and left the room. His foot had just touched the bottom step on his way to his bedroom, when Otis said, "The silence between us is intolerable, Vladimir. The quiet in my mind . . . it's deafening."

Vlad paused and glanced over his shoulder at his uncle. "I'm not the one who started it."

Otis's eyes shined with hurt. "True enough. Can we talk?"

Vlad shrugged casually, but inside, his muscles had already lost much of their tension in relief. "Sure."

Then, inside Vlad's mind, Otis's voice, warm and welcoming—something Vlad missed more than he would ever admit to. "*Not here. I was thinking of your house. You haven't been by to see it since the renovations were completed. I have things I'd like to show you, things I'd like to discuss with you.*"

Vlad's initial reaction was to jump at the offer—after all, he missed Otis's company, and very much longed for the opportunity to sit down and chat. But there was their last conversation to be considered. *"First promise me that you'll leave Joss alone, that you won't harm him in any way."*

Otis's jaw tightened. *"You know I can't promise that."*

He met Vlad's eyes, pleading aloud. "Please, Vladimir. Just a short chat between uncle and nephew. Let me have my say and you can go back to brooding."

Vlad winced. Maybe he had been moping more than was sensible lately. "Okay. But it can't take long. Henry and I are going to the movies."

Not that Henry had any inkling at all that they were hanging out. But Henry had proven to be enormously supportive ever since he'd come to the conclusion that being Vlad's human slave was pretty cool. He had no idea that Vlad had another drudge in Snow, since Vlad had insisted that he'd released the goth girl. It was a lie, but one Vlad had needed to tell. He didn't want anyone knowing about his continued feeding from a human's veins.

The problem was . . . sometimes he got the idea that Snow wanted to be much more than his drudge.

Vlad shook his head. The last thing he needed to be doing was thinking about Snow when Otis was lurking around in his head. He didn't block Otis, but definitely changed gears in his thought process, instead mulling over Joss and the ever-looming first day of school.

The walk to his old house was long and quiet. Occasionally, Otis would give him a sidelong glance, but neither spoke. Once they turned down Lugosi Trail, Vlad smiled. His house had been given a fresh coat of paint, and brand-new windows had been installed. Even the shrubs alongside the porch looked brighter, happier now that someone was calling his house home. He'd never asked where Otis got the money to fix the house. It didn't matter. What mattered was that it was being given new life.

It made looking at it easier to recall the memories he had of his life there, before the fire, before his parents' deaths, before everything he knew had disappeared in a whiff of ash and soot.

Otis's voice buzzed pleasantly in his brain. *"It's so good to see you smile. You haven't in some time."*

Vlad slowed his steps some, thinking, then he spoke to Otis with his mind. *"I haven't had much of a reason to."*

Otis took on a hopeful tone. *"And now?"*

They crossed the street, and Vlad cleared his throat. "The house looks nice. Mom would like the color you chose."

Otis raised his eyes to the house. The siding was a pale yellow—a warm tone compared to the gray that it had been. "Nelly picked it. She said that it was Mellina's favorite color."

An image flashed in Vlad's mind, an unexpected memory from years ago. His mom in a flowered skirt, a pale yellow sweater tied about her shoulders. She was laughing, running across the yard away from Tomas, away from Vlad. Something about them being out to get her, but Vlad couldn't recall it clearly enough. And just like that, it was gone.

He shook his head, smiling at the memory, and stepped forward onto the porch, following Otis's lead. Otis turned the knob and opened the door, gesturing with a small nod for Vlad to head inside. With a strangely light feeling of excitement in his chest, Vlad stepped into the house.

On some level, he'd expected that acrid, horrible scent of smoke and ash to assault his nostrils, but it didn't. Instead, it smelled like Otis had been baking cookies. A glimpse into the new living room revealed the source of the smell—scented candles had been placed on a new mahogany coffee table. The walls were in golden tones, warm, homey. And as Vlad moved from room to room, he marveled that this was his house—the same house he'd been born in, the same house he'd lived in for so long. It looked different. Way different. The furniture, the cabinets, the paint on the walls had all been changed. It looked like an entirely new place.

Vlad wasn't sure how he felt about that.

On the one hand, he'd assured Otis that a change was definitely needed, that maybe a new look would ease the pain of visiting his once-happy home. On the other, he felt somewhat intruded upon, as though Otis had tried to erase the memories of his parents by redoing the house—a stupid thought, but there it was. He flicked his eyes to his uncle, who was watching him carefully. "Is . . . is *everything* different?"

Otis continued to watch him for a moment, as if trying to gauge his reaction to the changes. Finally, seeming to accept that there was no way he could ease any concerns in Vlad's mind, he took a breath and said, "Not everything. Come upstairs."

Otis led the way through the kitchen to the back stairs,

then up. Vlad followed, taking in every inch of his renewed former home. The wood floors had been sanded and stained, and the distinct lack of that smoky scent continued throughout the house. It was a missing link in the experience—a bad thing that had been there for years and was suddenly gone. Vlad didn't miss it, but felt a wave of guilt at its absence, as if by not whiffing that scent, he were somehow trying to forget that awful day, the day he lost his parents forever.

Otis paused on the top step and peered over his shoulder at his nephew. The look in his eyes said he'd picked up on Vlad's tension, but he couldn't identify the source, wouldn't without reading Vlad's thoughts—something Otis had promised he would only do if Vlad granted him permission. He wet his lips as if to speak, to offer some sort of comfort, but turned his head at the last moment and continued his trek up the stairs and down the hall to the door of Tomas's office.

Vlad halted on the stairs, wishing for a moment that Otis *would* read his mind so he wouldn't have to say the things he was thinking out loud. After exchanging troubled glances with Otis, he followed, hesitant to see what now lay behind the door to his dad's sanctuary.

"This room was the most difficult to renovate." Otis waited, gesturing with his eyes to the doorknob.

With a deep, hesitant, hurting breath, Vlad reached out and turned the knob, opening the door.

Inside, the walls were exactly the same as they had been, down to the scrape where Tomas's chair had rubbed the paint away. His dad's desk remained, though the chair was new. Everything looked exactly the same as it had been before the fire. Only cleaner.

He turned to Otis with a questioning look.

Otis smiled, his eyes shining. "It was so difficult, in fact, that I left it as it was. Gave it a good scrubbing, of course."

Vlad ran the tips of his fingers across his dad's desk, looking around, taking it all in. Finally, he spoke. "Thank you, Otis. This means a lot to me."

"There's one more room that I left untouched." Otis's eyes moved to the hallway, to the door of Tomas and Mellina's bedroom. From his pocket he pulled a silver key and placed it in Vlad's palm. "The room is exactly as it was that day. I merely had workers seal it off to prevent the scent of smoke from pervading the rest of the house."

Vlad turned the key over in his hand. When he spoke, his voice was raspy, his chest full of gratitude. "Why?"

Otis's voice was kind and warm. "Because it's not up to me to decide when it's time to leave that moment behind, Vladimir."

Vlad couldn't help but notice that Otis had used the word *when*, not *if. When* it was time. As if there was no question that that time would come.

And he was right. Sooner or later, Vlad was going to have to let go of his guilt and say goodbye to the haunting memories of that day.

But not today.

Vlad nodded and slipped the key into his front pocket. "The house looks amazing, Otis. You've done a great job."

Otis was looking at him, a troubled expression on his face. "You ooze sorrow, Vladimir. What I would do to ease your every pain . . ."

Vlad tried to ignore his uncle's words, but couldn't. "I really like the floors. Dad always loved mahogany."

"Talk to me. Tell me what's troubling you so deeply. Is it Joss? Is it Meredith? You've been so distant since I moved to Bathory. Is it me?"

Vlad swallowed hard. "It's . . . nothing."

It wasn't a lie. Not exactly, anyway. The fact of the matter was that it was a combination of all of those things, and more. So much more than he could ever tell Otis.

Images of Snow flitted through his mind, of their monthly sessions in the alley behind The Crypt. Vlad had kept those moments secret, so secret that Henry was convinced that Vlad had a crush on Snow, and that was why he needed to frequent the goth club. He couldn't have been more wrong. The Crypt was an absolute blast to hang out at, and the only feelings Vlad had for Snow were reminiscent of how a human might feel about a Big Mac.

A really sweet, amazingly understanding, pretty Big Mac. A Big Mac that got what he was saying before he even said it. A Big Mac that listened in ways that Meredith never would have been capable of.

Otis furrowed his brow. "I will not lay a hand on the slayer unless he presents a threat. While I don't understand your feelings, I will respect them, Vladimir. If that is what it takes to heal whatever is broken between us, then so be it."

Vlad shook his head. "Thank you for that. But it's not you, Otis. I'm just dealing with a lot of unexpected stress."

"I'm not surprised. You haven't been eating right." Otis's voice softened, as did the expression in his eyes. "Nelly says you only manage four or five blood bags a day anymore—significantly less than you were eating."

Vlad's entire body tensed. "Yeah, well . . . I haven't been hungry lately."

"She's also commented that you have a new group of friends—"

"Your point?" Vlad snapped. He hadn't meant to, but he did. He was trying to stay calm. Otis knew. He knew about Snow. He knew Vlad had been feeding on a human. But how? Vlad had been so careful to hide his feeding sessions. Even Henry didn't have a clue. And Otis wouldn't dare break his trust by reading his thoughts unwanted.

Otis's tone was calm and somewhat pleading. "I just want you to know that you can always talk to me, Vladimir, about anything. I will never judge you."

Vlad's heart raced along with his thoughts. Otis couldn't know. There was no way. Vlad had guarded his secret too carefully for his uncle to find him out. Hadn't he? "Well, there's nothing to judge, is there? I haven't done anything wrong."

Otis grew silent. After a moment, he gave Vlad's shoulder a squeeze. "I know you didn't do anything wrong, Vlad."

He turned and headed down the hall, pausing at the top of the stairs. Without looking back, he said, "I know."

Vlad froze at his uncle's words. No truer words had ever

been spoken—Otis knew. Somehow, he knew all about Vlad's late night trips to The Crypt. He knew about Snow. He knew that while Vlad might be strong enough to stand up to D'Ablo and fight to the near death with a vampire slayer, he didn't have the strength to admit when he was wrong.

He stood there for a long time, listening to his heart pounding in his ears. After a while, he slowly made his way down the stairs to the kitchen. Otis was sitting on a stool next to the large island, a coffee mug of blood in his hand. He didn't bother to offer any to Vlad, almost as though he assumed that Vlad's hunger had been recently satisfied.

It had. Just a week before.

Vlad tightened his jaw and let another lie escape his lips. "I have to meet Henry now."

As Vlad hurried out the door, slamming it behind him, Otis called out, "See you at dinner tonight."

Great. Just what he needed.

4
MEANINGFUL CONVERSATIONS

"NELLY, THIS STEAK IS DELECTABLE!"

Nelly smiled her gratitude across the table at Otis. Vlad poked his steak with his fork. It was good. Nice and raw, warm enough to encourage the blood to pool on his plate.

But it wasn't human—a fact that was making it increasingly difficult for Vlad to finish his meal.

Otis met his eyes momentarily before engaging Nelly in some inane conversation that Vlad completely tuned out of. After several minutes of their chatter, Nelly cleared her throat, eliciting his attention. "You seem distracted tonight, Vladimir. Anything going on that I should know about?"

Plenty of stuff, Vlad thought.

Otis raised an eyebrow, but didn't speak. Vlad flashed

him a look. *"Lurking around in my mind, Uncle Otis?"*

Vlad turned his outward attention back to his aunt, balancing the two conversations—verbal and telepathic—with ease. "Nothing's going on. Just not hungry, I guess."

Otis took another bite of steak, chewing thoughtfully. *"Lurking, but not poking around. What's stuff, anyway?"*

"What time is Henry picking you up?"

"Around six. Movie starts at eight, so we'll probably wander the mall for a while. I might be back late though. I promised Snow I'd stop by The Crypt and bring her my copy of *Dracula*." Simultaneously, he spoke to Otis with his mind. *"It's . . . nothing, like I said this afternoon."*

"Just try to be back by ten. I don't like these late-night stays in Stokerton. Big cities are dangerous places at night."

Otis frowned slightly. *"Nothing . . . which is to say, nothing that is my business to know?"*

"You catch on quick, Otis." Vlad shook his head. "You worry too much, Nelly."

Nelly stood and cleared the dishes away, waving off Otis's efforts to help. When she disappeared into the kitchen, Otis met Vlad's gaze again. *"There is something I need to ask you. You walked out earlier and stole my opportunity away."*

Vlad shook his head sharply. *"Don't. Please."*

Otis furrowed his brow. *"I admit I'm a bit perplexed by your reaction, Vladimir. But nevertheless . . ."*

Vlad looked his uncle directly in the eye, defying him to ask about his dining habits again. He wouldn't admit to it. He couldn't admit to it, not after all the preaching he'd done to

Otis about how humans were people, not food. *"I know what you're going to ask and the answer is no."*

Otis sat back, stunned. It looked as if his heart had been ripped out. His words were merely shocked whispers in Vlad's mind. *"Just like that? No? Won't you at least give the matter some thought?"*

"What's there to think about? You obviously already know how I feel about it, and you have no right to ask me to change that. It's not your place and you know it."

"I am truly sorry. I thought you would be happy. I had hoped that you would give me your blessing."

It was Vlad's turn to act surprised. *"Wait . . . my blessing? For what, exactly?"*

"Vlad, it's likely that I won't make it out of this trial alive, but I want you to know that if I do, I intend to ask for Nelly's hand in marriage, and I would like to know that I would have your blessing if I did. It's no secret that I hold Nelly in the highest regard. I . . . I love her, Vladimir. I want to make her my bride. I was wrong to judge Tomas so harshly. I now understand what he was trying to tell me."

Vlad stared, unable to speak for a moment. Otis wanted to marry Nelly? He wasn't cornering Vlad about feeding on Snow? He took a deep breath, letting that sink in for a while. It wasn't that Otis was saying anything that he didn't already know, but the fact that Otis had finally admitted to it really blew his mind. Vampires, after all, didn't love humans. And if they did, they definitely wouldn't tell anyone, and they certainly wouldn't marry them. "What about Elysia?"

"What about it?" Nelly returned for more plates, and Otis smiled and watched her as she moved back to the kitchen. *I'm already a criminal. And there's no use fighting it anymore. I love her. And I want a chance at happiness with her. But . . . I won't marry her without your blessing.*

Vlad thought for a moment before speaking. It wasn't like he disapproved of his uncle marrying his guardian. But he had to watch out for her. *What about your trial? You told me that there's a huge chance you'll be put to death for betraying the Stokerton council and hiding me from them—I believe your exact words were 'I do not know of a vampire who has survived an Elysian trial of this magnitude.' You can't widow her on your honeymoon, Otis. It's not fair to her.*

I planned to wait until after the trial to propose. Call it a lucky charm. He smiled sadly, as if all of his hopes of surviving his trial in Elysia were resting on the notion that he might one day call Nelly his wife. *Maybe it will be enough to get me through the charges against me.*

There are a lot of them, Otis. I mean, we were lucky they never called me to trial, after all, but you . . . Vlad met his gaze. *I don't want to see her get hurt, Otis.*

I want nothing more than her happiness, Vladimir. You have my word. Honesty filled Otis's eyes.

Vlad smiled. *Then you have my blessing.*

He stood to leave the table and met his uncle's eyes once more. *Oh and one more thing. You look terrible. You should step out for a bite later.*

Reluctantly, hope crept into Otis's tone, as if he were worried Vlad might be pulling a fast one on him. *"Meaning . . . ?"*

Vlad shrugged. *"You know what I mean. Find yourself a hobo and chow down."*

Otis exhaled a sigh, his body visibly relaxing. *"Thank you. These past few months have been excruciating."*

"Just no one from Bathory, okay?"

"Fair enough."

A smile danced on Otis's lips. Vlad could tell his uncle was already daydreaming about rivers of blood pouring down his throat. "I've missed our talks. Is there . . . anything else you'd like to talk about before heading into Stokerton?"

Vlad stiffened before turning away. "No. Not at the moment, anyway."

He shouted a goodbye to Nelly. Luckily, Henry was just pulling into the driveway in his early birthday present, a gloss black Dodge Charger, as Vlad closed the door. Vlad would be lucky if he got Otis's piece of hand-me-down crap someday. It must be nice to be a McMillan.

In a few quick steps, Vlad was at the car. He opened the door and slid onto the soft leather seat with a sigh. "You have no idea how good your timing is."

Henry flashed him a questioning glance, but Vlad waved it away. Then Henry backed out of the driveway and slammed the transmission into drive, gunning the engine until they were barreling their way out of town.

After they'd passed the edge of farmland that counted as part of town, Vlad cleared his throat. "So . . ."

Henry glanced at him. "You're wondering about Joss, right?"

Vlad nodded. Dutifully, Henry spilled all the details: The enormous U·Haul, helping his aunt and uncle with a million and one boxes, avoiding eye contact with his cousin until the truck had been emptied. Henry hesitated for a moment, and Vlad said, "Anything else?"

It was only then that he noticed the puffy, purple bruise under Henry's right eye. "Dude, did you get in a fight with Joss?"

Henry grinned. "Busted his lip."

Vlad raised an eyebrow, suppressing a small smile. "Why?"

His hands tensed on the steering wheel. "Nobody calls my best friend a mosquito. Especially somebody too chicken to say it in anything but a muttered whisper."

Vlad allowed his smile to come through. "Thanks, Henry."

"Hey, man. I got your back."

The sky outside had faded from a soft blue to a mix of oranges and reds. Henry cranked up the stereo. Vlad watched out the window and wondered where Joss was now, what he was doing. Would he unpack before beginning his hunt for Vlad? Or would he be waiting in the shadows near Nelly's front porch when Vlad returned home tonight?

Joss's presence in Bathory was unsettling to say the least.

Henry turned the radio down again. "I forgot to ask you something. Melissa wants to know if you wanna go on a double date with her cousin Sara."

Vlad shook his head. "I don't feel like dating anyone, Henry."

"It's not a date. Not really. But it would do you some good to get out with other girls. Y'know?"

Vlad slumped down in his seat. The scene at last year's Freedom Fest played over and over in his imagination. The words he'd spoken to Meredith ripped apart his insides even now. *I don't love you. I never did. Now just . . . just get away from me.*

He cast a quick glance at Henry. "Girls other than Meredith, you mean."

Henry sighed. "Dude, what's the big deal about Meredith? She's just a girl. There's probably a couple hundred at Bathory High alone."

"She's not *just* a girl. She's . . . Meredith."

"You hardly know her, Vlad. I mean, it's just like with everybody else—you keep your distance."

Vlad balked. "I know her."

Henry said, "Okay, so what's her favorite color?"

"Pink."

"Anybody with eyes can see that. What's her dog's name?"

Vlad blinked. Meredith had a dog? "I don't . . . know."

"Beeper. Why did her family move to Bathory?"

"Well . . . I . . ."

"Her grandmother was sick and they needed to take care of her; they live in her old house."

Vlad's heart sank. The truth was he *didn't* know Meredith. Not really. "Okay."

"What does she want to do after graduation?"

"I said okay. You've made your point."

"Have I?" Suddenly Henry sounded enormously frustrated. "Because my point is that you may spend a lot of time fantasizing about who you think Meredith is, but you've never really made the effort to know who she is outside of your daydreams. And you've certainly never given her a chance to know who you really are."

Vlad shook his head. "That's not as easy as it sounds, Henry."

"So you can't tell her the vampire stuff. Fine. Don't. But dude . . ." The car slowed, pausing at a four-way stop, and Henry met his eyes. "Does she even know *your* favorite color?"

Vlad swallowed hard. He really hadn't noticed that he and Meredith were virtually strangers. He just knew that he loved her, and that her absence had left a huge, gaping hole at the center of his being.

Henry sighed as he pulled the car forward through the intersection. "She's just a girl, Vlad. They all are, until you take the time to get to know them."

Vlad rolled his eyes at the window, returning his attention to the sky. It was really annoying how Mr. Kiss Every Girl with a Pulse had morphed into Dr. Phil ever since he and Melissa had gotten serious. Clearly, a monthlong relationship was enough to fill Henry with an abundance of romantic wisdom. Riiiiight.

Vlad reached over and turned the volume knob on the stereo up, before Henry felt like sharing any more of his incredible insight on the opposite sex . . . or before he threw up. Whichever came first.

5

THE TROUBLE
WITH DRUDGES

HENRY PULLED INTO A PARKING SPACE at the edge of the parking lot, as far away from The Crypt as he possibly could, as if the distance made it easier to deny that he'd been to the goth club at all. He threw Vlad a glance. "Don't take all night, okay? I told Melissa I'd call her after we got back from the movies, and her dad freaks out if I call after ten."

Vlad resisted rolling his eyes, and then Henry cut the engine. "*Son of Psycho Slasher Chainsaw Guy* starts in about a half hour, so I figure you've got about twenty minutes before we bolt."

Vlad flashed him an irritated look and snorted. "So . . . what? You're not coming in?"

Henry softened some. "I kinda thought I'd wait out here."

"Come on, Henry. I put up with you being at Melissa's beck and call twenty-four/seven, the least you can do is put up with my friends wearing black eyeliner." He cast Henry a pleading glance. "They won't bite. Well . . . most of them, anyway. I'm almost certain."

Henry seemed to mull it over for a moment, and Vlad saw his in. Vlad smirked and said, "Y'know, you were much more adventurous before you entered the bonds of holy matrimony."

Henry slugged him in the arm and opened the car door, stepping out into the night.

They crossed the parking lot and Vlad opened the door to the club, leading Henry down the ramp until they entered the heart of The Crypt. It was a place that Vlad had come to know quite well over the summer. He felt at home here, nonjudged, accepted for who he was—or who they thought he was, anyway. Across the room, lounging on the velvet couches, were October, Sprat, Andrew, and Kristoff. Vlad offered a wave and scanned the room for Snow. He'd just fed two weeks before, but the tension between him and Otis was making him hungrier than he'd been in a long time. Besides . . . he rather enjoyed the sensation of feeding.

Not that he'd ever admit that to anyone. Least of all, Otis.

Plus, he enjoyed Snow's company immensely.

Not that he'd ever admit that to Henry.

Vlad turned his head and spied her, sipping a red syrupy drink from a plastic goblet at the bar. He smiled, willing her to notice him. She blinked, looking up, meeting his eyes, and smiled too. It was kind of cool, knowing that he could summon a girl by will alone. It made him feel kind of like Fonzie from that old *Happy Days* show that Nelly liked watching on Nick at Nite. Not that he was going to try the trick with the jukebox anytime soon. Come to think of it, when was the last time anyone had seen a jukebox?

He glanced at Henry, who was shifting awkwardly from one foot to the other, clearly uncomfortable with his surroundings. A girl in a tight, black corset walked by and Henry relaxed some, raising an eyebrow at Vlad as if to say, "Who knew goth chicks were so hot?"

It was nice to see that some things never changed. Now if only he'd stop being Melissa's lapdog.

"I'll be right back, Henry. I've gotta talk to Snow in private." He moved through the crowd, toward the back door, not bothering to meet Snow's eyes again. She would follow. He didn't need to look at her again to know that. On his way, he swore he heard Henry shout, "Is 'talk to' code for 'make out with'?"

He'd just touched the door when October grabbed him by the arm. "Hey, stranger!"

Vlad smiled, casually noticing Snow's approach. His heart picked up at the sight of her. "What's up, October?"

"Not much. Are you here for a while or just a quick in-and-out?"

"Just stopping by. Why? Miss me?"

"Not as much as Snow has," she chuckled. "So . . . why's Henry McMillan here? He looks lost."

Vlad shook his head. "Not lost, just waiting on me. Why don't you ask him to dance? He could use a babysitter while I talk to Snow."

"Talk. Riiiight . . ." October laughed, and walked off toward Henry, leaving Vlad standing by the back door. He opened it and Snow walked silently outside before he followed, licking his lips.

Snow had barely breathed a hello before Vlad's eyes were on her porcelain neck. She leaned back against the brick wall of the adjacent building and met his hungry gaze, smiling. Her lips were painted a deep red, her eyes lined heavy with black. "It hasn't been a month yet, has it?"

Vlad was focusing so intently on his hunger that it was difficult to hear her words over the sound of blood rushing through her veins. "Not yet. But I was hungry. You don't mind, do you?"

"Not at all." As he leaned in, she brushed her hair from her neck. Her eyes widened. "Wow, your eyes are purple. Cool . . ."

His fangs almost shot from his gums, and he closed his mouth over her flesh, biting down. She shivered at first and Vlad forced himself to slow down. He didn't want to hurt her. Nor did he want this to be over with quickly. He couldn't lie to himself anymore—it wasn't just the blood that had called him here tonight. It was the act of feeding that he had longed for. It comforted him. It made him feel complete.

After Snow relaxed, Vlad bit down harder, opening the artery. Delicious crimson splashed over his tongue to the beat of her racing heart, and Vlad slipped his arms around her, drinking deep, feeling her entire being shake with excitement . . . and fear. She tensed again and he clamped his mouth down, barely resisting the temptation to tear through her flesh completely, enjoying the taste of her blood, the sensation of her terror as he continued to feed. He heard her whisper his name, followed by the subtle breathy word, "stop," but even then, he continued to feed. Her heartbeats began to slow, but Vlad couldn't stop, wouldn't stop. It was his nature. It was his need. His need to kill.

No.

He pulled back hard, and stumbled backward, keeping his distance, gathering himself. Snow crumbled to the ground, dazed. He watched her, wondering if she had any idea how close she'd been to dying, and a wave of guilty nausea washed over him. He almost gagged, but took slow, deep breaths, calming his stomach, collecting his thoughts. What was wrong with him, anyway? He'd promised Snow, promised himself, that he would only feed when he physically needed to. He shook his head, feeling the nausea settle some. He had to get a grip, or he was going to become something that he couldn't stand to be. A monster. Just like Joss had said.

Snow stirred, rubbing her neck absently, and smiled over at Vlad. "Wow, hungry much?"

Vlad breathed. "I'm sorry."

"Don't be. You need it."

Not that time. Vlad hadn't been more than a little snacky.

But Snow had no way of knowing that. And he'd almost killed her, almost took her life without her even knowing. His veins filled with horror, his heart raced. He was an almost-murderer. A bloodthirsty maniac. A near-killer.

She struggled to stand, and Vlad moved across the alley and helped her, the beast within him contained once more. He dared a glance at her neck, which had healed already. "Are you all right?"

But she wasn't all right. She was still in the presence of the boy who'd selfishly taken her life-giving blood just to satisfy some stupid craving. She was like a cookie to him now, not a person.

What the hell was he becoming that he could treat her that way?

Snow nodded, her arms draped over his shoulders, her body still wobbly. "I'm fine. Just a little dizzy. I always feel weird after you feed. Like I'm floating through a haze."

"I'm sorry." He said it again, had to say it again. He *was* sorry. For hurting her. For changing her life. For needing not to stop.

A small smile turned up the corners of her lips. "There's nothing to be sorry for, Vlad. I actually enjoy it. It makes me feel close to you."

Vlad allowed himself a small smile. "I feel close to you too."

She tilted her head for a moment, eyeing him with uncertainty. "Something wrong? You seem kinda stressed tonight."

Sighing, Vlad said, "It's a lot of stuff. That slayer I told you about is back, Henry's acting way too noble for my tastes, and earlier I got the weirdest feeling that Otis knew about our meetings."

"Is that a bad thing?"

He ran his fingers through his hair, brushing his bangs from his eyes. "Bad? No. More like horrible. Because if Otis realizes that I've been lying to him . . ."

"Why are you lying to him, anyway?"

Vlad sighed, his heart heavy. "Sometimes I don't know."

"It's okay, Vlad. I understand." She met his eyes and Vlad's tension melted away. She did understand. At last, he had a friend who he didn't have to hold back with. She really, truly understood.

Without warning, Snow leaned forward and pressed her lips to his. He was surprised—she'd never done it before—but he didn't stop her, not at first. Her lips were warm and sweet. She was a great kisser, soft and giving, but not . . . not Meredith.

He pulled away—it was more difficult than he thought—and blinked at Snow, his terror over nearly killing her settling, replaced by confusion. "What are you doing?"

She rolled her eyes slightly. "Duh. Kissing you."

Suddenly Vlad was very aware of how close she was standing. Still, he didn't back away. Not yet. "But . . . why?"

Snow smiled. "Because I like you, Vlad. Why else? I don't go around kissing just anyone, y'know."

He didn't say anything, didn't move. And his inaction made him feel terribly guilty. What would Meredith think of him making out with Snow after he'd broken her heart in front of the entire population of Bathory? She'd be heartbroken. She'd be furious.

Snow leaned in again, her lips tempting him. Vlad pushed her back—a little more forcefully than he had intended—and growled. "Stop. Just stop. Just . . . let me think."

She immediately relaxed back against the wall, following a direct order from her vampire master.

Vlad stepped back, pacing some in the dark alleyway. "I think you're confused, Snow. This . . . this isn't a . . . a . . ."

"Relationship?" she offered.

Vlad nodded. "You're my drudge, my food source. You shouldn't be kissing me. You don't really like me; you're just confused."

She shook her head, serious. Hurt lurked in her dark eyes. "I knew and liked you for a whole hour before I became your drudge, Vlad. If you don't want me to kiss you, why not just order me not to?"

But that was the problem. Vlad didn't know what he wanted. Not exactly.

On one hand, it felt really nice to kiss Snow. But on the other . . . there was Meredith to be considered, and whether or not he was ready to be with another girl so soon. Not to mention that probably the only girl he'd feel safe being so close to right now would be Snow. She didn't seem to mind his urge to feed. But Meredith might. And he missed her. Missed seeing her, missed kissing her, missed holding her hand.

Plus, he wasn't entirely certain that he deserved to kiss any girl after the pain he'd put Meredith through at the Freedom Fest. He deserved little more than to be kicked in the face with baseball cleats.

He looked at Snow—pretty, small, sweet, understanding Snow—and shook his head. "I'd appreciate it if you didn't do that again, okay? Not . . . not yet. I'm just . . . I'm not ready."

Snow nodded slowly, thankfully not pointing out the obvious—that he hadn't ordered her not to kiss him ever again. She looked a little hurt, but Vlad turned away before he could examine her expression further. He yanked the door open and was enveloped by the sounds of the club. To his immense surprise, Henry was sitting on the edge of one of the velvet sofas, talking to Kristoff.

With a raised eyebrow, Vlad crossed the room, slugging Henry in the arm lightly. "What's going on?"

Henry's eyes widened at him. "Dude, who busted your lip?"

Oh no. Snow's blood.

Vlad kept his cool on the outside, casually rubbing at his lip with the back of his hand and mumbling something about tripping, but Henry didn't seem to be buying it, so he shrugged and said, "Lipstick."

At this, he earned a glare from Kristoff, who didn't approve of the idea of Vlad making out with anyone in their little circle. In fact, Vlad was pretty sure Kristoff didn't want Vlad in their little circle at all. Henry shook his head with a look of disapproval. Vlad shrugged. After all, who was Henry to judge what girls he kissed. "Are you ready? I don't wanna be late for the movie."

Henry muttered, "Are you kidding? I was ready to leave before we walked in the door."

October left the dance floor, nearly breathless. "Where's Snow?"

Vlad shrugged with one shoulder, fighting back the enormous guilt that was creeping up his spine. "She's . . . around."

Then, before anyone could speak, Vlad tugged Henry off the couch and through the crowd, up the ramp, and out the door. After they were in the car and driving down the road to the mall's movie theater, Vlad asked, "So what were you and Kristoff talking about?"

Henry furrowed his brow for a moment, confused. "Oh, you mean David? We were just talking about some of the stuff that happened when he lived next door to me in the second grade."

Vlad blinked. How could he and Henry have known each other their entire lives and he had no idea that Kristoff, once David, had ever lived next door to Henry? Shaking off the surprise, he looked out at the night, at the streetlights and taxicabs. It briefly crossed his mind that they were merely three or four blocks from the Stokerton council, but he didn't worry. Otis had assured him that D'Ablo and the rest of the council were busy with preparations for the coming trial—Otis's trial. Even though it wasn't scheduled until the spring.

Vlad's trial, it turned out, had never been scheduled. Call it a miracle. Vlad certainly did.

As they pulled into a spot in the mall parking lot, Henry cleared his throat. "So it looks like you're over Meredith, huh? That was fast."

Vlad raised an irritated eyebrow. "For your information, Snow kissed *me*. Not the other way around. And what's with the attitude? Weren't you just saying I needed to see other girls?"

"I was thinking someone less . . . scary."

That was it. Vlad raised his voice in protective defense. "Snow is sweet, smart, and pretty, Henry. The only thing scary about her are her military boots, and that's only because she could put a grown man down with a single kick."

Henry snorted. "Whatever. You've been acting so weird since you started hanging with the Halloween brigade."

"Kinda like how you've been acting weird ever since you became Melissa's pet?" As Henry opened his mouth again, Vlad shot him a glare. "I've changed my mind about the movie. Take me home, Henry. And don't say a word until we get there."

The drive home was quiet, and Henry didn't so much as glance at him, but Vlad couldn't care less. Henry was acting like a prime-time jerk.

By the time the car had pulled into the driveway, Henry

looked as if he was ready to explode. Vlad opened the door and got out, but not before Henry muttered something rather unpleasant in his general direction. Vlad ignored it. After all, Henry had called him out, and then he had called Henry out in return. They were pretty even, and saying anything back to his grumble as Vlad had exited would've only continued the tense moment between them.

As for directly ordering Henry to take him home and keep his mouth shut . . . well, it didn't make Vlad feel good to boss his drudge around, but he wasn't about to sit there while Henry insulted his friends. So what that they wore black? So what that they liked hanging out in cemeteries and lighting candles? They were nice. And perfectly normal, as far as Vlad was concerned.

He made his way up the porch steps and opened the front door, only then realizing that the lights were all off inside and a note was taped to the front door.

Vladimir—
It is of the utmost importance that you come to your parents' house the moment that you read this note. I will explain later why I did not contact you in the usual manner. Please make haste.
    Yours in Eternity,
    Otis

Vlad read the note over again, focusing intently on "in the usual manner." Otis hadn't wanted to contact him through telepathy, but why? His words had sounded shaky, nervous, frightened. Vlad could only imagine what kinds of things could manage to scare his uncle.

With a deep breath, Vlad turned from the door and made his way down the stairs, hoping that Joss hadn't had time to unpack his stake while he and Henry were arguing over Henry's really stupid prejudices. As he stepped from the porch, the scent of something carried by the breeze caught his attention. It was dark and ancient and made Vlad shiver, despite the warmth of the evening.

Vampires. There were vampires in Bathory.

6
THE VAMPIRE DORIAN

VLAD MADE IT ACROSS TOWN without incident. He'd been tempted to walk by the house that Joss now called home, just to see for himself that the slayer was now an official resident of Bathory, but his good sense won out over his curiosity. He found his way quietly to the back door of his old house. He knocked—which felt very weird to do, but something about his uncle living here made him feel that knocking was warranted—and when there was no reply from within, he pulled open the door and stepped inside.

Muffled voices were coming from the front of the house. He hesitated, then strode forward, making his way to the living room, where the voices were coming from. At the arched entryway to the living room, Vlad paused. The large room was host to a dozen or so vampires.

A few glanced at him, but otherwise, the conversation continued as if he hadn't entered the room at all. Vlad scanned the room and found Otis perched on the arm of the couch. He met Vlad's eyes and gestured to an empty seat near the entryway to the kitchen. With more than a few questions on his tongue, Vlad sat and spoke to Otis with his thoughts. *"Otis, who are all these pe—"*

But Otis cut him off abruptly.

Vlad looked at him, but Otis merely shook his head and returned to listening to one vampire in particular, who was speaking in Elysian code—something that Vlad still didn't quite understand. As if remembering this, Otis cleared his throat. "Please, Cratus, speak English so that we can all understand."

The vampire he'd addressed didn't miss a beat, picking up where he was in English. "The changes to the Stokerton council are greatly disturbing. Under D'Ablo's continued leadership—"

"A crime in its own right." A familiar voice sent Vlad's head around and his eyes searching for the speaker. When he found him sitting in an easy chair in the far corner of the room, Vlad couldn't help but smile. Vikas. It was good to see him again.

"—it seems that the Stokerton council is becoming less a system of government and more a religious sect. The vampires there follow D'Ablo blindly, as if he were a prophet whose wisdom were not based on fairy tales and hidden agendas. And it gets worse." Cratus swallowed hard, raking a trembling hand through his wavy, dirty blond tresses. "D'Ablo has somehow managed to weasel his way onto the Council of Elders."

The room erupted in shouts of disdain. Several vampires stood, making loud threats on D'Ablo's life. Through the chaos, Vlad met Vikas's gaze, which shifted from troubled to pleasant, as if Vikas was happy to see him. Vlad nodded, offering a smile, and turned to look at Otis, who had stood. "Please, my brethren. We must remain calm."

His voice was just that—calm, almost serene, but Vlad could sense the disquiet beneath Otis's cool exterior.

It took a minute, but eventually, they all returned to sitting and listening as Cratus continued. "His presence on the Council of Elders has upset more than a few Elysian councils, and yet, he remains, having taken Mortimer's place as the youngest vampire in the group. Vikas will speak further on this, I'm sure."

Vikas stood and an air of awe fell over the group. Clearly, Vikas was a highly respected vampire, someone whom they all trusted inherently. "Some background for those not so familiar with the Council of Elders."

Vlad shrank back in his seat. He was pretty sure he was the only one here who had no idea what they were talking about, so even though Vikas was doing him the favor of not pointing him out directly, it still made him squirm.

"The Council of Elders has been convening on rare occasions—that is to say, whenever a matter cannot be resolved by a single council—for centuries. We are, normally, the nine oldest vampires in existence. And as D'Ablo is but a *tuneya-dec*—" Vikas caught his abrupt shift into Russian and flicked an apologetic glance to Vlad. "Pardon me. I meant to call the dog a parasite."

The room erupted in laughter. Despite the tension in his bones, Vlad chuckled. Clearly, there was at least one thing they could all agree on—D'Ablo was a jerk.

Vikas continued. "D'Ablo has no place on the council. He is not among the nine oldest vampires, and his so-called wisdom has been questioned several times by those of us who do have a right to sit on the council. With rumors that Em, the oldest of our kind, has fallen in with his cultlike following, there is no question of how he managed to get his name to be listed among ours."

"Cultlike following?" Vlad hadn't meant to speak out loud, but when he did, all eyes turned on him, many with sympathy.

Cratus shook his head at Otis. "Enough coddling the boy, Otis. Tell him the truth. Tell him what's waiting for him in Elysia. Tell him about D'Ablo's twisted belief system."

Vlad glanced at Otis, but before Otis could speak, Vikas spoke for him. "Indeed, it is time that Vladimir knew about the divided factions in Elysia. I am certain, Mahlyenki Dyavol, that you know a bit about the division in vampirekind. There are those who believe as most do, that the prophecy of the Pravus is little more than a fairy tale, passed down through the ages like a ghost story. But there is another group, an ever-expanding group of vampires, who believe the prophecy to be real. These vampires believe that you are the Pravus and that you will assert vampirekind's place in the world. No more hiding from humans, no more limits on feeding. They believe that you will rise up as their leader and put humans in their place, along with all who oppose them."

Of course Vlad knew the story. He'd heard it from Vikas's own lips on a cold night in Siberia his freshman year, and had never forgotten it. "What's that have to do with D'Ablo?"

Otis, Cratus, and Vikas exchanged glances. It was Otis who spoke. "It's recently been discovered that D'Ablo . . . is the leader of this cult."

Vlad furrowed his brow. If that were true, wouldn't D'Ablo be trying to protect Vlad and raise him up as the Pravus, maybe suck up a little and get on his good side?

Otis nodded, as if he knew what Vlad was thinking without the use of telepathy. "Apparently for years, he was in full support of locating the person they deemed the Pravus and protecting him at all cost. But something changed—we don't know what, but whatever it was, it made D'Ablo rethink his plans and strive to take the so-called Pravus's place. Thus his little ritual last year."

Vlad shook his head. To think, if whatever it was that happened hadn't happened, D'Ablo might be kissing up to him all the time instead of trying to kill him. "Just how big is this cult, anyway?"

Otis looked to Cratus, who said, "Intelligence suggests the following has grown substantially over the years."

Vlad shifted his eyes between the two of them. "By how much?"

When it seemed no one was going to answer, Vikas spoke up. "We suspect roughly a third of Elysia follows this thinking, but there's no way to be certain. The followers are incredibly secretive."

"So what does it mean?"

Otis sighed heavily. "It means that you can trust virtually no one, Vlad. It also means that D'Ablo's presence on the Council of Elders most assuredly has something to do with you, as he's convinced that you are this . . . this Pravus."

"I *am* the Pravus." Vlad tightened his jaw and locked eyes pointedly with his uncle. "I am. But just because I am doesn't mean I'm going to become some psychopath."

He looked around the room at the other vampires. Some looked fearful. Most looked doubtful. "I'm not like the rest of you. You know that. A few of you have seen it firsthand. So call me what you will—Pravus, freak of nature—I'm different. Now what are we going to do about D'Ablo?"

After a long and poignant silence, Cratus sighed. "We wait. And we watch."

Vikas shook his head. "It is troubling, my friends, that D'Ablo should hold the thread of Otis's life in his treacherous hands."

The realization hit Vlad hard. The trial—they were talking about Otis's trial. The one that would decide if Otis lived or died, the one that would determine whether or not his uncle was a vampire of honor or a criminal doomed to death. And D'Ablo was one of the people who was going to make that decision.

He bit his bottom lip, dropping his eyes to the carpet.

Vikas's voice, deep and strong, continued to speak. "What's more, Otis's pretrial comes fast on the heels of D'Ablo's lust for vengeance."

Otis spoke, his voice gruff. "When?"

Vikas held Otis's gaze, his expression grim. "D'Ablo insisted that it be held this All Hallows Eve."

All eyes were on Vikas, whose mouth slowly curled into a smile. "But I insisted that it take place at the end of the year. And as he is but a babe and I am an old man, it seems the council is more apt to side with me. Otis has been granted a stay of execution, so to speak, until December twenty-sixth."

Everyone seemed to exhale at once.

Apparently, the pretrial was something you wanted to put off as long as possible.

"There is more," Vikas said in his thick Russian accent. "D'Ablo had planned for the pretrial to take place in Stokerton, but the other members of the Council of Elders and myself have determined that the pretrial—like the trial—must be held in the only city without a governing council."

Otis spoke, his voice just that of a whisper. "New York."

Vikas nodded. Several vampires looked uncomfortable, but most just looked relieved.

Vlad watched them with intrigue. He'd had no idea that

there was a town that wasn't governed by a council. He thought all cities were governed by the nearest council. Clearly, New York was not. Huh. That wasn't in the *Encyclopedia Vampyrica*. Nor was it something Otis had ever mentioned. Vlad pondered that for a few minutes, until Vikas took his seat and the conversation broke off into what was happening elsewhere in Elysia.

To Vlad's left, two vampires were telling what he thought were dirty jokes in French. To his right, one vampire recounted his last meal to another in plain English. Across the room from Vlad, a young, handsome vampire with copper-colored hair was staring intently, silently at him. Vlad shifted in his seat and was about to call Vikas over when the vampire stood and pointed a long, pale finger at Vlad. The other vampires fell silent. "You. The child of a vampire and a human, if the stories are to be believed. Tell me your name."

Vlad swallowed. The air in the room chilled. "Vlad. And they're not just stories."

Vikas spoke under his breath from his spot in the corner. "Tread carefully, Mahlyenki Dyavol. Dorian is . . ."

But he didn't finish his sentence, leaving Vlad to wonder just what Dorian was.

Otis looked guarded.

Dorian stepped closer, sniffing the air. He was handsome and young-looking, having made the change in his mid-twenties, with dark brown eyes and a pale bronze to his skin. He looked like an old friend that you just couldn't place, like anyone that you might have once known. Remarkable, yet completely forgettable. The perfect vampire.

Dorian moved slowly, smoothly, in a way that struck Vlad as feline. Vlad got the distinct impression that if he moved, Dorian would be on him like a cat. "Ah, yes. I can smell it in your veins. So . . . unique. Tantalizing."

Otis's jaw tightened. "Dorian."

Dorian ignored Otis, edging ever closer to Vlad. His tone was soothing and kind, and if Otis and Vikas weren't looking so concerned about his proximity to Vlad, he might not find the vampire alarming at all. "I bet you carry tasty delicacies in your veins."

Vlad blinked, suddenly realizing why everyone in the room was watching in fascination. Dorian wanted blood. Vlad's blood. Vlad sputtered, "But I'm a vampire. I thought that wasn't allowed. Feeding on your own kind."

Dorian shrugged slightly, smelling the air again. Then he smiled. "But you are also half human, and that makes you prey to my predator."

Vlad gulped.

Vikas took a bold step forward, "How forgetful I am. I brought with me several cases of bloodwine, and the bottles are just waiting to be uncorked. Vladimir, would you assist me?"

Before Vlad knew it, he was being ushered quickly into the kitchen. Dorian's eyes followed him the whole time—a curious smile on his lips. After a moment, Otis joined Vlad and

Vikas in the kitchen, looking more than a little troubled. Vikas spoke first. "That was close."

Otis nodded, "Too close. I hadn't thought of the repercussions. It's so easy to forget Vlad's human heritage."

Vlad looked at Otis. "Are you going to fill me in on what we're all doing here, and maybe explain why that Dorian guy wants to take a bite outta me?"

Otis grabbed several bottles of bloodwine and uncorked them, speaking to Vikas. "This may be a problem for us. Please, do what you can to keep the peace."

He looked at Vlad then, an oddly frustrated look on his face, and barked, "And you—stay away from Dorian." Then he disappeared back into the living room.

Vlad furrowed his brow. It wasn't like it was his fault Dorian thought he smelled tasty. He looked back at Vikas, who was smiling. "Your uncle is troubled. Pay him no mind, Vladimir. He is merely concerned that Dorian may force us to order his departure before he can fully help Otis's case. You see, Dorian is unlike any vampire in existence. He is skilled beyond all of us, and he has resources that we believe may free your uncle of the charges against him. But should we insult him by not catering to his every whim . . ."

Vlad's stomach shriveled up in realization. "Oh. So if he wants to feed from me and you say no, then he leaves and Otis . . . Otis . . ."

"Otis will face the justice of Elysia." Vikas gave Vlad's shoulder a squeeze. "It would be wise to keep your distance from

Dorian. It is rumored that he has a taste for rare and some-times even vampiric blood. I am certain the mixture of vampire and human in your veins appeals to his palate. It makes yours the most rare blood type in the world."

Vlad's throat suddenly resembled a desert. He tried to swallow, but couldn't.

Vikas, calm and cool, said, "Dorian is a vampire used to getting what he wants, and we cannot disappoint him. So let's make certain that what he wants is not you."

A worried crease settled on Vlad's forehead. "Should I go home?"

"I think the safest place that you could be tonight is under this roof, Mahlyenki Dyavol. After all, what's to stop Dorian from sniffing his way into your bedroom while you are alone and indulging in every last drop of your blood? At least here you will be watched after. You should remain here until the vampires depart, which will be in a few hours. If you grow weary, I will have Tristian watch over you. If he sees anything to be alarmed by, I will know it."

Vlad nodded, utterly freaked out that someone would want to bite him and drink his blood. He couldn't help but wonder if Snow ever felt this way. The thought sent a guilty shiver up his spine. "Why isn't anyone using telepathy?"

Vikas popped open a bottle of bloodwine and drank deeply, then met Vlad's eyes with a weary glance. "As I said, Dorian is skilled beyond any of us. If our minds remain open, there is no telling what he might dredge up . . . or do. Be on guard. But be polite. Dorian is our guest, and an important figure in Elysia. He deserves both our respect and our fear. But . . . do not let his presence taint the celebration for you, Vladimir. Besides, you should be celebrating, yourself. If Elysia has not yet called you to trial, you are likely free of the possibility. Enjoy your freedom."

He turned and made his way back into the living room with an armful of open bloodwine bottles.

Vlad uncorked a bottle that was sitting on the counter and took a swig. It was as delicious, tangy, and spicy as he recalled it to be. After another swig, he followed Vikas back into the crowded room.

He wasn't exactly sure what Vikas had meant by it being a celebration, so when he made it across the room to Otis, he said, "Vikas called this a celebration."

"He's right."

"What exactly are we celebrating, Otis?"

Otis blanched, growing silent for a moment. When he spoke, his voice was gravelly. "We are celebrating my life, as it were."

Vlad frowned, his heart suddenly very heavy. "Otis . . . you still have a chance. The Council of Elders might—"

He was going to say "find you innocent," but Otis shook his head and walked away, the threat of tears in his eyes, before Vlad could utter another word. Vlad stared after him, dumbfounded.

A heavy hand clasped his shoulder, and Vlad turned to see Vikas, who was watching after Otis with a troubled expression. "As I said, he is troubled, your uncle. It would do little good to attempt to cheer a dying man."

Vlad's heart felt heavy and shriveled. "But, Vikas, you're on the Council of Elders. Isn't there anything you can do?"

"Something you will soon learn about Elysia, Mahlyenki Dyavol, is that trials are but a formality." Vikas squeezed his shoulder once, lowering his voice. What he said next broke Vlad's heart in two. "You should enjoy your time with your uncle, Vladimir. It grows short despite my efforts to lengthen it."

Another vampire said something in Elysian code to Vikas, and he laughed openly before leading the vampire to the kitchen. When Vlad turned around, Dorian was there, waiting, wearing that same kind, expectant smile on his lips, that same harmless demeanor. "You will offer your blood to me."

At once, every eye in the room turned to Vlad. After a minuscule pause, several vampires, including Otis and Vikas, began to speak, to argue with Dorian over what he had just said to Vlad, or to plead with him not to do whatever it was that he was about to do. Vikas offered Dorian Tristian's blood— AB negative, as much as he'd like—in exchange for what he wanted of Vlad. Bemused, but insistent, Dorian whispered, "Hush now."

At his spoken words, the crowd fell utterly silent.

Vlad looked them over—none could move, none could speak, but by their blinks and the look in Otis's eyes, they were well aware what was happening. Vlad, however, had no idea what was going on. He only knew that Dorian had stopped their every action, their every sound, with a whisper. It made the tiny hairs on the back of his neck stand up in confused fear. He looked at Dorian but didn't speak.

Dorian stepped closer, a dark, hungry look in his eye. "You will offer your blood to me now."

Before Vlad realized what he was doing, he'd reached up with his hand and pulled the collar of his T-shirt back. He bent his head to the side, exposing his neck, and all the while, he had no control over his actions. It wasn't mind control—this was something else, something worse, something more powerful than Vlad had ever dared imagine could exist.

And he couldn't resist it.

Dorian looked at Otis and nodded. His demeanor was very apologetic. "Your pleading and absolute refusal makes this moment that much more enticing, I'm afraid. I really don't understand what the fuss is about. Vlad will likely survive. And if he doesn't . . . well, then, I am deeply sorry. But I must have the boy, you understand."

Vlad's insides turned to mush. Dorian was going to drain him of blood. And there was nothing anybody could do about it.

Except Vlad.

Panicking, he struggled with all his might to move, to let go of his collar and straighten his head, but the more he attempted to struggle, the more cooperative his movements became. Against his will, he stepped forward, coaxing Dorian to drink.

Dorian's eyes brimmed with apologies. "I am sorry, Vlad. But I must have your blood. It calls to me, and I shall heed that call no matter the cost."

Dorian stepped closer, ready to bite. He was poised over Vlad's neck when the answer came.

Otis couldn't move, couldn't speak, but only because Dorian had stopped him—not because Dorian was controlling him. Quickly, Vlad slipped into Otis's thoughts and, with an apology, took control over his uncle's actions. With his control, Otis stepped forward, shoving Dorian from Vlad. Dorian stumbled back, blinking in confusion.

His spell over the crowd broke, and angry voices erupted.

Vlad's heart raced, and he shot Otis an apologetic glance for having used mind control, but Otis shook it off in gratitude. Then Otis turned to Dorian. "You will leave my home and keep your distance from my nephew."

Vikas placed a hand on Otis's shoulder, but something about the way he looked told Vlad he was positioning himself to pull Otis back if a fight erupted.

Dorian's fangs slowly shrank back into his gums. He kept his eyes on Vlad, a strange blend of curiosity and confusion filling them. After a moment, he nodded and moved through the kitchen and toward the back door.

Otis shook Vikas off and stepped away. He was calmer now that he'd had his say, but Vlad couldn't help but wonder about the tension that seemed to ebb from his uncle in response to Dorian's actions. He also couldn't help but wonder why a vampire as powerful as Dorian would leave without even so much as an argument.

Otis turned back to Vikas. He looked worried, and equally as surprised as Dorian had. "I've never seen Dorian back down like that. I can't help but wonder why."

Vikas shook his head slowly, dropping his voice to just above a whisper. "The answer, my old friend, is simple. Dorian has never backed down before. Perhaps he is . . . conflicted."

As Dorian reached the back door, he called out to Otis, his tone shaken. "When you want my help—and you will, Otis—you know where to find me."

He opened the door, pausing long enough to meet Vlad's eyes. With a single nod, he stepped out into the night.

Two hours later, Vlad had tired of the vampire crowd and felt safe enough to be alone, but not quite safe enough to head home. He retired upstairs to his old room, where Tristian stood watch from the hall—but not before Otis stopped him to make certain he wouldn't leave without an escort. "Just stay here until our guests depart. Then Vikas or I will walk you home, all right?"

Vlad moved into his old room and before he closed the door, he replied, "I don't need a babysitter, Otis."

And he didn't. He was the Pravus, for crying out loud. But . . . he was really glad he didn't have to worry about Dorian, Joss, or anyone else who might be out for his blood on his walk home tonight. He didn't need a babysitter. But he certainly appreciated the company.

The room was painted in the same soft blue as it had been in his childhood. He wagered Otis had wanted to preserve those younger years for him in some way. As if color could do such a thing.

Vlad lay back on the bed, his eyes quickly fluttering closed. Drifting in that place between wakefulness and sleep, he thought about his mother and how she would sometimes enter his room at night, just to press her lips to his forehead. She'd whisper, "I love you, Vlad." And Vlad would pretend to sleep, cuddled all warm and snug and safe under his blue blankets, which matched the color of his walls.

Maybe there was something to this color thing after all.

He drifted off and was on the verge of deep sleep when he thought he felt a presence, warm and wonderful, in his room. But when he opened his eyes, his mother was nowhere to be found.

What a stupid thing to hope for. After all, just because he missed her, just because this was the first night he had slept in his house since that horrible day when he'd lost his parents . . . that didn't mean his mom would be here, watching over him from beyond death.

Did it?

Vlad looked around the room, at the shadowed blue walls, at the new carpeting, the new light fixture, at everything that wasn't his past and was his present.

No. She was gone. Gone forever. To someplace much happier, much brighter, and full of goodness, full of light. She had to be.

He curled up on his side, and as he gave in to the call of sleep he thought of his mother and all the wonderful moments that they had shared. For the first time since her death, he didn't think of smoke and ash and that horrible moment when he'd lost her forever. He thought only of happy times and the warmth of his mother's embrace.

A hand—warm, gentle—brushed the hair from Vlad's still-closed eyes. Following its light touch was Otis's voice, equally as caring. "Vladimir, I hate to wake you, but our guests have gone. We should get you home."

Vlad rolled over, content to sleep, and mumbled, "Five more minutes, Dad."

After a pause, Otis's only reply was to cover Vlad with a soft blanket. As his footsteps faded out the door and down the hall, Vlad snuggled into his blanket and slipped back into a deep and restful slumber.

7

A RUDE AWAKENING

VLAD SAT UP, STARTLED OUT OF SLEEP by the realization that his first day of school was today—his backpack, the clothes he wanted to wear, even his schedule was back at Nelly's house, and he was still at his house, resting peacefully, dreaming of his mother. Rubbing the remainder of sleep from his eyes, he dragged himself out of bed and through the still-dark room, stumbled down the hallway and stairs, and yawned several hundred times before checking the time (4:36 A.M.). He scribbled Otis a note that said he'd see him at school later and ducked out the back door.

It didn't take long for him to wind his way back to Nelly's place, and he'd just stepped up onto the porch when he realized that he hadn't given Joss a single thought on his walk.

That slowed his steps a bit. He'd better learn to be a bit more careful, what with a slayer on the loose ... one who knew his address, Vlad thought with a shiver. He made his way inside and upstairs, took a quick shower, ran through his morning routine, and dressed. By the time he sat down to breakfast, the clock on the wall said that it was 5:44 A.M. For once in his life, Vlad was on time and not rushing to get out the door.

Actually, he was early and not exactly sure what to do to kill time. He wasn't hungry in the least. He thought about playing some video games or watching television, but neither sounded very appealing in the wee hours of morning. So instead, he pulled out his journal and began jotting down all of his feelings about the impending day. He was feeling conflicted about Joss, apprehensive about Meredith, but mostly ... he was feeling lost. His life had changed dramatically over the past few years, ever since Otis had revealed himself to be not only a fellow vampire, but his uncle. Every moment since then had been full of surprises—not all of them good. And Vlad wasn't sure he could take much more.

The very thought of everything he'd faced in his life was enough to make even the strongest man weep. Vlad thought he'd handled his troubles with as much strength as he could, given the immense pain he'd experienced—both physical and emotional. Losing his parents at a young age, being picked on and bullied by his peers, suffering broken bones and bruises, getting terrified out of his mind, hunted by both a slayer and vampires, technically killed, betrayed more than once, and brokenhearted. His life had sucked. But it was his, and nobody who mattered would judge him for shedding a few tears.

Glancing at the clock again, Vlad slipped his backpack over his shoulder and headed out the front door. Like clockwork, Henry pulled up in his new car, and Vlad slid into the front seat with a groan of envy. "I thought you were driving Melissa to school."

Henry snapped, "I don't have to be with her every second of every day."

Vlad took a breath and made sure that anything that could possibly fuel Henry's temper was absent from his voice. "What happened?"

Henry sighed, and his anger seemed to ebb out of him. "Girls, man. Just . . . girls."

Vlad nodded, as if he had any idea what Henry was talking about. He didn't, but he thought it was important for Henry to feel like he could relate. "Hey, why are we driving anyway? The school is like four blocks away."

The corner of Henry's mouth rose in a smirk. "Dude. When you've got a car like this, you don't walk anywhere."

"Ohmigod!"

Joss grinned. There was a blur of pink and then Meredith was hugging him, hugging him so tight and close and happily around the neck that Joss's head, along with his heart, almost burst. If he'd known what her reaction would have been to seeing him again, he would have dropped by the night he and his parents had pulled into town. He squeezed her and spun her around a little, chuckling. When he sat her back down on the ground, he was sorry to let her go. "Miss me much?"

Meredith beamed. "Only tons!"

"Wanna walk together?"

She looked down the street for a moment, and Joss knew just who she was looking for, so he put on his best smile and said, "Or should I get outta here before your boyfriend shows up?"

She shook her head, her chocolate curls bouncing this way and that, and adjusted her backpack on her shoulders. There was a look in her eyes that Joss couldn't place, but he knew it wasn't a good one. "Trust me, that's not gonna be a problem."

They started down the sidewalk together, walking side by side, heading toward the high school on their first day of their junior year. After a minute or two, Joss cleared his throat. Nudging her playfully, he tried to keep his tone light. "So why'd you stop e-mailing me, anyway? The last I heard, you were going to Freedom Fest last year and then . . . nothing."

Meredith shrugged, her mood slightly somber. "I'm sorry, Joss. I've just been in a really weird place lately. Ever since Vlad dumped me, I just—"

"Vlad dumped you?" There was a hopeful, pleased tone in his voice, one he tried desperately to counter with a sympathetic glance. "That's awful. What happened?"

"Nothing."

"C'mon, you can tell me."

Meredith sighed, slowing her steps. "No, that's just it. *Noth-*

ing happened. One minute we were laughing and holding hands, the next he was pushing me away and telling me it was over."

Joss's thoughts raced. He knew, from the so-called friendship with Vlad two years before, that there was no way that he would break up with Meredith unless something had made him. Joss needed to find out what that was.

On the outside, he tried to appear cool and calm. On the inside, however, he was overjoyed. Not only because now he might have a real chance with Meredith, but because now he didn't have to worry so much that she would end up as the next meal of a monster. "So it's over between the two of you?"

Part of him was elated that there was no longer anyone standing in his way, but part of him—the part that had been sent by the Slayer Society—was intrigued by the bits of information he was gathering about his prey. This one wasn't like most vampires. In fact, Vlad was unlike any vampire that Joss had ever encountered. Past experience had taught him that. This one was crafty, how else could he have broken through Joss's defenses and gotten so close to him. This one would have to be dealt with carefully.

"Yeah. I guess." The look in her eyes was one of immense sadness, something that sent Joss's blood boiling. He wanted to ask if she knew what kind of monster Vlad was, or if she'd ever been bitten and infected as one of his human slaves, but he couldn't. Not yet. Not without breaking protocol. And after a year of reconditioning, of being reminded of what he was, and what the monsters he was hunting were, Joss was all about following protocol.

He cleared his throat and said, "If you ever want to talk— about anything—I'm here for you, okay?"

She smiled and said, "You're sweet, Joss. I'm glad you're back in town."

They backed down the driveway and Henry began a slow, leisurely drive to the high school. Vlad neglected to comment that they'd have gotten there faster if they'd walked.

As they approached the school, Vlad spotted a pink-clad figure making her way up the sidewalk. Meredith. He watched her, wondering if she hated him, wondering what she'd say when they inevitably ran into each other in the hall. He'd almost become lost in his wonderment when he noticed the person walking next to her.

Time slowed to a crawl, the music on the radio suddenly sounded warped and distorted. As the car pulled into the parking lot, the pace of everyone outside was like that of a snail; even the birds seemed to be flying in slow motion. Vlad instantly knew the familiar face, the lean frame, the backpack . . . which was undoubtedly holding the tools necessary to kill him.

A car passed on the road and as Joss glanced at the passenger, time slowed to a crawl. Joss would have known that black hair, those pale features, the dark eyes anywhere.

Vladimir Tod.

Just one of the vampires he'd been sent here to kill.

He narrowed his eyes, taking in the pale skin, the thin frame, obvious clues to what Vlad really was. He should have known. He should have recognized the beast for what it was and taken action immediately last year, but he was blinded then, blinded by the want of friendship.

He wasn't blind now. Every ounce of his being was seeing 20/20.

Vladimir Tod was going to pay.

Like the villain in an old movie, Joss glanced back, meeting Vlad's eyes. And in that moment, that microsecond, Vlad's question was answered. They were no longer friends. Joss was here to finish what he had started their freshman year. And what's more, the guy code was only upheld between friends. There was no longer reason for him to stay away from Meredith.

Time picked up again, and the car passed Joss and Meredith by. As Henry pulled into a parking space, he said, "Sorry about that. I didn't know Joss was walking her to school or I'd have said something. I didn't even know he'd talked to her yet. Man, that guy moves fast."

Vlad reached up with his hand, touching it lightly to his chest, remembering that glint of silver in the light of the moon. "Yeah . . . he does."

8

A LESSON LEARNED

VLAD FOLLOWED HENRY'S LEAD, opening the door and getting out of the car, even though what he really wanted to do was to sink down in his seat and wait for the first day of school to be over. Henry and his fabulous car were immediately surrounded by curious students, so Vlad walked across the parking lot to the school's front doors alone. Every step seemed to take an hour, but finally, Vlad pulled open the front door to Bathory High and stepped inside to the usual chaos of the first day of school. Several new freshmen were wandering the halls, looking lost and scared. He slipped around them and into the gym long enough to grab his locker number and combination, then ducked back into the front hall to locker

133. He'd just opened it and dropped his backpack inside when he heard a familiar giggle to his left.

Swallowing the lump in his throat, Vlad turned his head. About ten lockers down stood Meredith. Joss was whispering something in her ear. Something that made her cheeks flush pink. Something that set Vlad's face on fire with jealousy. Joss paused long enough to smile at Vlad over Meredith's shoulder, then went back to whispering.

Vlad slammed his locker door shut and was two steps on his way to shoving Joss into next week when Henry grabbed him by the sleeve. "Chill, Vlad. Don't give him what he wants."

Vlad pulled away, his furious eyes on Joss. "He's going to come after me anyway. At least right now I'm ready for a fight."

Henry sighed and stepped into Vlad's view. "You're angry and jealous and in the mood to do some forceful dentistry. So you may be ready to fight, but you're not ready to win. Not against Joss. You need a cool head for that, and you know it."

Vlad glanced over at Meredith, who was chatting friendlily now with his mortal enemy (well, kinda mortal—Vlad *was* a vampire, after all . . . well, half-vampire, anyway), and tried to let Henry's words sink in. His friend was right, no matter how much he wanted to beat that smirk off Joss's face. So instead, he slipped quietly inside Joss's mind and made Joss bite his tongue hard. He slipped back out again. Maybe next time he'd make him walk into his locker door or something. With a deep breath, he turned away and followed Henry down the hall to first period.

Once he could no longer see Joss's face—or that hint of smugness in his eyes—Vlad immediately felt better. Maybe it would be a good idea to keep his distance from Joss. After all, that kind of negativity couldn't be good for Vlad's already frayed nerves.

Then again, neither could trigonometry first thing in the morning. But at least he had Henry to keep him company.

Mr. Evans was already scribbling things on the board when he and Henry walked in. He paused long enough to offer them a polite smile, but then went right back to jotting equations down—equations containing so many numbers and letters on either side of the equal sign that they made Vlad's stomach flip over with unease. He and Henry found seats near the back and sat down as the rest of the class filed in. Thankfully, Melissa Hart was nowhere in sight. Vlad didn't think he could stomach watching Henry make moon-eyes at her every day, all year long. Unfortunately, Eddie Poe was there instead, happily cradling his camera and staring at Vlad with an intensity that made him squirm.

Then, as if it were any other day, just a run-of-the-mill class day, the first hour of his first day as a junior commenced. And Vlad was immediately bored out of his skull.

The rest of the day flew by, and he hardly saw Joss at all. Even lunch was blissfully Joss- and Meredith-free, though it was tainted by the occasional annoying click from Eddie's camera. It was starting to look like a pretty great day, and Vlad's last class was taught by his favorite teacher—probably favorite person—on the planet. Otis Otis, ultracool uncle and vampire extraordinaire. Nothing could stain the day now.

Vlad had just dropped his books in his locker and grabbed a notebook and pen, ready for a good dose of mythology, when he felt a nudge in his mind. Not a word, so much as a familiar prickle that told him Otis wanted his attention. He turned and saw his uncle standing at his open classroom door. Students greeted him and walked inside, but standing in the hall, having a quiet discussion with Vlad's uncle, was Joss. Neither of them looked particularly happy about it, and Vlad wondered why Otis had wanted him to notice. With a casual pace, he made his way down the hall to Otis's door.

Otis seized the opportunity, acting surprised to see him. "Vladimir, it's good to see you. Young Joss here is a bit confused and insists that he's in my class, when my roster shows no such thing. Would you mind keeping an eye on things here until I return from the office?"

Vlad couldn't help but notice that Otis had said "I" instead of "we," meaning there was no way he planned on returning to class with Joss in tow. He didn't make eye contact with his former friend, but faked a pleasant smile to Otis. "No problem."

With his thoughts, he said, *"What are you worried about? It's not like he can stake either of us between quizzes, Otis."*

"I know reconnaissance when I see it, Vladimir. By the way,

someone's waiting for you inside. You should say hello." Otis turned and headed down the hall. Vlad thought about asking who was waiting for him, but he had a sneaking suspicion he already knew.

He stepped inside Otis's new classroom and there she was, looking every bit as pretty as she had the night he broke her heart. She was looking right at him. Vlad released a tense breath and said, "Hi, Meredith."

Good. Keep it casual. The last thing Vlad wanted was deep questioning about why he'd called their relationship quits. There just wasn't any charming way to say that you couldn't shake viewing your girlfriend as a cheeseburger. Vlad knew. He'd spent all summer thinking about just that.

Even now, the scent of her blood was almost too much to bear.

She bit her bottom lip, as if contemplating what to say to him. She settled on "Hi."

He wet his lips, and kept his eyes on anything but hers. "So . . . you're taking mythology, huh?"

With any luck, he could fend off her questions with polite chitchat until Otis got back. So far, so good. But her blood—that delicious taunting of B positive that lurked within her veins . . . it called out to Vlad's thirst. It was all he could do to force his fangs not to answer its siren song.

"So that's it then? You don't have anything more to say to me?" She sounded mad.

Vlad dared a look into her brown eyes. Yep. She was definitely angry. But he still didn't know what he was supposed to say to improve the situation. So instead, he blinked and pretended that he had no idea what she was talking about, even though he knew exactly what she was talking about, which was, of course, him turning into a giant jerk and breaking up with her for what seemed like no good reason. Even though he had two very good, very sharp reasons threatening to poke out from his gums at just the sight of her. He shrugged slightly. "What should I say?"

Meredith's eyes shined with the threat of angry tears. She wasn't buying Vlad's act at all, which told him two things: 1) He shouldn't think about trying out for the school play anytime soon, and 2) Girls were a lot smarter than boys gave them credit for. After a moment, Meredith said, "You could start with 'I'm sorry.'"

And she was right. He could. But *I'm sorry* was usually followed by an explanation of sorts. And *that* he couldn't give her. So he blinked again and wondered how much longer Otis would be, hoping like crazy that something—anything— would distract Meredith from the conversation and get her across the room from him, where she might be a bit safer from his appetite.

"You owe me an explanation, Vlad." She shook her head, lowering her voice to just above a whisper. "You owe me at least that."

With a look of pained disgust, Meredith shook her head and took her seat at the front of the class, near the windows.

Vlad watched her and frowned. There would be no fixing this, no apologies, no making anything right between them again.

Behind him, Otis said, "Let's find our seats, shall we?"

Vlad wandered to the back, the aisle nearest the door, to one of the only empty desks left, and took his seat. A moment later, Joss passed and took the seat behind him. Vlad stiffened and thought to Otis, *"What's he doing here?"*

"Learning all that he can about us, I'd wager." Otis turned his attention to the class, introducing himself and running down a list of things they could expect this year. Vlad couldn't help but smile. Otis used almost the exact same words that he had used the first time Vlad had seen him in eighth grade, telling the class that they could call him by either his first or last name, so long as the obligatory "Mr." proceeds their choice.

"I thought he wasn't on your roster."

Otis passed papers out to the kids in the front row, who began the well-rehearsed routine of passing them back. *"As did I. But according to Principal Snelgrove, he is—no doubt some maneuvering on behalf of the Slayer Society. It's not as if they haven't hacked a computer or two in their time."*

Vlad shook his head, overwhelmed by stress at Joss's close proximity. The last time Joss was this close to Vlad's back, Vlad ended up in the hospital. He breathed out, "So what now?" then caught himself and thought those same words to Otis, who had a stark eyebrow raised.

"We do as he's doing. We wait. And we watch."

It was a sound plan.

Only one problem. Vlad had a feeling he and Otis weren't the only ones Joss was watching.

Across the room, Meredith smiled in Vlad's general direction, but Vlad would have bet his life that she wasn't smiling at him.

He slumped in his seat and prepared himself for the longest school year yet. The hour crawled by, but at the end, he'd relaxed some with the knowledge that Joss wouldn't stake him in school—if anything, he had to worry about his nightly visits to the belfry.

Once class finally ended, Otis bid them all goodbye, and Vlad ducked out the door. He was just opening his locker when Joss walked by. Joss muttered under his breath, "Don't you just love the color pink in the late summer sun, Vlad?"

Vlad whipped around, knowing Joss was making a snide observation about Meredith, but before he could do or say anything, Henry had picked Joss up by the collar and slammed him against the lockers. Joss merely smiled.

Mr. Hunjo ripped the boys apart. His voice boomed out into the hallway. "McMillan! And . . . McMillan! Office! Now!"

Joss blew a kiss at Henry, taunting him. Henry's fist flew through the air, but Joss ducked it effortlessly. Mr. Hunjo grabbed them each by the collar and dragged them down the hall, barking that he had had just about enough out of the both of them.

To be honest, so had Vlad. He was already tired of Joss's

presence, and Henry had been absurdly overprotective lately. After all, if anybody deserved to take a swing at Joss, Vlad did, but Henry was trying to beat him to the punch, literally. Actually, he had once already.

Shutting his locker door, Vlad headed out the front doors. After a glance around for Eddie Poe and his all too present camera, he hurried to the side of the building. Several kids were walking by, so he had to stand there and look casual until the coast was clear. Once it was, Vlad did something he'd never done before—he floated up to the belfry in broad daylight. When he reached the window, he landed lightly on the balls of his feet and stepped inside.

The room was just as he'd left it. His father's leather chair was placed against the wall to his left, a small table covered with half-melted candles nestled beside it. Two large bookcases had been painstakingly lifted in pieces to Vlad's sanctuary and reassembled. The books that had once graced the room in high stacks were now lining the shelves neatly, but for one or two that Vlad had shoved haphazardly on top of the others on his way out after a long night of reading. Beside the bookcase Vlad had hung the framed picture of his father. He could see Tomas's face no matter where he stood in the room, and he rather liked that. He smiled briefly at the picture as he dropped his backpack to the floor. "Hi, Dad."

He pulled his journal from his backpack—pausing only briefly to remember the night Meredith had given it to him—and a pen. After plopping down in his dad's chair and rereading every entry he could find about Joss, he flipped to an empty page and began formulating the best way to take a slayer peacefully out of commission.

After an hour of staring at the blank page, Vlad gave up and closed the book.

9
Same Dog, New Tricks

VLAD CLOSED HIS LOCKER after anatomy and physiology and released a very deep breath. So far, he'd managed to avoid both Joss and Meredith all day long, and he was nearing the home stretch, quite literally—one more class and he'd be home. Two days of high school down. Only about five million to go.

Beside him, Melissa and Henry were mashed together in a make-out session that wasn't quite hidden by Henry's open locker door. Two teachers had passed by and said nothing to the slobbering couple. Vlad frowned, hoping they'd get caught. It wasn't that he wanted Henry to get in trouble, but it seemed at least a little unfair that he and Meredith had gotten caught and subsequently punished after innocently kissing in a broom closet last year, but Henry and Melissa were practically swallowing each other in public and nobody seemed to care. Just one of the perks of being popular, Vlad surmised. Still, it was annoying.

A girl that Vlad didn't recognize walked by, raising an eyebrow at the attached couple. Vlad smirked and jabbed a thumb at them. "Zombies. Can't you tell?"

The girl laughed and walked away, and Vlad's shoulders straightened just a little.

Finally, likely because they remembered they needed to breathe, Melissa and Henry parted. It sounded a bit like two suction cups being pulled apart.

Henry breathlessly whispered, "About tonight . . ."

Melissa pulled a small compact mirror from her purse and slathered on some lip gloss, shaking her head. "Sorry. Gotta cancel. But maybe Friday. I don't know."

Vlad watched Henry's ego visibly deflate. It was all he could do to bite his tongue.

As Melissa wandered off to join her friends—Meredith included, Vlad couldn't help but notice—Henry muttered, "So, Friday then."

After debating whether or not he should let him spend the rest of the day like this, Vlad decided that he couldn't stomach the barrage of high fives that would inevitably accompany Henry all the way to class, so he said, "You've got lip gloss on your cheek, dude, and Passion Pink is not your color."

Henry's mood clouded as he rubbed the pink shiny stuff away with the heel of his hand. To Vlad's immense surprise, he said, "I'm thinking of breaking up with Melissa."

Vlad just stared at him, hoping that it wasn't some kind of sick joke. "Really? Why?"

Henry retrieved his English book and shut his locker door. "I feel like she's using me. All she wants to do is make out when we're together, which is great and all, but that's it. Nothing else. No talking. No spending time getting close. Just . . . kissing."

Vlad snapped his mouth shut. Far be it for him to point out the irony to Mr. Make-out-with-any-girl-who's-willing-and-then-dump-them-right-after. When Henry looked at him, seeking his opinion, Vlad just nodded supportively.

Henry wasn't buying it. He wrinkled his brow in suspicion. "What is it?"

Vlad shook his head. "Nothing. I didn't say anything."

"You didn't have to say anything for me to know something's up. I may not be a mind reader like *some* people, Vlad, but I know when you're hiding something. What gives? You think I should reconsider?"

"No!" Vlad backtracked in an attempt to hide his joy at Henry's decision to break it off with Melissa, which wasn't easy. "I mean, no, that's not it at all. I just . . . well . . . Henry . . . haven't you noticed that you tend to treat girls exactly how Melissa is treating you now?"

Henry stared at him blankly.

Vlad ran a frustrated hand through his hair, brushing his bangs from his eyes. "You've probably kissed three-quarters of the girls here at Bathory High, Henry, but have only really dated one. Do you see what I mean?"

Henry nodded with confidence. "I'm a good kisser."

"No."

"Trust me, I am."

"That's not what I mean, Henry." He took a deep breath and restrained the urge to strangle his best friend. "I'm just saying that . . . look, does it hurt when Melissa wants to kiss you but not spend time getting to know you, even though you want to get to know her and just be with her?"

"Well, *yeah.*" Henry used the same tone he always used to say "Well, *duh.*"

Vlad waited for Henry to piece together the logic in his mind. When he didn't, Vlad said, "Did it ever occur to you how many girls you've made feel the same way you're feeling now?"

Henry stood there for a moment, blinking. Then his shoulders sank, and all the puzzle pieces slowly fit together for him. "Oh."

Vlad slapped him on the back. "Chew on that awhile, Romeo. I'm late for mythology. We'll have to explore this new revelation in our next session."

He made his way down the hall and moved inside Otis's classroom casually, not letting anyone who might be watching see his growing tension at what awaited him there. It wasn't paranoia. He knew he was being waited for, and when he glanced at Joss on the way to his desk, he could see that he was right. Joss was smiling that cool, superior smile that he'd added to his armory ever since his return. Vlad felt himself brace, felt himself ready a glare, but stopped and just looked at Joss, at this boy who had been his friend. For a moment, he forgave Joss for staking him, for threatening him, and for flirting openly with Meredith. For a moment, he just looked at Joss and tried to let him know with his eyes just how badly he wanted things to go back to the way they were.

Joss's smile slipped, and all the anger and resentment melted away for a microsecond, replaced by regret. Then Joss looked away.

Maybe there was hope. Maybe somehow, through all the hatred and threats and betrayal, maybe their friendship could survive. Maybe Joss—the real Joss, the Joss he knew—could be saved from the Slayer Society somehow.

Or maybe Vlad was just stubbornly clinging to a ridiculous, unfounded sense of hope. He wasn't sure. But one thing he did know: even though he positively loathed Joss the slayer . . . he missed Joss the friend.

Vlad took his seat, fighting the urge to turn around, to talk this all out with Joss and make everything okay again. Sure, he was still furious that Joss had tried to take his life a year and a half before. Sure, he still suffered the occasional nightmare, always accompanied by that fateful whisper: "For you, Cecile." But what it boiled down to was that Joss had been told all sorts of horrible lies about vampires, and maybe, if

Vlad tried hard enough, he could get Joss to see the truth. It was possible, wasn't it? No matter how unlikely, it was possible. People had been saved from cultlike groups before. Couldn't Joss be saved too? Couldn't Vlad save him?

He looked up as Otis hurriedly entered the room. After a second, the door closed behind Otis, who paused and closed his eyes for a moment, as if berating himself. Vlad thought back to the last day of school his eighth grade year, when the door had mysteriously closed just when it seemed Otis had wanted it to. He mulled over the two moments, so similar-looking, and wondered if Otis had a skill he'd not yet shared with Vlad. Flipping open his mythology book to where they'd left off yesterday, he decided to ask his uncle after class if the ability to move objects with but a thought were possible. But he didn't know if Otis would own up to it, even if his theory was correct.

He was mulling this over when he felt a distinct, familiar poke in his back. Sharp. Wood. A stake. Joss had a stake.

Without thinking, without considering any other possibility at all, Vlad stood and whipped around, yanking what Joss held in his hand away and shoving him over, sending his desk tumbling onto its side. It was only then that Vlad realized that Joss had been poking him with a pencil. He dropped it on the floor and glanced at Otis. "Sorry. I . . . sorry."

Otis pursed his lips. "Office. Both of you."

The word had barely formed in his mind before Joss stood and spoke it aloud. "What?"

Otis barked, "OFFICE!"

Not daring to question, Vlad huffed down the hall, keeping Joss in his peripheral vision the entire time. He hated that he wanted to fix the friendship they'd had, hated that he wanted very much to rescue Joss from the twisted web of the Slayer Society, and completely loathed the idea of trying to reason with Joss when he was acting like a lunatic. He tried to ignore it, but there it was, burning a hole through his chest—what Vlad wanted more than anything, but couldn't have: for him and Joss to be buds again. What's more, he wanted to beat some sense into Joss, and that wasn't a wise idea either. Especially since they'd probably just earned at least one afternoon of detention.

Principal Snelgrove met them in the outer office. "I don't care what happened. I don't want excuses. I don't want blame games. You'll both have in-school suspension tomorrow. I will not tolerate fighting! Is that understood?"

Vlad nodded. Snelgrove growled at Joss, "I said is that understood, Mr. McMillan?"

Finally, Joss nodded too. "Yes, sir."

The rest of the day was a blur. Suspension? It didn't matter if it was in school or not, Nelly was going to kill him. And Otis . . . what was he thinking, sending them to the office? He had to know it was Joss's fault.

One thing was for sure. Vlad was done tiptoeing around something he'd wanted to ask Otis for years now.

Once the final bell had rung, Vlad grabbed his backpack from his locker and headed to Otis's classroom, where he perched on the edge of his uncle's desk, watching Otis tuck things neatly into his old leather doctor's bag. Making sure to speak quietly, calmly, Vlad said, "Otis, how do you close doors without touching them?"

Otis snapped his eyes to Vlad, looking very much caught. He didn't say anything for a long time. Finally, as if coming to the conclusion that his nephew deserved an answer, he said, "It's something that I realized I could do only about six years ago . . . after I'd fed on vampire blood."

Vlad felt like he'd been punched in the chest. He mulled over a few theories, then settled on the obvious choice. "Dorian's idea?"

Otis breathed out a sigh and ran a trembling hand through his hair. "After Tomas left Elysia, I was lost. Dorian took me under his wing, tried to show me what more life had to offer. It was foolish of me—I knew the kind of man Dorian was . . . is—but I went along with him to a party full of vampires and humans. We killed the humans, drank them dry. And in my drunken state of bloodlust, I relented to Dorian's will and fed on a vampire as well. Dorian finished him off."

Vlad gasped, and not just at Otis's actions. "He killed a vampire?"

Otis closed his bag and met Vlad's eyes. "Yes, but the Council of Elders won't touch him. No law can. Dorian is . . . protected."

Vlad mulled this over for a bit. He couldn't imagine Otis feeding on a roomful of people. But then, he couldn't imagine

Otis feeding on anyone. He'd only ever seen his uncle feed on one person, on Henry, and that was out of necessity, not greed. "What was it like, feeding on a vampire?"

"It was wrong. And wonderful. Nothing compares. It was powerful . . . like pure light inside my veins." Otis's eyes went wide, then horrified at the memory of however that blood had made him feel. "Dorian's palate disgusts me, but I understand his tastes."

"And the telekinesis?"

"It started the next day. I try not to use it in front of other vampires, for fear they'll learn that I've fed from one of our own. I don't know if it's a common side effect or not." Otis wet his lips. "Have you experienced anything like that since I gave you my blood after Joss staked you?"

Vlad thought it over for a moment, but nothing unusual came to mind. "As far as I can tell, I haven't changed at all."

Otis nodded thoughtfully. "Perhaps it was Dorian's blood— the vampire we drank from was his creation, his son, after all."

Vlad gawked. "He killed his son just for a snack? That's seriously twisted."

Otis squeezed Vlad's shoulder and steered him toward the door. "Stay away from him, Vlad. Dorian is brilliant and cunning. He's also extremely dangerous, and he's taken a liking to you."

They entered the hallway, and Vlad watched as Otis locked his classroom door. He couldn't help but ask, "In the same way he took a liking to you?"

Otis turned, leading him down the hall, toward the front

doors of the school. "No. In the same way he took a liking to his son."

Vlad gulped and decided that staying away from Dorian would be top priority, right alongside steering clear of Joss when he was in a staking mood. Which was probably always. Maybe it was better if Vlad just wasn't alone again . . . ever.

As they made their way down the steps, waving to the janitor on their way by, Otis said, "I won't be dropping you off at home today, Vlad. Vikas is expecting you."

"Expecting me?" Vlad racked his brains but couldn't recall having arranged anything with Vikas.

Otis nodded, unlocking the rusty door of his crappy car. As he slid into the driver's seat and Vlad slid in next to him, he said, "You'll be training for two hours every afternoon. Vikas wants to get you sharp. Especially with a slayer in town."

Vlad frowned at his heavy backpack. "I suppose you expect me to do homework too."

Otis laughed. "Of course."

The car turned this way and that, until it found its way down Lugosi Trail and Otis brought it to a stop in front of Vlad's former home. Once inside, Otis excused himself upstairs to grade papers. Vikas was waiting in the kitchen with a stern expression on his face. Vlad immediately wondered if he was in trouble.

"Today, Mahlyenki Dyavol, I will teach you what I know about the Slayer Society. Then we will practice how to effectively dispatch a slayer."

There was no question in Vikas's tone, no possibility that Vlad might not want to know these things. He had to know them, and Vikas was determined to teach him. Just in case. Vlad nodded slowly, and dropped his backpack to the floor.

Vikas pointed to the chair across from him. "Sit."

Vlad sat, feeling all the while like he was in trouble, like he was being punished. When he spoke, his voice was gruff. "What if I don't need today's lesson, Vikas? What if Joss changes his mind?"

Vikas's brow furrowed, as if what he was about to say was enormously difficult for him. "I have seen his thoughts, Vladimir. He thinks of nothing but taking your life. You must learn how to defend yourself against your enemy. You must know how to kill Joss when the time comes."

When. Not if.

Vlad stood, his heart racing. "No matter what he did in the past, Joss is my friend. I'm not going to—"

Then suddenly, he felt Vikas in his mind. As Vikas spoke, he nudged Vlad, forcing him to follow his simple, firm instruction. "Sit."

Vlad sat, but not of his own free will.

"This is vital knowledge that you must have if you are to survive another encounter with this slayer. I have promised your uncle that I would ensure your safety and I shall. Though it would bring me great pleasure to dispatch this slayer myself, I have been told that I cannot unless he first breaks the peace between us. Therefore, that task falls to the first of us to be attacked. Should that be you, Mahlyenki Dyavol, you will need what I will teach you today. I will teach you and you will learn, even if I have to hold you here with my mind the entire time."

Vlad swallowed hard, vowing never to mention to Vikas or his uncle that Joss had already made the first move. Or that he was determined to find a way to free Joss from the Society's clutches.

Vikas released his hold on Vlad's mind and began his lesson, despite Vlad's protests. "The Slayer Society is a relatively small group of humans—all but a few male, all but a few middle-aged—who are bent on the destruction of vampirekind. We have no one to blame but ourselves, of course, as it was a vampire who created the slayers."

Vlad raised his eyebrows in surprise, but remained silent, very much irritated at Vikas's use of mind control.

"As you know, there are laws. The highest law being that no vampire should dare take the life of a fellow vampire. However, that is not to say that there are not certain vampires that deserve death, or that there are not those who would use the death of another to increase their own standing in Elysia." A puzzled look crossed Vlad's face. Vikas answered the question that Vlad had not yet asked, "Politics are the same in all cultures, it matters not what type of government they follow. To work around this law, which brings with it the absolute punishment of death—"

Vlad's heart all but stopped. Otis had killed Ignatius last

year. He could only imagine what that meant for his uncle.

"—a vengeful vampire by the name of Terryn took it upon himself to inform a small group of humans that vampires existed, with the explicit purpose of training them how to take down his vampire enemies. Revealing the truth of Elysia is a high crime, yes, but with his new group of assassins behind him, no one on the council dared to defy him. So Terryn lived several happy years after organizing his group of slayers, until they killed him."

Vlad, intrigued by the history lesson, finally found his voice. "But why wouldn't Terryn have just turned the slayers into his drudges and command them to obey him?"

"You're quite astute, Mahlyenki Dyavol, for that is exactly what he did, and he blinded them to the fact that he was a vampire." Vikas smiled to see that Vlad had decided to turn this into a discussion rather than a lecture. Vlad could feel Vikas's control release. He trusted Vlad to stay put. "However, that too is a violation of Elysian law. You see, a vampire is only allowed to bind himself to two humans. Any more than that and our connection with them becomes too diminished to maintain control over all of them at once. Terryn's original group consisted of thirty-four. And he trained them so well to recognize a vampire's characteristics that they eventually saw through his control and realized his true nature. He became a victim of his own creation."

Vikas had barely moved since he started talking. He was still sitting at the kitchen table with his hands clasped in front of him. Vlad noticed that the expression on his face had soft-ened, but only just. "You knew him, didn't you?"

"Yes. There was a time that I had called Terryn my friend. But that was before he lost touch with Elysia. Before he de-cided to lift himself to a position of power that he knew was not meant for him." A hint of remorse flashed in his eyes. "Even so, I was sad to hear of his death."

"So, then what happened?"

Vikas finally shifted in his seat and regained his compo-sure. "Ever since that day in 1835, there has always been a Slayer Society, though their beliefs have warped and twisted over time to the point where their goal—the destruction of vampirekind—borders on religion. They believe that new slayers are not chosen, but that the small piece of Terryn which was put into each of the original members shows itself in a member of their own family. The society members that exist now are all direct descendants of the original slayers. They believe that vampires are evil monsters, who drink ba-bies' blood and sleep in coffins. They are persistent, resilient, and will stop at nothing to do us in. They are our enemies. And as we created them, it is our right, our duty, to rid the world of them."

Vlad chewed his bottom lip for a moment before saying, "I understand your concerns, Vikas, but why are you telling me all of this?"

Vikas met his gaze. "Because you've made it quite clear that you do not understand the severity of the slayer's presence. To your uncle or me, dispatching the boy would be a fairly easy task. But to you, you who are still committed to a nonexistent friendship with him, it won't be quite so simple."

Shaking his head, Vlad stood at last. "Joss isn't going to try to kill me."

"It is your denial that will end your life, just as sure as his stake." Vikas stood and crossed the kitchen to the window. As he stared out at the backyard, his fingers traced the lines on his forehead. After a moment of quiet contemplation, he turned back to face Vlad. "Prepare yourself for what will come, Vladimir, or you will die, and neither Otis nor I will be able to prevent it."

Vlad was looking at the man who had been his friend and mentor for two years now—one of the very few people on the planet who knew his secrets (well, most of them anyway) and who he knew he could trust, and had, trusted with his life. Even though he stared directly into Vikas's eyes, they both knew that Vlad was somewhere else, lost in his own thoughts.

Vikas was right. No matter how much Vlad hoped and wished that he wasn't, he was right. The Joss he knew from his past was muted by the Joss he'd become, and clinging to the memory of the boy he knew two years ago was putting Vlad and those he cared about in danger. He would never hunt Joss, nor would he allow anyone else to. He would cling to the hope that a new friendship could be built between them, and that Joss may yet be saved from the cultlike ways of the Slayer Society. He would cling to the tense peace that existed between them. But if Joss should break that peace, Vlad needed to be prepared.

And he would be.

Reluctantly, he sighed. "Okay. Tell me what I need to know."

10
MONSTERS

IN-SCHOOL SUSPENSION was clearly invented by someone who really, really despised the idea of kids doing anything but homework and who thought that staring blankly at the wall without speaking was just about the most entertaining thing in the world to do. They were obviously evil to the core, and Vlad was cursing their unknown name during his entire trek down the hall and over to the old wooden door at the end of the hall, just past the cafeteria.

The door was scraped up and ugly—fitting, considering it opened up to a fate worse than most prisons. And lucky Vlad, he wasn't serving this sentence alone. Bad enough he'd be spending the day doing schoolwork in a forced silence that many monks would envy, but he had to do it all in the company of the one boy who'd already come close to killing him once and probably would try again.

With a deep, depressed breath, Vlad turned the knob and opened the door.

He'd never seen the inside of the ISS room, so he really had no idea what to expect. Immediately, there were three small steps to climb and once his feet hit the wooden floor, he recognized what the room had once been. He'd heard that many years ago there had once been a stage attached to what now served as the cafeteria, but that it had been walled off and turned into storage. Apparently, that storage room was also home to ISS. Boxes and various odds and ends lined three of the walls. Five desks sat facing an empty one. Two were occupied by boys that looked like bad news. Vlad took his seat nearest the door.

A moment later, the door opened again. Joss took a quick look around and approached the desks. After a glance at their rather scary-looking company, he begrudgingly took the seat next to Vlad.

Vlad chewed the inside of his cheek absently. He very much wanted to say something to Joss, something that would break the tension, but nothing came to mind.

The ugly door opened and Mr. Hunjo wedged his immense shoulders inside. He went straight to the small desk at the front of the room and barked, "What are you staring at? Get to work!"

Vlad finished up his schoolwork relatively quickly, and afterward, sat quietly, waiting for the day to come to an end.

The room's silence was only broken by the soft snoring of Mr. Hunjo, who'd succumbed to boredom and had decided that his best defense was a good nap. Vlad looked over at Joss and dared to whisper, "Why are you in Otis's class? What do you want?"

Joss shrugged halfheartedly. "What else, but to learn mythology? You know ... unicorns, trolls ... vampires."

He met Vlad's eyes then, and Vlad resisted the urge to read his thoughts. He didn't really want to understand how a slayer thinks, what a slayer feels. He just wanted to be left alone.

Remembering they weren't the only ones in the room, Vlad said, "So you have an interest in the make-believe, eh?"

Joss leaned closer and, after they both jumped at a particularly loud snort from the sleeping gym teacher, he responded, "I believe in truth and justice and the good of mankind. No matter how much bloodshed it takes to protect those things."

Joss's eyes were full of an eagerness that sent a terrified chill through Vlad. He shook his head in shock. "You're a monster."

Joss was quiet for a while. Then he sat back and returned to his schoolwork, but not before uttering, "It takes one to know one, Vlad."

11
A Snap

SPRAT BOUNDED FROM THE CAR to the door of The Crypt, dragging October along behind him. Kristoff was already inside and Andrew was following at a leisurely pace. Vlad was bent over, tying his shoe near the car.

He was relieved to be back at The Crypt for a night, as the past month of classes with Joss were already seriously stressing him out and he needed to blow off some steam. Plus, it had become a regular thing to do with his goth friends.

Friends. Vlad had friends. He shook his head, smiling.

As the door to the club closed behind Andrew, Vlad stood and moved toward it, ready to feel the thumping of bass in his chest and smell the adrenaline in the dancers' veins.

"It does smell delicious, doesn't it?"

Vlad clamped down on his thoughts and turned. He knew that voice. His eyes scanned the shadows until he noticed something dark moving within them. His chest tightened— partly from fear, partly from surprise. "What do you want?"

D'Ablo stepped into the street-lamp light. He was dressed in black from head to toe, complete with black leather gloves. Gloves. Plural. Which meant that D'Ablo had somehow sprouted a new hand. Vlad slanted his eyes, examining the hand. The fingers didn't move. The muscles didn't flex. When realization hit him, he said, "You're wearing a false hand. How does the council feel about that? After all, vampires aren't big fans of weaknesses and scars, are they, D'Ablo? It's a wonder they haven't removed you from office."

D'Ablo pursed his lips. "They're happy enough in their ignorance."

Vlad tilted his head in disbelief, thinking about the gathered group of angry vampires at his old house just five weeks ago. "I know several people who aren't so happy that a disfigured vampire is still president."

The corner of D'Ablo's mouth rose slightly in a small smile. "I assure you that *none* of those people matter."

Vlad's eyes traced D'Ablo's face for any sign of scars. When he saw him last, flames had all but melted his face away, but now the skin was smooth, flawless, as if that maniacal moment in the sun had never occurred. "The sunlight . . . it didn't damage or scar you at all?"

"With enough blood, healing is possible, even from the

likes of the sun. But you . . . you didn't burn at all. Did you, Master Pravus?" His eyebrows went up. It was as if he were defying Vlad to once again insist that he wasn't the child the prophecy had spoken of.

Vlad set his jaw. "No."

"So you've finally accepted that you are the Pravus?"

"Yes." What did D'Ablo want, anyway? It wasn't like they were friends or anything. "I'm assuming you didn't come here to chat, so what is it you want, D'Ablo?"

D'Ablo chuckled under his breath. "You know what I want. My ritual is not yet complete."

Vlad froze. The ritual. D'Ablo had said that the last part of the ritual required Vlad's sacrifice. He darted his eyes to the front door of The Crypt and silently wondered if he could outrun D'Ablo, or if D'Ablo would chase after him if he did. "So you're here to kill me?"

D'Ablo sighed, somewhat troubled. "Unfortunately, no. It seems I've misplaced my dagger. In order for the ritual to be completed correctly, the dagger is required. But never fear, Master Pravus. I am here to offer you a truce."

Before Vlad could bite his tongue, he snapped, "In your dreams, D'Ablo. That is *never* going to happen."

D'Ablo raised an eyebrow. "I am no threat to you without the dagger, and if I cannot be the Pravus I can at least assist him."

Vlad shook his head, filled with loathing. "You've 'assisted' me enough. Almost into an early grave."

D'Ablo held his palms out, pleading. "Hear me out."

Vlad turned back to the club, tossing bitter words over his shoulder as he left. "Bite me."

He'd barely taken a breath before D'Ablo was beside him, wrapping his hand tightly around Vlad's throat. Vlad tried to inhale, but couldn't. D'Ablo lifted him slowly off the ground and growled into his ear. "Of course, there's always the appeal of killing you just to silence that mouth. All it would take is a snap."

He squeezed tighter before letting Vlad go. A warning.

Vlad coughed, rubbing at his sore neck. In a hoarse, raspy voice, he called after D'Ablo, who was once again disappearing into the shadows, "You'll never be the Pravus, D'Ablo. I don't care what any ritual says. And a truce? You're out of your mind."

"A snap, Master Pravus." He chuckled again, causing Vlad to shiver. "A snap."

12
NOBODY

A SOUND TO VLAD'S RIGHT, SHARP AND FAMILIAR. Vlad turned his head toward it, as did D'Ablo. Dorian was standing there, an expectant smirk on his face, his hand held up as if he'd just snapped his fingers. "Nothing? I did snap, after all."

At the sight of him, Vlad's chest grew tight. Fear. Intense fear. He was now standing in the presence of the two most dangerous vampires he'd ever encountered, both of whom wanted his blood for one reason or another. He swallowed the lump in his throat and fought back the urge to run.

D'Ablo's jaw tightened. "Dorian. I wasn't expecting you."

"So I presumed. If you were, you likely wouldn't have been threatening this boy. *This* boy, in particular, now would you?"

Dorian tilted his head, his eyes slanting. It was as if D'Ablo had been caught playing with one of his toys. Vlad shrank back, revolted. Is that what he was to vampirekind? Just an object to argue over, just a freak who might fulfill their needs?

D'Ablo flicked his gaze to Vlad with a warning. "I assure you, it was no mere threat."

No surprise there. D'Ablo hadn't exactly been shy about trying to kill Vlad in the past.

"You're telling me." Dorian took what seemed like a casual step closer to D'Ablo, then another, and another. With each, D'Ablo appeared a bit more on edge. It was nice to see him afraid, for once. "You're actually telling me that you would kill Tomas's son? You, who once preached that Tomas was deserving of a seat on the Council of Elders?"

D'Ablo said nothing in reply.

Dorian clucked his tongue, quieting his voice as if they shared a secret. "I think we both understand why that would be a poor choice."

Vlad had been ready to back away and break into a run, but now he furrowed his brow in slight confusion, the thought of running suddenly evaporating in the cool night air. "What about my dad? What are you hinting at?"

Dorian and D'Ablo looked back at Vlad, looking like they'd only just remembered his presence. Dorian moved his eyes back to D'Ablo and nodded toward Vlad. "Tell him."

D'Ablo scowled. He wasn't about to tell Vlad anything.

But then Dorian's expression grew serious. He repeated, "Tell him."

Immediately, D'Ablo turned to Vlad and spoke. "If I took your life, everyone who ever loved your father would not stop until I was tortured and killed. A life for a life. I would lose my position as president, my belongings would become the belongings of your loved ones, and my name would be mocked for centuries to come. Your father was a very power-ful and influential man. If I were to murder his son, I would regret it."

Once the final word passed over his lips, he seemed to re-gain control of himself. His face reddened in anger and ha-tred, and if his eyes could have shot lasers, they would have burned a hole right through Dorian.

Dorian merely smiled, obviously enjoying his control over D'Ablo. "That wasn't so bad, was it? It's fun to tell the truth. Is there any other truth you'd like to share with Vlad?"

A curt reply, one filled with venom. "No."

Dorian raised a sharp eyebrow, as if defying D'Ablo to speak. "Nothing about his father? Nothing about your plans?"

Vlad shot a look between the two older vampires. Plans? How did any of D'Ablo's plans have anything to do with Vlad's dad?

D'Ablo's scowl deepened, hatred spewing from every pore in his body. "No."

"Very well, then." Dorian turned back to Vlad, then glanced

over his shoulder at D'Ablo in an afterthought. "You may go now."

D'Ablo stalked off without another word, dismissed, like a household servant.

Dorian sighed, shaking his head at Vlad like they were old friends. "I have never liked that guy."

Now Vlad was alone with Dorian. Immediately, Vlad's heart picked up its pace. As if listening to a symphony, Dorian closed his eyes, his head swimming with the sound of Vlad's heartbeat. In an effort to snap him out of his daydream, Vlad said, "Nobody likes D'Ablo. At least, nobody I know."

"You'll be surprised."

Vlad furrowed his brow. *You'll* not *you'd*. As if Dorian knew something he wasn't telling Vlad.

"Less people like me than our friend D'Ablo, I'm afraid."

"Something tells me you're never afraid. Of anything." In an afterthought, Vlad took a step back.

A strange smile lit up Dorian's face and he shrugged casually, almost sheepishly.

Several seconds passed before Vlad said, "So . . . what do you want?"

"I've come to proposition you. It is within my power to save your uncle's life, but he is too stubborn to agree to a trade. So I implore you. Give me your blood and I will help your uncle survive his trial." He spoke so matter-of-factly that it sounded as if he'd rehearsed his speech all the way here, as if he'd practiced it over and over again, perhaps out loud, until it sounded perfect, until his demand seemed sane and rational, everything that Dorian most certainly was not. His eyes told Vlad that he was completely serious, but his eager nod seemed almost childlike. He waited, and when Vlad failed to give him a thumbs-up on the idea, he sighed, troubled. "If I have to take your blood by force, Otis will die. I'm sorry, Vlad, but I cannot control this urge. I must have your blood, at any cost."

Vlad's heart rammed against his ribs. As if it wasn't bad enough that Dorian wanted his blood, now he was left to choose between his life and Otis's. He swallowed hard, wondering how both Dorian and D'Ablo had chosen this exact night to get on his case, and if they were somehow working together. After all, they both seemed to be after the same thing. "Why ask? Why not force me right now?"

After a moment, it hit him. Vlad took in a shaky breath. "You're afraid you'll fail again. I beat you before, and that scared you. Because no one beats you, do they, Dorian?"

Dorian's mouth settled slowly into a frown, as if he were uncomfortable with the idea of anyone knowing his secrets. The irony did not escape Vlad. An all-powerful vampire, afraid of anyone finding out his deepest fears? That was one for the books. Dorian cleared his throat before speaking. "That's not all. I . . . derive pleasure from the idea that the boy who would be Pravus would bend to my will."

Vlad's stomach turned. "Not just hungry for blood, but

power too, eh? You're just like some spoiled kid, used to getting his way."

Dorian grew quiet for some time, finally breaking it to whisper, "You might say that."

Vlad shook his head. "The answer is no. You can't have my blood. Not one drop. I've had enough excitement for the night, thanks."

As Vlad turned to walk away, he felt his body stiffen. Before he knew what was happening, he turned to face Dorian again . . . but not of his own free will.

Dorian nodded apologetically. "I am sorry, but you do force my hand."

Against his will, Vlad moved closer, bending his head to the side, beckoning Dorian to drain his veins dry. Dorian's fangs slipped from his gums, ready, eager to partake, his eyes locked on the throbbing blue vein on Vlad's neck.

Inside Vlad's skull, Vlad ranted, raved, screamed, but there was nothing he could do to stop this moment from happening.

To his left, there was the familiar squeak of the club door, followed by October's voice. "What's taking you so long?"

Without a word, Dorian released his mental grip and stepped back. Strangely, he looked almost as relieved as Vlad felt. He moved down the street, disappearing into the night, but not before his voice echoed in Vlad's mind. *"That girl just saved you. She saved us both."*

Vlad's hands were shaking. That was close. Too close. And

what had Dorian meant, saved them both? He wasn't the one in danger of being drained here.

He turned back to October, who had a sharp eyebrow raised. "Who was that?"

Vlad rubbed absently at his neck, wondering silently what the look in Dorian's eyes, what the words in Vlad's mind, had meant. "Nobody. It was nobody."

13

OUTSPOKEN ENEMIES

VLAD CHEWED A BITE of his peanut butter, jelly, and blood-capsule sandwich and swallowed, but it didn't go down easy. He couldn't stop watching the exchange that was happening two tables over and wishing like crazy that he had some kind of supersensitive hearing. Unfortunately, vampires were nothing at all like superheroes. So Vlad watched, trying to learn on the spot how to read lips and failing miserably.

He kept fighting back yawns, completely exhausted by his recent training sessions with Vikas, who had promised him that they would only get more difficult. Not to mention how much sleep he'd been losing since his encounter with both D'Ablo and Dorian two weeks before.

After a few more seconds of squinting at Joss's moving lips, he almost smacked himself in the forehead, wondering how exactly a vampire momentarily forgets about that whole mind-reading thing. He laid his head on the table and closed his eyes, slipping stealthily into Joss's head, content to linger long enough to learn what Joss and Eddie were discussing.

Joss's head hurt. He was tense and anxious, but not uncertain in the least. He was doing the right thing . . . for the good of mankind.

Vlad rolled his eyes. Whatever you gotta tell yourself to sleep through the night, Joss.

Eddie's voice came out in a breath. "I can't believe it. I mean, I can. I knew he was a vampire, but I had no idea you knew. Who else knows?"

A picture of Henry popped into Joss's thoughts, but he couldn't out his cousin, couldn't endanger Henry's life because he was being stupid and reckless . . . and was likely under Vlad's control. "Just us. And we have to keep it that way."

"So what do we do? I mean, he has to be stopped. And . . . I want proof to show people."

Joss raised an eyebrow. "You don't believe me?"

Eddie leaned forward, excitement in his tone. "No, I believe you. But I want the newspapers to believe me. I want the television programs to believe me."

"You want to be famous for proving to the world that vampires exist?"

"Yes."

Joss tightened his jaw, disgusted. If Eddie weren't proving to be useful, he'd walk away from this conversation and deny it had ever taken place. But he did seem to be of use, which is why Joss had confided in him in the first place. Joss wet his lips and a lie escaped his mouth. "Give me time, and I'll make you more famous than you have ever dreamed."

Eddie sat back, looking more than a little pleased. He shook his head and chuckled. "I'm glad nobody's listening to us talk. They'd think we were both crazy whack-jobs."

Vlad pulled out of Joss's thoughts, sat up, and chuckled. At the same time, Joss looked at him and pursed his lips. The look in his eyes said he knew Vlad had been listening, even if he wasn't entirely sure how. Vlad smiled pleasantly and waved.

It wasn't that he was happy about what he'd overheard, but at some point, his sanity was bound to break at the ridiculousness that was his life. Why not now?

"Why are you smiling?" October had a thin black eyebrow raised and was looking at Vlad in the way that said she was pretty sure he'd lost his mind, and she was totally cool with that.

Vlad shook his head. "The voices in my head said something funny. So what are you up to tonight?"

"Hanging at The Crypt with the guys . . . and Snow." She pursed her purple-painted lips as if her next words were delicate ones. "She likes you, you know. And I think you like her. So why aren't you two dating?"

Deep inside Vlad's chest, something twitched. He was pretty sure it was part of his heart—probably the part that had really liked the way it felt when Snow kissed him. He shrugged slightly. "What makes you think she likes me?"

"Because when you're not around, you're all she talks about. And when you are around, her eyes light up and she looks genuinely happy. I know that look in Snow's eyes, because it's something rare to see." She snatched a cookie from his hand and took a bite, chewing thoughtfully. "You've met her father, Vlad. You've gotta know Snow's home life is nothing to smile about. Her school life is stressed, and until you came along, our nights at The Crypt were just about the only thing Snow had to smile about."

Vlad pulled his collar away from his neck. Was it hot in here? He glanced around nervously, desperately looking for a change in conversation.

October pointed the half-eaten cookie at him. "I know she likes you, because she's my best friend. I don't have to hear her say it—just like I don't have to see you two kiss to know you've done it."

With every word she said, Vlad sank down in his seat just a little bit. If she kept talking, he was going to wind up on the floor, feeling like a jerk for having let Snow kiss him.

Finally, October sighed. "So . . . why aren't you dating?"

"Because . . ." Vlad tried to resist, but his eyes flicked to Meredith as she passed their table.

October shook her head. A subtle anger burned on the

edges of her frown. "Oh, I see. She's good enough to make out with, but she's not Meredith Brookstone?"

"This has nothing to do with Meredith. I like Snow, but we're friends. Just friends." But even as he spoke the words, he wasn't confident that he believed them. Admitting that to October, however, wasn't going to help things at all.

"I swear, Vlad. I know that Henry McMillan is your best friend, but I really didn't think that you were that much alike."

Vlad winced at the thought of sharing Henry's reputation. Was he that bad? Was it so obvious to the world that he was allowing his inner monster to use Snow, and treating her like less of a person than she actually was? Guilt gnawed at his insides. Eddie and Joss were right. He was an inhuman beast. He had to be stopped.

October picked up her tray in one hand and gathered her books into her free arm. "You'd better tell Snow that you've got her stuck firmly in the Friend Zone, Vlad. Because she's falling hard for you, and I don't want her to get hurt."

Vlad gulped. He was pretty sure he was more afraid of October's fury than D'Ablo's ritual and Dorian's cravings combined. "I will."

Before she walked away, she leaned down and hissed into his ear, "And if you think I buy that 'this has nothing to do with Meredith' crap, you're dreaming."

Vlad laid his head back on the table. October was right. Something had to be done about Snow, and not just because she had a huge crush on Vlad. Ever since she'd kissed him,

Vlad found himself lingering for hours in the alley after feeding sessions. He found himself spending more time around her, which wasn't a bad thing. But he also couldn't shake Meredith from his thoughts, which was completely unfair to Snow. He couldn't date one girl knowing he still loved another. And he did love Meredith.

Didn't he?

He liked her, cared deeply for her, couldn't stop thinking about all the hand-holding they did, all the meaningful kisses they exchanged. He missed her. But did he love her still?

Vlad looked over at Meredith, who was giggling at something Joss said and twirling a lock of her hair around one finger.

Yes, he decided. Yes, he did still love Meredith. And probably always would.

And that meant he needed to take a step back from Snow. Maybe a lot of steps.

The rest of Vlad's day crawled by in a clouded mist of contemplation. He barely paid attention to his teachers. And surprisingly, he didn't think much about his feelings for Meredith. He thought about Snow, and which was more important to him, her blood or her feelings. He liked Snow and really enjoyed their long conversations about anything and everything—her rotten home life, his struggles with Elysia—but she confused him in ways that no girl ever had. They were friends. But something more than friendship was starting to burn around the edges and it scared Vlad.

He couldn't be with Snow the way he'd been with Meredith. He still loved Meredith. And Snow . . . she deserved better.

Besides, she was just his food source . . . wasn't she?

No. She was a person. A person who deserved better than a monster like Vlad. When the last bell rang, Vlad grabbed his backpack and headed out the front doors, but he didn't get far.

Two sets of hands picked him up, one by his arms and one by his legs, and carried him around to the back of the school, to the grassy area surrounded by shrubs, where a few teachers went to smoke during lunch. It wasn't until those hands threw him down on the ground that Vlad could confirm they belonged to Bill and Tom, the resident bullies who had been a constant thorn in Vlad's side since before kindergarten. He wasn't surprised in the least.

But when they wordlessly duct-taped him to the small maple tree . . . that gave him cause to raise an eyebrow. He didn't bother protesting—he'd just tap into his vampire strength and snap free once they'd gone. It was just an annoyance, a minor setback to his afternoon plans.

Eddie stepped into the clearing, and Vlad's eyes darted to Bill and Tom. After a moment of awkward silence, Bill said, "Where's our twenty bucks, Poe?"

Eddie held up a bill and Tom snatched it. "Man, you got ripped off. We'd have done it for free."

The bullies guffawed and made their way back to the front of the school. Eddie's small face wore a smirk as he crouched in front of Vlad, a superior, knowing look in his little weasel eyes. "Comfy?"

Vlad glared. The last thing he wanted to do was spend even a moment in the presence of Eddie Poe, vampire paparazzo extraordinaire. He pulled his hands forward, ready to tear through the tape that held him in place, and was hit by a wave of nausea that ripped away his strength required to break the bonds. He looked at Eddie, narrowing his eyes, and put some real effort into it, yanking at the tape, but still he couldn't break it. Confused, he tried again, but failed. A terrible ache was settling into his stomach, and Vlad knew that if he didn't lie down soon, he was going to throw up all over Eddie's camera.

With a smug smile, Eddie unzipped his backpack and pulled out a string of garlic. He held it up for Vlad to see. "Does this answer any questions for you?"

Vlad shrank away as much as he could, but there was no escape. So that was why he suddenly felt so sick, that was why he was feeling so weak. He made a mental note to give Eddie a permanent wedgie the moment he escaped. "Eddie, what are you doing?"

Eddie tied the end of the string, making a loop, and despite Vlad's struggling, placed it over Vlad's head and around his neck.

It was the most dangerous necklace that Vlad had ever worn.

Unless the garlic got into a wound or Vlad swallowed it, he'd be fine—Otis had assured him of that. But the real danger was that Eddie knew the garlic would subdue him long enough to . . . to . . . to do whatever it was Eddie planned to do.

The scent of the garlic was choking him, but Vlad managed to repeat his words. "What are you doing?"

He'd meant for them to come out threatening, but they sounded more like a whimper.

Eddie fiddled with his lens, occasionally pointing his camera at Vlad and adjusting something. "I'm just making sure you stick around long enough for me to take a few pictures."

Vlad tried to push into Eddie's mind, but no matter how hard he pushed, he couldn't get inside—the garlic must have weakened that too. His voice shook, but he tried to remain calm. "You should know I'm really allergic to garlic, Eddie. We've been going to school together since kindergarten."

"It's a good cover, Vlad, and not entirely a lie. Aren't all vampires allergic to garlic?" Eddie smiled a strange, sadistic smile. He pulled a pocketknife from his back pocket and opened it, revealing a small, sharp blade. His actions were so casual that Vlad found himself frightened—frightened! Of Eddie Poe. He never saw that coming.

Despite his fears, despite his nausea, Vlad shook his head and tried hard to act cool and casual. "You still think that? Man, Eddie, you should see a shrink. Seriously. Vampires aren't re—"

He was going to say "real," but then Eddie drew the blade across his palm, splitting his pale skin open. Bright red blood blossomed from the cut, and Vlad's eyes locked on Eddie's self-inflicted wound. Vlad's stomach, despite the queasiness-inducing garlic, rumbled with need.

Eddie poked at his cut with his finger, enticing it to open, to bleed freely. Blood drew a lazy line down his palm, and with prodding the line thickened. He waved his bleeding hand in front of Vlad's face and smirked. "Not real, huh? So why do you look so hungry all of a sudden?"

Vlad forced his eyes away. He had to get a grip, or the garlic wasn't going to be enough to keep him down. He was going to tear through Eddie Poe's little neck and devour every drop of his blood. And even Eddie didn't deserve that . . . no matter how much Vlad wanted to do it.

Eddie snapped a few pictures of Vlad, then sat down just a few feet in front of him and said, "I can wait all day. Sooner or later you're gonna have to show me fangs."

The smell of Eddie's blood—oh man, it was AB negative—filled Vlad's nostrils. He could feel his will breaking. He was going to bite Eddie and get a taste. He had to. Eddie had practically invited him to dine. Fueled by hunger, Vlad pulled on his restraints and felt the duct tape stretch and begin to break. The garlic wasn't enough to keep him away from the taste of the rubies hidden within Eddie's small veins. Vlad needed it. Just a taste. Just a small taste.

A familiar voice entered the clearing. "Eddie, are you crazy? What are you doing?"

Eddie was snapping tons of pictures, but the voice was

enough to distract Vlad from his momentary weakness. Barely, but enough. He looked up and saw Joss dropping his messenger bag on the ground beside Eddie. Joss looked at Vlad, tilting his head curiously. "Your eyes are purple. Why do they do that?"

Vlad blinked, collecting himself. "I . . . I don't know."

Joss spied Eddie's hand and clucked his tongue. "Is that what's causing all the commotion?"

As Joss took Eddie's hand and examined the cut, Eddie yanked it away. "It's the only way to get proof."

"By sacrificing yourself?"

Eddie wilted, but Joss patted him on the back. "The garlic was a good idea, but not enough, I think. Vlad isn't like other vampires."

Joss glanced back at Vlad and said, "Are you, Vlad? You're something else. Something . . . special."

Vlad pulled at the tape again, but it refused to break. Every cell in his body felt ill.

Joss crouched down and smiled, withdrawing his stake from the bag—the same stake that had been buried in Vlad's chest a year and a half before. His words were but a whisper. "So let's find out what."

Joss ripped the garlic away and flung it over the shrub. As he did so he jumped back, but not fast enough. Vlad snapped through the duct tape like it was tissue paper and moved so fast that Eddie had barely taken two quick breaths before Vlad crushed his camera with one hand and turned to face Joss, fully at the ready.

If they wanted a fight, they were going to get one.

Eddie looked scared; Joss looked mildly concerned. Joss's voice was smooth and calm as he spoke, but tinged with surprise. "You move faster now. Something your uncle taught you?"

Vlad growled, ready to rip Joss's limbs from his body. "No. Something my enemies taught me."

A small smile tugged at the corner of Joss's mouth. "What else have you learned?"

Vlad's fangs shot from his gums. The smell of Eddie's blood was making him crazy, but Joss's presence, his taunts, were worse. He snapped his teeth at Joss, only barely hearing a tiny whimper from Eddie, and said, "Why don't you come find out?"

"Vlad! Don't!" Henry stumbled into the clearing, breathless.

Vlad whipped around, completely on edge. He could smell Joss's blood now too—A positive, tangy. If he didn't feed soon, he'd go mad. "Henry, just get out of here. I'm handling this."

But Henry didn't leave. Instead, he moved to the most dangerous spot in the clearing—directly between Vlad and Joss. He looked from his best friend to his cousin and back. "Not like this. If you two want to kill each other, fine. But not out in the open, in the middle of the day, where anybody could see. You owe me that much. You both do."

Joss kept a firm hold on his stake, staring Vlad down. He wasn't about to quit, no matter what he owed Henry.

And the blood . . . oh man, Vlad needed that blood.

Vlad looked at Henry, who was pleading with his eyes, and

his fangs shrank back into his gums. As his sanity slowly returned, he realized that Henry was right. He did owe him that much. Never mind the fact that he'd been ready to do just that, to extinguish their lives completely. Self-loathing wormed its way into his chest and settled there, festering. Though his famished hunger remained, he shook his head and tugged Henry's sleeve. "Come on. Let's get outta here before I drain Eddie dry."

As they passed Eddie, Vlad noticed that he had paled in terror. He also noticed that there was a new scent on the air. Eddie had wet himself.

For some reason that made Vlad smile.

14

A FRIEND'S BETRAYAL

VLAD FLEW ACROSS THE BASEMENT AND TURNED, his vampire speed making him a blur in the dim light. He threw a roundhouse kick to knock the stake from Vikas's hand. Vikas stepped back, just as fast, and Vlad missed. Vikas smiled, allowing Vlad a moment to catch his breath. "Much better today, Mahlyenki Dyavol. You're no longer holding back."

Vlad slipped his sweat-drenched T-shirt over his head and tossed it on the basement stairs. "Let's go again."

Vikas shook his head. "That is enough training for today. Now tell me what clouds your mind; what has brought this fury to your attacks?"

Vlad didn't want to talk about it, but he knew Vikas wasn't

about to drop the subject. He sat on the steps and ran a frustrated hand through his slick hair. "You were right, okay? Joss isn't going to walk away from Bathory without killing me."

Vikas sighed and dropped the makeshift stake to the floor. He walked over to where Vlad sat, squeezed his shoulder, and took a seat beside him. "Do you recall our conversation in the hospital after you were staked?"

Vlad nodded. "You said you'd been betrayed by a friend too."

Vikas was quiet for a while, then, in a gruff voice, he said, "I believe the time has come that I share with you my story of friendship and betrayal."

He stood and moved up the steps. A heartbeat later, Vlad followed.

Vikas barked at Tristian, who was standing quietly in the kitchen. "Blood, Tristian. Warm. Then leave us."

Tristian hurried to the freezer and collected bloodbags, and as he was pouring them into mugs, Vikas looked at Vlad, who stood there watching Vikas order his drudge around as though he was nothing. Vlad frowned and a glimpse of guilt crossed Vikas's eyes. As Tristian sat the now-steaming mugs in front of them, Vikas spoke again, his voice much softer. "*Bol'shoe spasibo*, Tristian."

Vlad took his seat across from Vikas and blew the steam from his mug before taking a sip. Vikas didn't touch his, but the moment Tristian was out of the room, he said, "I have held many friendships over the centuries that I have lived, Mahlyenki Dyavol, and I have been betrayed by those friends more times than I can count. But few truly ripped at my soul. In truth, only one instance pained me in that way. I did not believe that I would ever forgive my friend. I did not believe I would let my friend live should I see him again. But time, as they say, heals all wounds, and my wounds mended long ago."

Vikas took a deep breath and released it slowly. He met Vlad's eyes, his irises a cool ice blue, and after a long, silent moment, said, "It was Otis, your uncle, that betrayed me in the worst way possible."

Vlad almost choked on a mouthful of blood. He coughed, trying to keep it contained. Vikas handed him a towel and nodded. "Shocking, I know, to think that Otis, my dearest living friend, would be the cause of great pain. I almost killed him. I would have, but . . ."

Vlad dried his mouth and said, "But?"

He almost couldn't believe that Otis had betrayed Vikas at one point. Vikas was the one man Otis knew he could count on. Their friendship seemed unbreakable.

Vikas looked away, staring into the contents of his mug. "But I didn't."

"What happened?"

"Your father was not the first vampire to love a human. Roughly two centuries ago, in Paris of all places, I met and fell deeply in love with a woman named Nadya. She was a good, Russian woman. Fair hair, hazel eyes. She was lovely, striking for a human, with a figure that—" Vikas's lips spread into a smile and Vikas shook his head, realizing he was getting into the TMI area. "We shared an instant attraction for each other and, despite the laws, planned to marry the spring after she came into my life. But Otis discovered our love affair and reported my treachery to the nearest council president. It was decided that either Nadya would die and I would be punished, or she would have to be turned, reborn as a vampire. I wanted neither for her, as Nadya had made it clear that while she loved me with all my vampiric charms, she did not wish to undergo the change herself. So I refused to change her."

Vikas paused to take a drink of his blood. His eyes found a window, and they lingered there for several moments.

Vlad's voice finally broke the silence. "And?"

"With barely a breath, thinking that he was saving my life, Otis volunteered to turn Nadya. The council guards held me back as I screamed my protests. He left the room, returning only moments later with her blood on his lips to proclaim the deed had been done."

Vlad gasped. Otis had the best interest of his friend in mind, but he never even considered his feelings.

"I demanded to see my Nadya, to beg her forgiveness. Otis led me to her—her wounds had not yet healed, so new to the vampire world was she. When I saw her, I fell to my knees and begged her to forgive me, promising that she would have a life unlike any other, one that I would give everything to fill with love, laughter, and joy." Vikas's eyes shined with the threat of tears at the memory. "But Nadya . . . she was furious and thought that I had betrayed her. She threw bitter words at me like daggers and ran from the room. Dawn was too close. I chased after her, but she ran into the light as it spilled over the city. I reached the end of the building, reaching out to pull her back, but my arm caught fire. Tomas and Otis pulled me from the sun, saving my life, though I was determined to extinguish it. Once we were inside, safe among the shadows, I turned on Otis, but Tomas stopped me from taking his life. Your father saved Otis's life that day, and I did not speak to Otis for fifty-three years."

"That's . . . horrible. What made you forgive him?"

"Two words. Two words that it took him fifty-three years to say and me fifty-three years to hear." He stood and collected the empty cups from the table. "He said 'I'm sorry.'"

Vlad raised an eyebrow. It couldn't be that simple. "That's it?"

"No." Vikas swallowed hard and met Vlad's eyes. "He meant it."

Vikas moved across the kitchen and rinsed the mugs in the sink. Vlad was quiet, lost in his own thoughts. Vikas had cleaned the mugs, dried them, put them away in the cupboard, and returned to the table before Vlad spoke, his voice hushed, his thoughts troubled. "Joss is so different now. It's like he's not even the same person I was friends with two years ago."

"That does not surprise me, Mahlyenki Dyavol. Your friend has undergone purification by the Slayer Society."

That gave Vlad pause. "Purification?"

Vikas nodded. "In order to remind Joss what it is that he is fighting against, to recondition him, the Society has purified your friend with a month's long barrage of their customs and laws ... and pain."

Vlad winced. He could only imagine what twisted things Joss had undergone. Of course, that explained the shift in his personality.

Vikas went on, as if to make sure that Vlad understood. "Intense and frequent pain so the things he is told will not easily be forgotten. It's a practice that they learned from early vampires, though we found it to be far too barbaric and abandoned the practice several centuries ago."

So that was it. Joss had been brainwashed by the Society, and their friendship was likely gone forever. Vlad wouldn't apologize for being what he was; that was ridiculous. He was good enough to be Joss's friend when Joss thought he was human; it shouldn't matter that he was a vampire. If anyone owed anyone an apology it was Joss, and Vlad was starting to think that it would be at least fifty-three years before that would happen.

If it ever did.

But ... if Joss had been brainwashed, there was always the chance he could be *un*brainwashed.

Vlad just had to figure out how.

15
A SLAYER'S DUTY

T HE WHITE FEDEX TRUCK BACKED OUT of the driveway and turned onto the road, then shifted gears and sped off down the street. Joss stood in the doorway, clutching a plain white shipping envelope. It was here, at long last. No more waiting. No more reconnaissance. He could move forward with his assigned plan of action.

"Is that the new calendar I ordered?"

He turned his head to his mom, who was peering over his shoulder at the envelope. She was smiling—something she hadn't done on a regular basis in a long time, not since Cecile was murdered. The move to Bathory had been good for her; being around family had really lifted her spirits. If he could rid the town of vampires, it could be good for all of them.

"Nope. Just something from Uncle Abraham. I asked him for help with that research paper in history. Guess he sent some stuff to help me out."

She nodded, so trusting, at his lie. Joss was good at lying. He had to be. His parents knew nothing about the Slayer Society. His dad's job was a clever cover set up by the Society, but they really had no clue that Joss was the one doing the real work . . . the necessary, honorable work. "Well, Abraham would be the one to ask, wouldn't he? College professor, world traveler. I'm glad to see you taking your education seriously and working so hard on your grades, Joss. School is important."

Joss offered her a reassuring smile. Clutching the envelope to his chest, he slipped by her and headed down the hall and into his bedroom, closing the door behind him.

He pulled the tab, tearing open the envelope, and slid his hand inside. When his fingers brushed against the familiar feeling of parchment, he closed his hand over the letter and pulled it out, dropping the shipping envelope to the floor. In his hands he held a small parchment envelope, held closed by a red wax seal which bore the Society's crest. He ran his fingertip over the seal and turned back to the door, locking it. Then, sitting on the edge of his bed, Joss turned the envelope over in his hand and pulled the back flap, breaking the seal. He withdrew the letter, unfolded it, and read over the words with eager eyes.

His growing smile dropped. The Society wanted more information about the vampires he'd come here to kill.

So much reconnaissance for such a minor infestation. But it was the oldest one, the one called Vikas, that they needed to know more about, and the youngest . . . Vlad. Once Joss had his answers, once he'd satisfied the Society's curiosity, he'd be free to rid the world of each and every one of them.

The photograph on his dresser, enclosed in a small silver frame, caught his attention. A pretty girl, only five years old when the photo was taken. Her blonde curls framing her cherubic face, her green eyes huge, her smile dazzling. Joss had loved her from the moment he'd touched his mother's stomach and the baby had kicked at his hand. His little sister, his reason for fighting so hard against the bloodthirsty creatures of the night. Cecile. Every vampire he'd killed, every pain he'd had to endure . . . it was all for her. It was all worth it. Just to know that he was, in some small way, avenging her wrongful death. He'd do anything for her.

Even if it meant killing the boy he'd once called friend.

16
OUT FOR A BITE

VLAD BUTTONED HIS JACKET and braced himself against the chilly autumn breeze as he moved down the sidewalk toward home. He'd just spent the last two hours in the belfry reading everything he could find about the Pravus in the *Compendium*, but discovered nothing that really pointed to anything definite on what the prophecy really said. It all seemed like a bunch of hearsay, with quotes from one vampire's theories and quotes from another vampire agreeing with those theories. Sadly, even though Otis removed the glyph that had prevented Vlad from reading the Pravus passages, Vlad was left just about where he'd begun—having no idea exactly what the prophecy said and even less of an idea of where he might find it.

"I know where the prophecy is."

Vlad's steps came to an immediate halt. His thoughts had been closed to anyone who might try to read them—something Otis had urged him to practice—but the intruder on his nightly trek had seemingly read them without any effort at all. He turned slowly and looked into Dorian's eyes.

Dorian shrugged slightly. A small smile touched his lips. Bemusement, or something sinister, Vlad couldn't tell. "Call it a talent, one of many. I can read anyone's thoughts, no matter how they might resist."

The center of Vlad's chest tightened as he tried to force all of his secrets from his mind in a blind panic.

The smile slipped from Dorian's lips and he shook his head, almost apologetically. "But I'm a man of principle, Vlad. I never share the secrets I collect."

Vlad shook his head defensively, wondering just what Dorian was doing in Bathory. He didn't have to wonder for long, though. The answer was obvious: he wanted Vlad's blood at any cost. "Not everyone has secrets."

"I assure you, everyone has at least one thing that they would like to hide from the world. Even me."

Vlad wet his lips. He couldn't help but wonder if Dorian was bluffing. After all, there were people in the world who were trained to profile people, to guess what it was that made them tick. Maybe Dorian was just a good guesser. "What about me?"

"Where to start?" His smile returned as he seemed to tick through a list of Vlad's greatest secrets. He tapped his lips with his pointer finger as he thought. Then finally, he seemed to settle on one. "Ah, yes . . . you feed on a human girl named Snow and lie to everyone—including your uncle—about it. What's more, you think you might have strong feelings for the girl, but can't bear to fathom loving anyone but Meredith. Of course, she's with Joss now. The slayer boy. That does complicate things, doesn't it?"

Vlad's jaw hit the ground. He sputtered and stumbled over his words, but all that managed to leave his lips was something that sounded vaguely like a choking noise.

Dorian shook his head again and smiled. "Don't worry, Vlad. As I said, I never share the secrets I collect. Your sins are safe with me. Of course, your sins are not why I've come."

Vlad believed every word he said. But he didn't trust that belief, remembering what Otis and Vikas had told him about Dorian's immense skills. He looked around them, at the dark windows of houses lining the street, and wondered if Dorian would try to take his blood where someone might see, and if he did whether Vlad could stop him again. With a nervous jitter, he said, "Why *have* you come?"

Dorian licked his lips, sending a frightened shiver down Vlad's spine. Then he offered an apologetic smile. "Our first encounter was rather rudely interrupted, and our second too short, don't you think?"

"Otis and Vikas seem to think you'll hurt me if we spend time together. I think they're right." Vlad tried to appear strong and confident, though he knew that Dorian could sense his fear.

Dorian smiled again, and this time it was definitely out of bemusement. "As it happens, I don't wish to harm you in any way. I merely want to drink from you. No death will come of my actions, I swear."

"Did you promise your son that same thing before you killed him?"

Vlad expected Dorian to react out of fury and insult, but instead, Dorian's face dropped in sorrow. "Touché, my young friend. No, I did not promise my son anything that fateful night, and I miss him more than I can bear. Otis . . . he told you about feeding from my son. He told you of the power he now possesses. As terrible as it seems, some good has come of Aidan's death. And so, if you died, if I were unable to control my appetite and took your life in the midst of feeding, I imagine some good would come of yours."

Aidan. Why did that name seem so familiar to Vlad?

Pursing his lips, Vlad said, "I won't let you feed from me."

"The trouble is that I find your blood irresistible. I'm afraid you will give me your blood or I will be forced to take it from you. I cannot stop this hunger, Vlad." His eyes dropped to Vlad's throat, causing Vlad to gulp. Dorian's chilling words rang out into the night. "I can only barely control it."

Vlad instinctively took two steps back, but Dorian did not follow. He wondered if the distance would help Dorian control his thirst.

Dorian smiled. "Unlikely, but it's good of you to try."

"You said you know where the prophecy is."

"That I do. In fact," he said with an air of burden, "I possess it."

Vlad suppressed a gasp. He eyed Dorian for a moment, wondering if it were possible that Dorian was trying to trick him.

Dorian put his palms up, shaking his head. "No tricks. I swear."

He set his jaw, eyeing the unassuming vampire with distrust. "What do you want from me?"

Dorian wet his lips, as if the thought of Vlad's blood was making him parched. When he spoke, his voice sounded gruff. "Why ask questions to which you already know the answers?"

Ignoring his quip, Vlad hurried to stay on subject, to keep Dorian distracted from his veins. "Can I see it?"

Dorian paused for a moment, that hungry light leaving his eyes. It didn't look as if he was considering Vlad's request, but rather pondering whether or not such a simple request was actually possible. After several seconds, he said, "No. You cannot."

Vlad ran a frustrated hand through his hair. "Then, what exactly was the point in telling me you have the prophecy if you weren't planning to share it?"

Dorian shook his head. "I never said that."

Vlad raised an eyebrow. He thought for sure Dorian had implied just that, but okay. "Then at least tell me where it is."

"I don't suppose you'd consider a trade?" Dorian grinned. In any other light, it might have seemed charming.

"No trade."

"I am torn, my young friend. Torn between duty and an insatiable appetite." Dorian glanced at Vlad's neck and the bizarre combination of horror and hunger flooded his expression. "I'm afraid my appetite seems to be winning, and my patience is waning. Please don't make me force you. I may not be able to stop this time."

Vlad shook his head slowly, setting his jaw. Clearly, this was all some kind of sick game for Dorian, some cruel way of getting what he really wanted. He probably had no idea where the prophecy was. "I resisted you once. I'll do it again."

"You give me no choice." Dorian lunged forward with a speed and ferocity that Vlad had never before encountered. In a panic, Vlad did all that he knew to do, he shoved his way into Dorian's mind.

It didn't stop Dorian, but it did make him hesitate long enough for Vlad to book it out of there. To his relief, and immense surprise, Dorian did not follow.

17
HALLOWEEN

"ARE YOU GONNA BE MAD IF I GO?"

Vlad shook his head. Henry was already dressed as a zombie, with chunks of rotting flesh hanging off of his face. Where else could he go dressed like that, but Matthew's annual Halloween party? "Nah, I won't get mad. You go ahead. I just don't feel like watching Joss and Meredith's first official date unfold before my eyes, y'know?"

Henry nodded, but looked pretty bummed out. Vlad wondered if he was thinking about how he'd ditched Vlad for last year's party. "So are you just staying in tonight?"

Vlad shrugged with one shoulder. He knew his answer wouldn't make Henry the happiest guy in the world, but that was just how things were. "October's picking me up. We're going to The Crypt for a while. They're having a vampire bash."

Henry grew quiet, and Vlad couldn't help but wonder if Henry thought he was choosing the goths over him. That would never happen. Henry wasn't just his drudge, he was his best friend. But still, he worried Henry might think so. After a moment, Henry nodded. "Fitting. Bet you win for best costume."

"I'm not dressing up."

A smile cracked Henry's expression. "Still."

Vlad knew it couldn't have been easy to be around him since he broke it off with Meredith. He'd been grouchy and withdrawn, for sure. Henry deserved better from his best friend, but Vlad just couldn't face Joss and Meredith tonight. He shifted in his seat on the couch and silently vowed to make his absence from the party up to Henry. "Where's Melissa?"

"We're over. I dumped her on my way here." Henry shrugged, as if it were no big deal.

Vlad mulled this over for a moment before he said, "Tell me you didn't break up with her in a text."

"Yeah, why?" Henry shrugged again, casually, though the sting of the fresh breakup lurked in his eyes.

"Dude, that's brutal."

"But necessary. If you dump them in person either they get all weepy or mad. Either way, it's a bad situation. And I couldn't risk smearing my face paint with tears . . . or blood, whichever happened to be flying around." Henry smacked Vlad playfully on the back with his rotting, pus-oozing hand. "Anyway, I'd better bolt."

"See ya, man."

"Have fun sucking face with Snow."

Vlad rolled his eyes. There was no use arguing. No matter what he said, Henry and October were convinced that he and Snow were making out in the alley behind The Crypt. But it wasn't her face that he was looking forward to sucking—it was her blood. Though it was something he still wasn't really comfortable admitting to.

The phone rang, so Vlad snapped it up in his hand. "Hello?"

Silence on the other end, and then, "Hi, Vlad. It's Meredith."

Vlad's stomach shriveled into a tiny, hard ball.

"I know you're wondering why I'm calling, so I'll just get right to it. Any minute now, Joss is going to show up at my door to take me to Matthew's party."

Great. Rub it in. That's helpful. The hard ball that had been his stomach quivered a little inside of him.

"So the reason I'm calling is to ask you . . . to ask you if there's any reason that I shouldn't go with Joss tonight."

A thousand reasons raced through Vlad's mind, but two remained at the top of the list: 1) Joss was a killer, and 2) Vlad still had feelings for her. But Vlad spoke neither aloud. Instead, he said in a raspy voice, "Nothing comes to mind."

She was quiet for a long time before uttering "Okay" and hanging up on her end.

Vlad stared at the phone in his hand for a full minute, kicking himself for not saying what he'd really wanted to—that Joss was a manipulative jerk and she should stay far, far away from him at all costs—before returning the phone to its cradle. He couldn't tell her that, because what came next? Ditch Matthew's party and come hang out with me at The Crypt tonight? I can introduce you to Snow, who happens to be my enormously hot drudge? No way. Not happening.

Besides, Meredith was safer not being around him. She was safer with Joss.

October pulled up and honked her horn, and suddenly it felt like everyone in the world but Vlad had their own car. Shouting a quick goodbye to Nelly, Vlad bolted out the door. He piled into the back with Sprat and Andrew, and with a jerk, October managed to get the car into gear and drove them all into Stokerton, music blaring on the radio, dashboard lights making Kristoff's silver hair glow slightly blue. By the time they pulled up in front of The Crypt, Vlad was feeling much better about missing out on Matthew's party. Once they stepped inside and descended into the club, he'd forgotten that Matthew was even holding a party.

The entire room was decorated in red and black, with hundreds of tiny, fuzzy bats hanging from the ceiling. The normally empty picture frames on the wall held artwork depicting famous vampires: Dracula, Count Chocula, the Count from Sesame Street, and more. And everyone—everyone but Vlad, that is—was dressed as stereotypical vampires. Some wore capes, some dressed in Victorian finery, but every single one of them had a pair of fangs. Vlad smiled and let his own fangs slip from their hiding place behind his gums. No wonder he loved it here.

Standing by the bar was Snow, dressed in a slinky black dress, with a small silver bat hanging from a chain around her pale neck—paler than usual, which Vlad attributed to rice powder. Her black hair was pinned up, with several loose curls hanging down, brushing lightly against her skin. She smiled at him and he smiled back.

October tapped him on the shoulder and said, "Tell her, Vlad. If you're not interested, tell her tonight . . . or I will."

After debating just what to say for several minutes, Vlad walked over to Snow and said, "Having fun?"

Snow could barely contain a grin. "Good music, my favorite night of the year, room full of vampires . . . I'm having a blast."

"Can we talk?" Vlad swallowed a lump in his throat. "Outside?"

Snow nodded, taking Vlad's hand in hers, leading him to the back door. When she touched him, he secretly reveled in her warmth. He could get used to this feeling, Snow's skin against his. But didn't Snow deserve better than a beast who only wanted her for what she could give him? That wasn't a relationship. That was a tragedy waiting to happen. He slipped his hand from hers and avoided her questioning glance.

No. He couldn't get used to it, to any of it. He was getting too close to Snow for her own good.

As they passed October, she handed Snow her jacket and shot Vlad a look that said she meant business. It turned out while guys would not only stand by and watch as their friend volunteered to help out the lion tamer, and hand him a steak as he was entering the cage, girls were fiercely protective of their friends. Vlad couldn't ever imagine threatening a girl's life for making out with Henry. Besides, that would be *a lot* of girls, and Vlad wasn't sure he could even remember all their names, let alone threaten them with bodily harm for making Henry grin like an idiot. As far as he was concerned, Henry could make out with anybody he wanted. Except for Meredith. And maybe Snow.

They stepped outside and Vlad's fangs throbbed within his mouth, as if they'd become accustomed to feeding in the cold. It wasn't why he'd come here, but his body, that monster that lurked within him, known only as thirst, reacted immediately.

She smiled at Vlad once the door closed, sealing them off from the club. "You've been really hungry lately."

"It's not that. I mean, it is, but we need to talk." His eyes found her neck and that delicious blue vein. At once he was seized by hunger, all sense and reason gone, lost in his blood-thirst. "Maybe it's better if I feed first."

"Why? Worried whatever you have to say to me will make feeding awkward?"

Vlad blinked, tearing his gaze away from her neck. It would make it easier to focus on the conversation at hand. A little, anyway. Her tone sounded hurt, as if she already knew what he was going to say, that they should just be friends, that the feeding sessions didn't mean he had any real feelings for her. Her cheeks flushed, and Vlad couldn't tell if it was out of anger or embarrassment.

"Snow . . . we're friends, right? I mean, you're my drudge, but that's it, right? Just my drudge? Just my friend? You don't think we're . . ." But the look in her eyes said it all—she didn't view him as just a friend. October was right. Snow had a crush on him. A big-time crush. And what's worse, Vlad wasn't entirely sure she was the only one with attachment issues.

She shrugged, trying to keep it casual, but he could tell she was hurting . . . and lying through her teeth. "Of course. Just friends. Why?"

Vlad wet his lips, his hunger drowned out by his concern for Snow's feelings. Quietly, he brushed a stray curl from her cheek and said, "Do you like me as more than a friend? Tell the truth."

She glared at him then and held it for a long time, as if she didn't like feeling weak or vulnerable. Just as Vlad was about to ask again, she said, "Yes. I like you. As more than a friend. But you don't feel the same way, so why does it matter?"

The last thing he wanted to do was to placate her, to give her false hope, but he didn't want to lie either. The truth was, he really enjoyed their stolen moments together. But those moments were always tainted by guilt—guilt for feeding on her, guilt for spending intimately close time together with a girl that was not Meredith.

Always Meredith. She was haunting him in ways he'd never realized she would.

A strange battle was going on inside of him, between his vampire side and his human side. Part of him wanted to cease his prattle and sink his fangs deep into Snow's vein. Part of him retched at the thought. She was a person, after all. She was his friend. And since when did the vampire side of him start making sense? He tore his gaze from her neck and took a deep breath, trying to block out the scent of her blood on the air. "Snow, you're one of the prettiest girls I've ever seen. You're funny, smart, and really cool to hang out with. But—"

"But?"

Vlad gulped. It was his turn to feel vulnerable. "There's . . . this girl."

"There usually is. What's her name?" Her tone grew bitter, jealous. It kind of amused Vlad a little. A girl, as sweet and caring as Snow, jealous over a guy like Vlad? That was one for the record books.

He breathed out her name in a whisper, as if uttering its purity here in the place where he fed in secrecy were a sin. "Meredith."

"Do you love her?"

Vlad barely let the question slip from her mouth before he answered. "Yes."

Snow blinked, looking a little surprised at Vlad's quick reply. "Does she love you?"

Vlad pictured Meredith in his mind and recalled the way her smile lifted his spirits, the way her very presence made his heart expand. He nodded slowly. "I think so. I mean, maybe. I think she did once, and there's always the hope that she will again someday."

Snow's eyes dropped to the ground. Her shoulders sagged some. She looked defeated. All Vlad wanted to do was to make her eyes light up again. Her voice was calm, but hushed. "Does she know that you're a vampire?"

He shook his head. "No. I haven't told her. I just don't know if she could handle it."

They stood there, so close, for so long that it seemed that time had actually disappeared and the world had completely forgotten them.

"Maybe you need to find that out, Vlad. If you love her, you've got to give her a chance to know you. And if she loves you, she'll love everything about you." Snow's voice was soft, but full of meaning. She took a breath and whispered, "The way I do."

Then she leaned forward and her lips found Vlad's. This time, he welcomed it. This time, he kissed back with abandon. Her kiss was sweet, her lips tasted like peppermint lip balm, and for the first time in a long while, Vlad didn't once think about Meredith or Joss or Otis's impending trial. He didn't think about D'Ablo or Dorian or anything else.

He only thought of the pretty girl named Snow and her peppermint kisses.

18
A BAD DAY

VLAD TURNED THE CORNER ONTO LUGOSI TRAIL with heavy steps. It wasn't that he wasn't looking forward to his training session with Vikas—in fact, he'd been enjoying them immensely over the past few weeks—but school had been particularly grueling today. All he was really in the mood to do was go home, camp out in front of the TV, and maybe kill a few dozen people on *Vampires Attack!*, the Xbox 360 game Henry had bought him for his birthday last year. But that, much to Vlad's chagrin, wasn't going to happen.

As he crossed the street, he took a glance around, wondering to himself what exactly it was that had sent Eddie off his trail recently. It was nice not being followed home every day, but Vlad didn't trust why Eddie had stopped. Maybe Joss had warned him about the unpredictable temperament of vampires. Or maybe Eddie hadn't really, truly believed that Vlad was a bloodsucking monster until Joss confirmed his theory. Or maybe he had just run out of clean pants. Either way, it was kind of nice to be alone again, though he couldn't help but wonder if he truly was alone or if Joss was his new constant shadow.

But then, it was only a matter of time before Eddie would return to his old habits. After all, even for vampires, there was no stopping the media.

Stealing around to the back of the house, Vlad pulled open the door and stepped inside. Immediately, something felt very wrong.

"Vikas? You home?" He reached out with his blood, the way that Otis had taught him last year, and felt his teacher's presence upstairs. Something felt . . . wrong. Vikas's blood felt off, somehow. Different. As he climbed the steps, his pace hurried, and with worry, he opened the door to the guest bedroom.

Vikas was lying on the bed. The dark circles under his eyes and his sunken cheeks made his face look like a skull. He was always pale, but now he looked like a sickening combination of gray and green. His eyes were closed, and if Vlad didn't know any better he would have thought that Vikas might be dead.

Tristian was standing over him, dabbing his forehead with a cool, moist cloth. Vlad's face darkened to see his actions.

They only confirmed his fears that Vikas must be terribly ill. Vlad stepped inside the room, careful to keep his footfalls hushed. He exchanged glances with Tristian, who looked so worried that it made Vlad's heart skip a beat. "What happened?"

Tristian parted his lips to speak, but Vikas opened his eyes and spoke in a gruff, stubborn voice. "I'm fine, Mahlyenki Dyavol. Just a bit under the weather."

Ignoring Vikas's grumblings, Vlad sat on the side of the bed and met Tristian's gaze.

In a hushed, timid voice, Tristian said, "I brought him a glass of bloodwine from the open bottle on the counter, like I do every afternoon. He gets peckish around three, you know." A worried crease had taken up permanent residence on Tristian's forehead. He looked down at his master, whose eyes were closed again. "Even if he eats a late lunch, he's always hungry around three. So I brought him a glass. He took a sip and just . . . just crumbled to the ground."

Worried tears filled Tristian's eyes. "All I could think was that something was wrong with the wine. So I put my finger down his throat to make him throw it up. He vomited and retched up every drop of bloodwine, so I gave him as much of my blood as I could and put him in bed." Tristian took the cloth from Vikas's head and dropped it into a bowl of water on the bedside table. "I tried to call Otis, but he told me not to."

"Stubborn old man." Vlad shook his head. Vikas opened

his eyes and gave Vlad the best 'I heard that' look that he could muster. It was like Vikas to be the strong one, even when his life was on the line. Vlad squeezed Tristian's shoulder and offered him a comforting smile. "You did everything right, Tristian. I can see why Vikas values you so much as his drudge. Could you please go get me the bottle so I can take a look at it?"

After Tristian left the room, Vikas clutched Vlad's arm and pulled him closer, his voice raspy. "He poisoned me."

Vlad's eyes widened and his heart thumped hard inside his chest. "Who? Tristian?"

"No. The boy. The slayer." Vikas fell back on the bed, barely able to open his eyes. He looked so weak, and in so much pain. He swallowed hard, as if it were a challenge to call a slayer by his given name.

"Joss." Vlad almost hissed the word. He should have known. But why use poison? Why not a stake? It seemed like a cowardly way to take down one of the oldest vampires known. One would think that such a task would give the slayer who accomplished it bragging rights among his psycho slayer friends. "How do you know it was Joss?"

"Who else would wish the death of me in this town and take such a cowardly approach to achieving that end but a slayer? I should have smelled it, but I never thought the blood-wine could be tainted. It seemed like one of the neighbors was cooking something foul. One of the downfalls of living among humans, it seems." Vikas coughed and then caught his breath. "I took a sip. Just one sip. Luckily, I vomited it all up, or you and I might not be having this conversation. Tristian . . . he saved my life."

As if on cue, Tristian returned to the room, bottle in hand. Vikas moaned at the sight of it, and Vlad nearly gagged at the scent. Garlic juice. Probably so little that Tristian couldn't pick up on its faint scent with his human senses. But to Vlad and Vikas, the nauseating stench was overwhelming. As if realizing this, Tristian ran the bottle back downstairs. Vlad heard the back door open, so it was likely he was throwing it in the trash. Smart guy.

Turning back to Vikas, Vlad said, "If Joss did this . . ."

He didn't have to finish his sentence, and really, there was no "if" about it. Vikas could be right. Joss could've somehow slipped inside unnoticed and poisoned Vikas's drink. The very idea both enraged and sickened him.

Vikas chuckled. It sounded strange coming from someone who looked to be lying on his deathbed. "If this is all the boy has, if this is his best weapon against us, then let him have his moment, Mahlyenki Dyavol. In three days, I will be well and on my way to living forever. In just eighty years, he will be dead. If someone doesn't kill him first."

Vlad couldn't be sure if that last sentence was meant as a suggestion or not, especially with the way Vikas raised a single eyebrow at him. In an effort to squash the same old conversation before it started, Vlad smiled. "So no training session today, huh?"

Though it seemed to pain him to do so, Vikas laughed heartily. "No. Not today, my friend."

There were hurried steps on the stairs and, just as Vlad had begun to doubt they belonged to Tristian, Otis burst into the room. "You are a damned fool, old man! You should have allowed Tristian to contact me. What if the garlic had gotten into your system before you could throw it up, or had entered a cut in your mouth? You could have died."

Vikas made a sound that sounded like "bah" and waved Otis away, but Otis wasn't going anywhere. He checked Vikas's pulse and frowned when he placed his palm against Vikas's glistening forehead. "You'll live. This time. But you're rather lucky I don't kill you myself for being so stubborn."

Otis smiled at Vlad. "Tristian is a good drudge. Much like your Henry. If he hadn't been here . . . well, needless to say, I'd be on the hunt right now for whoever did this. Any thoughts to who that might be?"

Otis and Vikas exchanged looks that said they shared the opinion that it had been Joss. No reply to Otis's question was required.

As much as the idea of Otis hunting Joss repulsed Vlad, he totally understood the urge at the moment. After all, Vikas was incredibly important to him. Not to mention how important he was to Otis and Tristian. Joss would have to be dealt with.

Vlad just wasn't sure exactly how to deal with him.

Vikas looked at Vlad. "What is to be done about your friend, Vladimir? It's only a matter of time before he turns his attention on you."

"You're worried about me? Vikas, he just tried to kill you."

"Perhaps. But I think he was merely trying to distract us all. The question is . . . from what?"

Vlad chewed his bottom lip for a moment. "What else is there that he could want here in Bathory? He just wants to get rid of the vampires."

Otis watched them both for a moment before speaking. "If Joss were sent here to kill us, he wouldn't be taking so long to try something. As I said before, I know reconnaissance when I see it. Joss is looking for something. Something that the slayers yearn for."

Vlad furrowed his brow. "What's that?"

In unison, Otis and Vikas replied. "Information."

A spark lit in Vlad's mind and his chest grew heavy. Picking up his backpack and throwing it over one shoulder, Vlad hurried out the door. Otis called after him, but Vlad didn't answer. He had to hurry. He had to confirm that Joss hadn't invaded the one place in town that nobody knew about but him.

As he rushed out the back door and around the house, Otis's voice invaded his thoughts. *What's your hurry, Vladimir? Is something wrong?*

I just have to check something. With that, he clamped down on his thoughts. Where he was going, he wanted to be completely alone.

It took him only minutes to cross town to the school and after a quick glance around, only seconds for him to float up to the ledge of the belfry and step inside. But then time slowed. Sound slowed as well, and what might have been his heart drumming in his ears in a panic sounded much more like the slow, steady beat of a bass drum. Heavy. Loud.

Someone had violated his sanctuary.

Someone had been here.

Someone knew about his secret place and had ransacked every inch of it.

Vlad would have bet that that somebody was either Eddie Poe or Joss McMillan. And his money was on Joss.

His father's chair was sliced open, the off-white stuffing inside puffing out of the cut. Books were thrown from his bookcases, revealing bare shelves. Candleholders were tossed across the room. In the corner, something shimmered in the moonlight. Vlad didn't have to move any closer to know that the picture of his father had been smashed.

He took it all in, trying to be angry, but feeling more violated than anything. When he spoke, his whispered words were a gray, breathy puff in the chilly air. "What were you looking for, Joss?"

Only one thing in the room appeared untouched. Vlad carefully stepped over books and debris and opened the drawer of the small table that sat next to his dad's chair.

It was empty.

Joss had stolen the most important thing to Vlad in the belfry. His father's journal.

Slowly, Vlad slid the drawer shut. Then he picked up the table and threw it across the room with a scream. Furious, he stepped from the belfry and jumped to the nearest treetop, hopping between trees all the way home.

He slammed the front door closed behind him, and Nelly snapped her eyes to his face. "What's wrong?"

"Nothing." Nothing that kicking Joss's butt couldn't cure, that was.

The look in her eyes said she didn't believe him in the least, but she wasn't about to push the issue.

Vlad sighed, brushing his bangs from his eyes. "I'm just glad we have a long weekend. I could use a break from school and all the drama."

And Joss, but he wasn't about to bring that up.

"Speaking of Thanksgiving weekend . . ."

Vlad's eyes went wide. He knew that tone. "Nelly, what did you do?"

"Nothing. Nothing, really." But her eyes gave her away completely. Whatever it was, she knew Vlad wasn't going to be happy about it. "Matilda and I were talking earlier, and she invited us over for Thanksgiving dinner tomorrow. Actually, she insisted that we come."

Vlad blinked. "We're having dinner at Henry's? That's all?"

"Yes, that's all." She gave him an awkward smile. "Basically."

"Basically? What does that mea—oh no." His eyes widened. Vlad moved to the closest chair and sat down, his head falling into his hands. When he spoke again the sound was muffled. "Please tell me Joss isn't going to be there."

He raised his head to look at her. "Please tell me you didn't agree to have dinner with the only vampire slayer in town!"

Vlad had stood up from the chair, and his voice had risen to a shout. He knew, but didn't care. "I can't believe you!"

He all but flew up to his room and barely had time to register that Nelly was saying that she'd had no idea until she'd already agreed and that it wouldn't be all that bad before he slammed his door shut so hard that he splintered the wood.

So much for the slayer's search for information. Joss had his father's journal.

And somehow, Vlad had to get it back.

19

A WAKING NIGHTMARE

VLAD WOKE FROM A SOUND SLEEP, but he didn't open his eyes right away. He wasn't exactly sure what had woken him, and he didn't exactly feel like getting out of bed at oh-my-glob-o'clock, so he laid there in the darkness, somewhere between awake and asleep, and tried to stop thinking about whatever it was that had shaken him from his dreams.

As if coaxing him further from sleep, Vlad's throat went dry, urging him to slip from his comfy bed into the bathroom for a sip of water. Reluctantly, Vlad opened his eyes.

Above him, seemingly suspended in midair, was a dagger. A familiar dagger, one that Vlad instantly recognized from the dark, bloody room that invaded his dreams every night, one filled with memories of a terrible ritual. Its blade gleamed some in the moonlight as it came down hard, aiming for Vlad's chest. He dove out of bed, hitting the floor hard. As he did, his eyes adjusted to the darkness and he could see his ever-present nightmare standing beside his disheveled bed.

Vlad gasped, "D'Ablo."

D'Ablo, holding the ritual dagger tightly in his good hand, merely smiled. "The time has come, Master Pravus. Or should I say *your* time has come."

He swung forward with the dagger again, and this time the blade caught Vlad's sleeve before he could move. Once Vlad was across the room, he spoke quickly. "I let you live!"

D'Ablo wasn't coming after him again—not yet—so Vlad seized the opportunity to explain. "Last year in Stokerton. I had the Lucis in my hand. I could've killed you. Otis urged me to kill you, but I didn't. And then, when we were outside in the sunlight, you were on fire. I warned you that you were dying so you'd hurry into the shadows. I could've blown you away or let you burn, but I didn't. Have you ever asked yourself why?"

For a moment, D'Ablo lowered the blade. But he did not speak.

Vlad's heart rate settled some, but just barely. "You knew my dad. You were close to him, you said it yourself. In a twisted kind of way, we have something in common. Wouldn't you say?"

A low chuckle, full of superiority. "Master Pravus, you presume too much."

"About what? About you?"

D'Ablo sighed impatiently. "Yes, about me. About your father, our relationship, your role in this world. It is your presumption that makes you weak. I despise weakness."

Vlad wasn't about to bring up the fact that D'Ablo had been weakened by the lack of a hand. He knew he could run out the door and speed his way to the safety of Otis and Vikas, but this wasn't something they'd understand. Whatever it was between him and D'Ablo was between him and D'Ablo. They had to settle this on their own. Like men. Like vampires. "So set me straight. What am I presuming?"

D'Ablo sighed again. His tone was that of a weary adult explaining something to a young child. "The pieces are in place, Master Pravus, but this game is far from finished."

Vlad shook his head. "You sound like Dorian. He never makes much sense either."

D'Ablo shot Vlad a look that said that he very much disliked Dorian. With a raised eyebrow, he frowned. "Perhaps you're not the only one guilty of making presumptions."

Vlad kept a keen eye on the dagger, but lightened his tone. He had no doubts that at any second, D'Ablo would attempt to finish his ritual. "Why do you want to be the Pravus, anyway? Believe me, it won't exactly solve all your problems."

"To be the Pravus is to be godlike. It is a gift unlike any other. Many have searched for a way to claim that status. All have failed. But for me." He looked at Vlad then, his expression softening some. "Surely you've studied the elements of the prophecy well enough by now to understand that a time will come, Master Pravus, when you will be forced to rule over the very humans you love. This is not something you wish to do. After all, you are just a boy. But I . . . I would take great pleasure in this act. Step aside. Allow me to rule."

Vlad set his jaw. "As tempting as your offer is to give up and die, to let you enslave my family and friends and do who knows what to Elysia . . . I'm afraid my answer is no."

Silence hung in the air for a moment. Then D'Ablo sighed. "Very well then."

For a while, neither of them moved. Then, just as Vlad was beginning to wonder what D'Ablo was thinking, D'Ablo lunged at him with the dagger raised high, a terrible growl emitting from his throat. Instinctively, Vlad ducked to the side, barely escaping the blade. When he looked back at D'Ablo, he couldn't resist quipping, "It's nice to know you're no longer getting your cronies to do your dirty work for you."

D'Ablo whipped around faster than Vlad anticipated. The blade sunk into Vlad's shoulder, buried deep into his flesh. He screamed and fell to the floor, Nelly's presence in the house an afterthought.

D'Ablo pulled the weapon out, sending a spurt of Vlad's blood to the floor. With a smug smile, he slowly wiped the bloodied blade on his pant leg. "I wouldn't deny myself the pleasure of killing you, boy."

Vlad cupped his wounded shoulder with his palm. Strangely, the burning, the stinging, the pain of it disappeared. Normally it would've taken three days for a cut like that to go away, but this time . . . it had taken only moments.

He flicked his eyes to D'Ablo, who didn't seem to have any clue at all that Vlad wasn't wounded anymore. D'Ablo shook his head and crouched in front of him. "What does it feel like to know that you've lost, Master Pravus? What does it feel like to know that you've lost to a better vampire?"

Vlad took a deep breath and slanted his eyes. "You tell me."

Before D'Ablo realized what was happening, Vlad kicked the dagger from his hand, sending it flying to the other side of his bedroom. It clattered against the wall and fell with a thump near the secret door to the attic.

Infuriated, D'Ablo howled and reached for Vlad, but Vlad dove over him, past him, reaching for the dagger. Once he had it, he stood and gripped it tightly in his trembling hand.

D'Ablo stood as well, that air of smug superiority never leaving him. He approached Vlad slowly, but confidently, and chuckled. "What good will it do you? It's not a stake. My life is intact. Wound me? Yes. But I will always return to claim what is rightfully mine."

D'Ablo spun around with vampire speed, but it was just what Vlad had been hoping for. He spun too and plunged the dagger deep into D'Ablo's shoulder. Through muscle, tendon, bone. The point of the blade stuck out of D'Ablo's back. D'Ablo hissed, but didn't scream.

Vlad gripped the hilt tightly and growled, then pulled the dagger upward in one clean jerk. His hand was covered in D'Ablo's blood and still gripping the handle . . . but the blade had broken off and was buried in D'Ablo's flesh and bone.

D'Ablo cried out and fell to his knees. When he looked up at Vlad's hand and realized that his ritual dagger—the one thing that might steal Vlad's status as the Pravus for him—had been destroyed, his eyes filled with a venomous evil that Vlad had never witnessed before. Slowly, he stood again, and, digging into his wound before it could begin the healing process, he gripped the blade with his fingers and ripped it from the sinewy tissues of his shoulder.

The sound it made sent a shiver up Vlad's spine. But Vlad managed to keep his voice both even and strong. "Get out. Now."

To his utter shock, D'Ablo left without another word.

It took Vlad an hour to clean up all the blood. And Nelly didn't make as much as a peep the entire time.

20
GIVING THANKS

THE CAR WAS COMPLETELY SILENT on the drive over to Henry's house. The only one who seemed remotely relaxed was Nelly, but even she wasn't talking. Maybe she knew if she did, Otis and Vlad would snap at her for agreeing to drag her vampire boyfriend and half-vampire ward to a Thanksgiving feast with the one person in town who they knew wanted blood more than they did. Otis was usually incredibly giving when it came to Nelly, but even he looked irritated beyond belief. Vlad folded his arms in front of him, slumping as far down in the backseat as he could. He had no idea what Nelly had been thinking when she told Henry's mom, Matilda, that they'd love to come. Granted, this was all Matilda's idea. But still.

Maybe Matilda thought that if she could get Joss and Vlad together over the holidays, they'd get along just dandy once again. For some reason, Matilda was just crazy enough to think that some pumpkin pie and cranberries were enough to heal a rift as big as the one between them. But she was wrong. There was no way Vlad was forgiving anything that Joss had done—not after he'd invaded Vlad's sanctuary and stole the most precious thing Vlad owned. Maybe once that would have been possible, but after the attack on Vikas, and the conniving thievery, Vlad had come to realize that there could never be a peace between them. And by the look on Otis's face, Vlad would have bet he felt the same way.

Vlad sighed and decided he'd be the first to break the silence. "What am I supposed to eat for nourishment while we're there, Nelly?"

"I told Matilda you were fighting a stomach bug, so you wouldn't feel much like eating. She's just happy you're feeling up to joining us."

"I think I'm coming down with a bug too." The corner of Otis's mouth rose in a smirk as Nelly shot him a glance. "It's a vampire bug. You wouldn't have heard of it."

"Would you two stop whining? It's not going to kill you to sit through dinner with Joss." She grew quiet for a moment, as if contemplating the possibility that her sentence might contain at least a smidgeon of irony. Then she shook her head. "Really. It's not."

Vlad shook his head, amazed by her innocence of the severity of the situation, her unfailing belief that good really lurked inside the hearts of everyone. *"She really doesn't get it, does she?"*

"What human does?" Otis smiled. By the look on Nelly's face, she knew a conversation was going on that she couldn't be a part of. He reached over and squeezed her hand reassuringly. *"She just wants everyone to get along. No matter how impossible that might seem."*

Vlad folded his arms in front of him and sank down in his seat. *"I'm not sitting by Joss. She can't make me forgive him for all he's done. Why would she even want that?"*

"I don't think that's what she's trying to accomplish, Vladimir. I believe she's merely looking for a sense of family around the holiday season. And we . . . not to mention the McMillans . . . are her family. No matter how dysfunctional that idea might be to you, Joss, or me. Blood doesn't make a family, Vladimir. Love does."

"So what do we do?"

"We do what all families do. Grin, bear it, and pass the mashed potatoes."

Otis turned the wheel, pulling his car into Henry's driveway. Vlad had pulled into this driveway countless times before in the seat of many different cars. Only this time, it felt different. This time it felt less like Vlad was arriving at his second home and more like he was about to enter the Temple of Doom. Holding his breath, Vlad opened the door and stepped out into the chilly November air.

It took Otis and Nelly a few seconds to exit the car. Vlad would have bet that Nelly was taking a moment to tell Otis that it meant a lot to her that he was joining them for Thanksgiving, and that Otis was reassuring Nelly that he'd be on his best behavior. Vlad, however, wasn't about to make that promise. He'd keep his distance from Joss, but so help him if his former friend whipped out a sharp hunk of wood . . .

It wasn't that he hated Joss—he didn't. And it wasn't that he felt that vampires were better than slayers—they weren't. It was the fact that he and Joss were being forced together by their own aunts, the two people in the world who should've wanted them to stay as far apart as possible. After all, Nelly knew what Joss had done—she'd seen the bandaged wound, had wept at his bedside as he healed, still flinched whenever Vlad talked about his time in the hospital. She'd listened to Vlad when he'd needed to talk about his friend's brutal betrayal, and she'd spoken words of comfort when Vlad needed to hear them. Most importantly, she backed off when he needed to be alone with his thoughts, understanding that no one else on the planet could make things a hundred percent okay for Vlad . . . not even her. So it hurt that Nelly had agreed to dinner with the McMillans, knowing that Joss would be there. In a weird way, it felt like she was choosing Joss over Vlad. That bugged him . . . and he wasn't sure why, exactly, except for the fact that she was his guardian. She was the one who was supposed to have his best interest at heart. Why she would want him to spend the day with the person who had tried to kill him? But deep down, Vlad knew that she would never put him in harm's way. He couldn't put his finger on exactly why today bothered him so much. Maybe it was because Joss had claimed Bathory as his hometown, the McMillans as his family, and Meredith as his girl. He couldn't have Nelly. She was all Vlad had left, apart from Otis, and Vlad was pretty sure that Joss didn't want him.

Otis and Nelly joined him and the three made their way up the steps to the front door. Otis stood protectively with his hand in the small of Nelly's back. Vlad rang the doorbell, but only for a microsecond, because Matilda had whipped open the door and rushed them all inside, greeting them each with warm hugs and holiday wishes.

It was impossible not to smile with Henry's mom in the room.

In moments, their coats were off and Nelly and Matilda were chattering about a new stuffing recipe that Matilda was trying out this year. Henry was nowhere to be seen, so Vlad excused himself, slipped his shoes off, and headed upstairs to look for his best friend. When he reached Henry's bedroom door, he paused at the raised voices within.

"You're family, Henry. I care about what happens to you."

"Joss, if you give me that crap one more time, I'm gonna punch you so hard your toes are gonna bleed. You're not doing any of this because of some ridiculous need to protect your family. You're doing it because you have a screwed up perception of what vampires are and Vlad got in under your radar, proving that perception wrong. It's spite and you know it."

"You only say those things because he has you confused. That's what they do, Henry. They mess with people's minds and get them to act in ways they normally wouldn't. You're better than this, Henry. You're better than his mindless drone. And I'm going to set you free, one way or another."

Vlad heard Henry step twice and then he exited the bedroom, his face flushed, his entire being seething with anger. When he saw Vlad, he calmed down a bit. "Let's go eat turkey before I beat the crap out of my cousin."

The way he said it, Vlad wasn't sure if Henry wanted to eat *instead* of beating Joss to a pulp, or if he just didn't want to do it on an empty stomach.

Once downstairs, they were met with the scent of a succulent Thanksgiving dinner. Henry's dad, who everyone called Big Mike, and Otis were in the living room, exchanging opinions about human politics with a good-looking tan man who looked like a thirty-seven or thirty-eight-year-old version of Joss. It could only be Joss's dad. Nelly and Matilda were chattering away in the kitchen, finishing up last minute preparations. A rail thin, pale woman, her cheeks somewhat hollow, the expression in her eyes haunted, placed warm rolls in a basket. She flinched as Vlad and Henry entered the room, knocking a butter knife to the floor. Vlad bent and retrieved it, giving her a smile as he dropped it in the sink. When he met her eyes, he realized that Joss didn't just look like his dad. Her eyes mirrored her son's. Vlad took a seat on the stool next to her, but slowly. Any faster and he was afraid she'd bolt. She seemed so tormented, so on edge. He felt bad for her. "You must be Joss's mom. I'm Vlad."

Immediately, her eyes brightened, but only for a moment. "Vladimir Tod. Joss has told me about you."

Vlad debated that sentence for a moment, before she patted him on the hand and said, "You know, Joss never has had many friends. Just his cousin, Henry, really. Losing his sister really left him . . . broken."

That haunted look returned to her eyes. Vlad forced a smile. "Joss is a nice guy. He's been a good—" He swallowed hard and forced the word out. "—*friend* to me. I'm glad I finally got a chance to meet you."

It took her a second, as if she were remembering how, but finally she smiled.

When Vlad glanced over at Nelly, she was smiling too. For a moment, the venom that he had for Joss lessened a little bit.

He looked up and met Joss's eyes as he walked into the kitchen. His slow steps and the look on his face said it all. Get away from my mom, you bloodsucking freak.

But Vlad didn't move.

As if relenting, Joss came over to where Vlad and his mom were sitting and said, "You okay, Mom? Can I get you a drink or something?"

By "a drink," Vlad was almost certain Joss meant "a wooden stake to jab Vlad with," but he kept his mouth shut.

His mom shook her head and stood. "No, but you and Vladimir could get the veggie tray ready while I go wash up."

Vlad looked around for Henry, but he had disappeared to who knows where. Nelly and Matilda grabbed a couple of platters and disappeared into the dining room, leaving Joss and Vlad completely alone. Vlad wished that he could talk to Henry's mind the way he did with Otis. He would tell him that he needed to get back to the kitchen, now. Right now. Before his cousin did something stupid.

Joss picked up a sharp knife and stabbed it into the cutting board in front of Vlad. Instinctively, Vlad flinched. Joss glared at him and muttered, "To cut the vegetables with."

Feeling more than a little stupid for having shown a sense of fear to a slayer, Vlad silently berated himself and reached for a carrot. After slicing four of them, as Joss worked on the celery, Vlad decided to break the silence. "Your mom is really nice."

Joss tensed and growled, "Don't talk to me."

"I wish I could do just that, Joss, but there's the matter of my father's journal to discuss. I know you took it, and I want it back."

Joss was quiet for a long time, and finally barked, "I have no idea what you're talking about."

Only one problem: Joss was lying. He had to be.

Returning to silence, they chopped the rest of the veggies and laid them out on a round glass tray, surrounding a small bowl of ranch dip. Then Joss picked the tray up and headed into the dining room without another word. Joss had changed, that much was for certain. Vlad washed his hands, torn between the conflict of missing the old Joss and utterly despising the new one.

The dining room was about as picturesque as it could be, with a cornucopia at the center of the table and small candles in amber-colored glass holders placed here and there all over the table and room. The place settings were in various autumn colors, burgundy, bronze, gold, and pumpkin. Food sat in beautiful bowls and atop gorgeous platters. The turkey, a perfect golden brown, commanded the feast near the head of the table. It looked like a scene out of a movie, and it smelled a million times better than anything Nelly had ever prepared. So much so that Vlad found himself actually mulling over the idea of eating some human food, sans blood.

Big Mike was sitting at the head of the table, with Matilda to his right. Next to her were Joss's mom and dad, then Joss. At the other end of the table sat Henry's older brother, Greg, and to his right Henry, then an empty chair, then Nelly and Otis. Vlad went to the empty chair, but just as he'd begun to pull it out, Joss stood. "Don't sit there!"

Joss's dad said, "Joss, it's fine."

"No, it's not, Harold." His mom looked even paler than before.

Vlad froze. He knew he'd been about to do something wrong but wasn't sure what.

Joss, still glaring at Vlad, snapped, "Sit somewhere else. That's Cecile's seat. We always leave an open seat for Cecile."

Matilda clapped her hands together. "Oh, that's what we're

forgetting! Henry, there's an extra chair in the kitchen. Why don't you grab it for Cecile? Her place can be between Greg and Joss."

At Matilda's nod, Vlad took his seat. Once everyone was seated and a spot was reserved for the spirit of Joss's dead sister, Henry's dad said, "It's tradition in the McMillan house that we go around the table by age, oldest to youngest, and say what we're thankful for. As I'm fairly sure I'm the oldest here—"

Vlad could barely contain a smile. He glanced over at his uncle who seemed to have the same problem. Otis won that prize for sure, but neither of them were about to argue the point.

"—I'll go first. This year, I'm thankful first and foremost for the health and happiness of my family and good friends, as I'm certain you all are as well. I'm also thankful for my new position at the Bathory *Gazette* as editor-in-chief and for Greg making it home from college for the holidays."

Vlad shifted in his seat. He wasn't sure what he was thankful for, but after hearing Mr. McMillan's speech, he knew it had to be for something far more meaningful than chocolate chip cookies.

Joss's dad spoke, then Otis did. After him, Matilda talked about how grateful she was that everyone had joined them today and what a blessing it was that Joss's family had moved to Bathory.

Vlad knew it was stupid, but he was starting to feel all

kinds of pressure to figure out something that he was thankful for. The truth was, other than surviving Joss's stake and dodging every death blow D'Ablo could throw him, Vlad couldn't think of anything unique to be thankful for.

Nelly paused for a moment and everyone waited for her to speak. Finally, she smiled and said, "I'm grateful that Vlad survived that horrible accident a year and a half ago and that his health is sure and strong now, despite the fact that we almost lost him. I'm so thankful that he has all of you, his friends, because without that kind of love and support, he might not have made it. I'm thankful that Joss is back in his life, and I'm certain that their friendship will find a way through whatever darkness envelops it."

Vlad glanced at Otis, who wore the same surprised expression that he did. Huh. Maybe Nelly wasn't so blind to the lingering danger that Joss brought with him.

She was looking at Joss, and he was looking back. More meaning crossed that table in their eyes than Otis and Vlad could have ever managed with telepathy. Nelly had forgiven Joss for almost killing Vlad. And now she was asking Joss to forgive himself.

Joss blinked away what looked like the threat of tears and Nelly smiled reassuringly. Beside her, Otis's expression was blank. Vlad was guessing that Otis wasn't brimming with forgiveness for Joss just yet.

After a short pause, Greg gave his reasons for being thankful—Vlad wasn't really listening, but it sounded like something having to do with his college baseball team. Henry only out-aged Joss by about a month, so he went first, mumbling that he was thankful that we were almost done giving thanks and could eat soon. Matilda berated him, while Big Mike just laughed. Then it was Joss's turn.

Joss, like Nelly, was quiet for a moment. When he spoke, his tone was hurting and full of venom. Vlad knew instantly that it was a message meant for him and him alone. "I'm thankful for the safety of my family, and if anyone dares to cause any one of them harm, I'm going to hunt them down and teach them what it is to feel pain."

Mouths fell agape around the table, all but Vlad, Otis, and Henry. Then Henry mumbled something foul that ended with "you, Joss" and Matilda sent him to his room without dinner, grounding him from video games for two weeks. Once silence and order had been restored, Matilda said, "It's your turn, Vlad. What are you thankful for?"

Vlad thought about it for a minute and then it came to him. This was it. This was how he was going to reach Joss, how he was going to cut through the distorted web of the Slayer Society and make him see the error of his ways. He made sure to meet Joss's eyes as he spoke. "I'm thankful for you, Joss, and . . . for Cecile."

Joss clenched his jaw. It looked like he was doing everything he could not to leap over the table and stab Vlad with a carving knife.

Vlad held his gaze, meaning every word, hoping something

would break through Joss's cold exterior. Even if it backfired, at least Joss would know how he felt. "Seeing the way you talk about her makes me realize how much I missed out on not having any siblings. Luckily, I've found a brother in Henry . . . and in you. Thank you."

The rest of dinner passed with casual conversation. The only two who didn't speak were Joss and Vlad.

After dinner, Joss disappeared into the guest room. Everyone else retired to the family room for after-dinner drinks and conversations about whatever it is that adults talk about when kids aren't around. With permission from Nelly, Vlad said goodbye to everyone, making sure to stop upstairs and thank Henry for having his back and sneak him a piece of pumpkin pie from the kitchen. He hurried back downstairs and out the door, thankful for the solitary walk home.

The air was brisk, so Vlad pulled the collar of his coat up around his ears and moved down the sidewalk, stopping only to gaze up at the clear sky and the bright, twinkling stars. He was so entranced by the beauty of the night that he didn't hear the familiar footsteps on the frosty ground. Nor did he hear the shuffling steps as Joss moved into a roundhouse kick. His chest exploded with pain and Vlad stumbled back, his tone surprised as he forced air back into his lungs. "Joss!"

"I can't kill you yet but that doesn't mean I can't kick your ass." His eyes were red, as if he'd recently been crying. He hissed, "How dare you say her name."

Vlad stumbled for words, but before he could find them, a

large hand closed over Joss's throat. Joss stiffened and Vikas smiled at Vlad over Joss's shoulder. "You would do well to treat this boy kindly, slayer. He saved your life, after all. If not for him, my friends and I would have feasted on your marrow months ago. Now find your way home."

Joss swallowed and Vikas tightened his hand. "This creature and I have business to attend to. Release me."

Vikas whispered in his ear, "Or you'll what?"

For a moment, Vikas tightened his grip, as if to give Joss a taste of what awaited him should he refuse to leave. He opened his hand and Joss fell to the ground. "Go home, little one. Spend time with your family. Forget about Vladimir and enjoy your holiday weekend."

Joss's eyes had remained fierce throughout the encounter, though Vlad could see fear hidden in them. He stood up, brushing the dirt from his jeans. Relief took the place of fear in Joss's eyes, and he started to back down the sidewalk toward Henry's house. He called out to Vlad. "Do yourself a favor, Vlad. Don't you ever say her name again. Your bodyguard won't always be there."

Then Joss turned and broke into a run.

Vikas shook his head. "That boy is a fool."

Vlad shook his head too, but for different reasons. "That boy is my friend . . . or was, anyway. He's been through a lot. He and his whole family have had their lives ripped apart by a vampire. No wonder he hates me. No wonder he is the way he is."

After a moment, he looked back to Vikas. "Shouldn't you be eating Thanksgiving dinner about now?"

Vikas smiled, and for the first time Vlad noticed the small trail of blood on the corner of his mouth. "I just finished, actually. Suffice it to say, Bathory no longer has a homeless problem."

Vlad groaned and tugged Vikas's sleeve, guiding him toward home. "Yeah, about your appetite while you're here in Bathory . . . we've got to talk."

21
Not-So-Distant Memories

V LAD RAN HIS FINGER THOUGHTFULLY ALONG the thin, silver chain around his neck until he reached the key that Otis had given him. He'd been wearing it ever since that day, always tucking it into his shirt so nobody would question what it opened.

But Vlad knew. And today, for some reason, the thought of opening the door to his parents' bedroom was consuming him.

He'd argued with himself all through first and second period about how stupid it would be to go wander around a room that really held no clues at all to how the fire had started, but the closer it got to the bell ringing at the end of third period, the less his internal arguments made sense. By the time the big hand on the clock ticked toward the number twelve and the bell rang out through the halls of Bathory High, Vlad had decided to sneak out and see if there was anything there, anything at all that might help him determine exactly how his parents had died and who, if anyone, was responsible.

It didn't take him long to exit the front doors or to get across town. As he opened the back door, he thought of Vikas, who was likely resting peacefully upstairs. It was weird to think of someone being there in his moment of possible discovery, but it wasn't like he could shake Vikas awake and ask him to step out for a moment while he strolled down memory lane with the ghosts of his mom and dad. He moved inside quietly. It sounded like the TV was on in the living room, which he immediately attributed to Tristian. Without making a sound, Vlad made his way upstairs and, as he moved past Vikas's door, pulled the chain over his head, holding the warm key in his palm.

He stood at his parents' door for several minutes.

He might have been gathering courage; he might have been mentally preparing himself. But mostly, Vlad was fighting to keep the memory of that day—the morning he found them—from the forefront of his mind.

It was a losing battle.

He closed his hand over the small, silver knob. At the same moment, in his mind's eye, he saw his hand, his ten-year-old hand, closing over the same knob. Together, both hands swung the door open. Both hearts beat out of control at the smell of ash and soot.

Shaking his head, trying hard to remain in the present, Vlad stepped over the threshold. His younger self stepped inside too, and turned as he did to face the bed.

"Mom! Dad! NO!"

Vlad closed his eyes, blocking out his younger self's voice. No, Vlad. Don't go down that path. Stay in the present.

But when he opened his eyes again, all he could see was his younger self's point of view. It was strange, as if he was watching a movie. Occasionally, the real world, the present world, would leak in and he'd see what he was really faced with, but mostly, he relived that day, moment for moment.

Instead of dust and cobwebs lying atop the soot and ashes, the ashes were fresh, some embers still glowing brightly. Instead of the quiet of a haunted, forgotten place, the sounds of sirens and voices filled his head. The room was filled with smoke, still overwhelmed by a heat that Vlad could barely stand to be near, but he had to see, he had to know. His chest rose and fell both from the run from school and from what he was seeing.

On the bed were two figures. Figures that had once been people. Figures that had just kissed him good night not ten hours before. All that remained were black, sooty shapes. All that Vlad could identify was an arm and what might have been an open mouth. He reached out, his fingers making contact . . .

Vlad jerked out of the memory, streams of tears coating his cheeks. He didn't want to remember, didn't need to remember. He'd come here looking for evidence, not pain. That he had an abundance of.

He looked around the room, his eyes searching for something, anything that might offer a clue as to what had happened. But when his eyes fell on the bed again . . .

He reached out, his fingers making contact with the ashen form closest to him. It was his mother. It had to be. That was exactly where she'd been lying when he'd turned off her alarm. As his fingers brushed against her, her body—her burned, fragile remains—crumbled into a pile. Vlad screamed.

He closed his eyes again, willing away that memory with deep, shaking breaths. The tears were coming too easily now. He brushed them away with his arm, but his efforts were useless. Determined, he opened his eyes again and focused on the present.

At first, he saw only dirt and dust over more dirt and dust. Then his eyes settled on a spot on the wall, near his father's nightstand. There the soot was smudged, as if someone had wiped it away. Vlad moved around the bed to get a closer look. He knelt and leaned forward, taking a good, long look at the glyph on the small panel there.

He'd never noticed it before. But then, he'd never spent much time in this room since the fire.

He reached up slowly, the glyph glowing at his close proximity, and touched it. The panel opened inward. When he peered inside, he saw nothing.

Another dead end.

Vlad cursed under his breath, but then bit his bottom lip and placed his hand inside the compartment. He felt all along each wall, then reached up and felt carefully along the top.

Nothing. The compartment was completely empty.

Vlad's shoulders sank.

As he pulled his hand out, his finger stung. He yanked it back, fearing a spider bite. Blood bubbled from the tip of his finger. A paper cut. Vlad sucked the blood away and reached back in with his other hand. Carefully, he moved it across the top of the compartment. With the tips of his fingers, he touched the corner of a slip of paper, wedged into a seam. It took him several tries, but finally, he withdrew the paper and sat back on his heels, holding it curiously in his palm.

He unfolded it and there, in his father's handwriting, was "Aidan" and a phone number.

It was probably nothing, probably meaningless, but Vlad tucked it carefully into his pocket and stood, looking around the room some more.

As he was going over the bureau's top drawers—or rather, what remained of them—Vikas's voice broke in from behind him. "What are you looking for, Mahlyenki Dyavol?"

He didn't miss a beat. "Answers. I want to know what happened to them. I want to know who did it. And I want to know why."

Vikas stepped closer, placing a caring hand on Vlad's shoulder. "What answers can you possibly find in the cold ashes, Vladimir? The men who did this must have had their reasons for doing so, but they've left nothing behind. Only bad memories."

Turning to face him, Vlad said, "Vikas? What makes you think it was more than one man?"

Vikas grew quiet for a bit, then gave his shoulder a squeeze before turning to leave the room. "Just a feeling I have, Mahlyenki Dvayol. It most likely means nothing at all."

Vlad took no comfort in his words, but his tears at last ceased.

22
A TAINTED EVENING

VLAD BUTTONED THE LAST BUTTON on his pewter-colored shirt and sighed. He didn't much feel like dressing up, and he certainly didn't feel like going to a dance tonight, least of all *this* dance, Bathory High's annual Snow Ball. He slipped on his black vest and smiled at the tiny skull buttons. If nothing else, at least he looked sharp.

Still, he really, really didn't want to go. Joss and Meredith would be there as a—Vlad gulped—couple. He didn't need any more reason to avoid the school at all cost. The very idea of those two dancing closely and ignoring the fact that he was once a big part of both of their lives sent a wave of nausea over him. But then . . . maybe he hadn't been a big part of their lives. Maybe they'd just been a big part of his.

Vlad shook his head. He couldn't start down that path of thinking, or the evening would be a total loss.

With one more glance at his reflection, Vlad walked out of his bedroom and down the stairs to where Nelly was waiting. At the sight of him, she smiled. "You look very handsome. So who's the lucky girl?"

"Her name is Snow."

Nelly's voice took on a tone of mock irritation. "And how come I haven't heard of her before?"

Vlad did his best to match her inflection with a sarcastic quip. "Because, she lives in Stokerton and I haven't mentioned her to you."

"So, when do I get to meet her?" Much to Vlad's annoyance, Nelly had that I-told-you-you'd-get-over-Meredith look on her face.

"Not tonight."

Nelly's jaw dropped; she let out a playful gasp. "You are so grounded to your coffin."

A smile fought its way onto Vlad's face. It didn't matter how hard he tried to avoid it or how much he wanted to wallow in his self-induced pit of despair, Nelly could always make him smile.

"I'm meeting her at the dance. October's giving her a ride." Vlad opened the front closet and grabbed his coat and shoes.

"Do you want me to drive you? Or would you like to take the car?"

"I'm not ready to drive in the snow yet." Vlad shuddered. "I'm not sure our neighbor's mailbox is ready either. Besides . . ."

Outside, Henry's horn honked, so Vlad opened the door and waved. As he slid on his jacket, he smiled at Nelly. ". . . Henry's driving me. I'll be back by midnight, okay?"

She nodded and Vlad walked out the door, closing it behind him. Once he was inside Henry's car and moving down the road, he grumbled, "I don't understand how you and October think it's okay to pressure me into taking Snow to this dance."

Henry was busy checking his mirrors, speedometer, and blind spot. It was obvious that he was avoiding Vlad's protests.

Vlad glared. "Dude, you know I'm trying to keep my distance from her and neither one of you are bringing dates."

Henry chuckled. "Quit whining. We're doing you a favor. You should've seen Snow when I dropped them off at the school."

"Wait, you drove them? I thought October was picking her up."

"Yeah, that was the original plan."

"So, what happened?"

Henry shrugged. "Plans changed."

"Thank you for explaining that so clearly. So, why didn't you just bring them over to Nelly's?"

"Because when a girl looks as hot as Snow looks tonight, you don't want your parental figure to see."

Vlad didn't argue, because for once in his young life, Henry sounded full of wisdom.

The car came to a stop just across the street from the school and, thanks to the chill of late December, it didn't take long for the boys to make their way inside. The hall was decorated in a thousand different snowflakes. Some dangled from the high arched ceiling; some were pasted onto lockers and walls; some littered the floor. A silver, white, and soft blue path led their way to the gym, at the doors of which stood a girl. A girl Vlad couldn't take his eyes off.

He thought he heard Henry say something about having fun as he moved down the hall and into the gym, but he couldn't remember how to speak, so his reply was merely silence.

She was dressed in black from head to toe. The top of her luxurious silk gown was strapless, baring her flawless, pale shoulders, and corseted, revealing just a hint of something that made Vlad's face flush bright red. The skirt of her gown was layered and full. Her hair was pinned up in messy curls, tiny bats dotting the barrettes, matching the tiny, glittery bats on her nails. Vlad took a step closer and breathed her name. "Snow . . ."

Her nervous smile relaxed. Vlad couldn't help but wonder what it was she had to be nervous about. He was the one who felt like a stuttering idiot. He walked down the hall in what felt like slow motion, and when he reached her, her smile faltered. "Listen, Vlad. I know I'm only here because October forced you to take me. So we don't have to pretend we're dating or anything. We can just be here as friends."

Vlad shook his head, a smile fixed on his lips, unwilling to let reality spoil the already magical evening. "You look amazing."

Relaxing her shoulders, Snow beamed. "You look pretty hot yourself, mister."

He held out his elbow and she looped her arm in his, then they walked arm in arm through the open gym doors into a winter paradise. Wide, wondering eyes turned toward them, and though Vlad was certain most of them were questioning who exactly was the beauty on his arm, he was happy to speculate that maybe a few of the gathered crowd had no idea who he was. He felt like a different person, oddly confident, ready to shine, and very, very aware of the feel of Snow's arm on his own.

One couple in particular caught his eye. A good-looking guy in deep blue and a pretty girl in white and pink. Joss and Meredith. And for once, Vlad didn't care about what Meredith might be thinking. He was too wrapped up in the shocked expressions that had greeted them.

But there it was, on the cusp of the other kids' thoughts. Meredith's words in his head. *Is that why he broke up with me? To be with her?*

Vlad pushed her thoughts away and with them, his anguish at seeing the heartbreak in her eyes.

Though the rest of the goth kids were nowhere to be seen, Henry was standing by the punch bowl with October. Vlad steered Snow toward them, smiling the entire time. October grinned. "You're the perfect couple."

Henry nodded. "Our work here is done."

He and October clinked their plastic cups together and smiled. Vlad was happy to see his two friends getting along and working together toward a common goal. Even if he was the reason that they had to work so hard.

The evening proceeded with much more grace than Vlad thought was possible. He and Snow danced to almost every song, when they weren't hanging out with Henry and October, who seemed to have developed a sort of friendship when Vlad hadn't been looking. The music was incredible—a perfect selection of songs. The food was amazing. Even luck seemed to be on his side, as he didn't see much of Joss or Meredith at all. Halfway through the night, a slow song came on, and Snow tugged him onto the dance floor with a gleam in her dark eyes.

As they danced, Snow stepped in closer and Vlad let her. They swayed side to side, so close and warm, and Vlad's heart fluttered happily. Then, without warning, his gums throbbed and his fangs elongated. Tensing, he snapped his mouth shut.

Not here. Not now. Not when he was trying so desperately to quit drinking from Snow.

Snow looked at him, concern filling her eyes. It took her a second, but when she realized what the problem was, that Vlad needed to feed and he needed to feed *now*, she tugged him out into the hall. Henry emitted a howl from across the room, which made Snow roll her eyes right along with Vlad. Once in the hall, Snow pulled him into a semidark corner, bent her neck to the side, and whispered, "Hurry. Before someone sees."

Vlad nodded, unable to speak, unable to refuse, only capable at the moment of hungering for what lay within Snow's delectable veins. He pulled her closer, trying to be gentle, and bit firmly into her jugular. The sweet taste of warm blood splashed across his tongue, and Vlad almost moaned with pleasure. Out of the corner of his eye, he saw a flash—Eddie, probably, and his stupid camera—but he didn't care. The hunger had him now. He drank deeply, filling himself with her essence, feeling his body growing stronger as hers grew weaker. For a brief moment, he opened his eyes, and over Snow's shoulder he saw a face that he knew very well.

Meredith's brown eyes were wide, but not terrified. She muttered, "I'm sorry. I didn't mean to interrupt," and turned to walk away, her eyes shimmering.

He'd hurt her. Again, he'd hurt her.

Vlad pulled back, withdrawing his fangs. They shrank into his gums immediately. He wiped the blood from his mouth with his palm. "Meredith, wait . . ."

Snow crumpled to the ground, weak from his feast. Vlad crouched down, his eyes full of concern. He'd done it again, despite his determination not to. He'd fed from Snow. He'd treated her like nothing more than a cheeseburger. He'd hurt Meredith again and once more, he was hurting Snow. He couldn't get anything right.

He didn't deserve either one of them.

He met her eyes and she mouthed, "Go after her."

After a pause, a long pause, filled with doubt that seemed to stretch on forever, he bolted down the hall, back to the gym. Meredith was hurrying across the room, heading straight for Joss. Vlad reached out and grabbed her by the arm. "Wait. Would you just wait?"

She stopped suddenly but didn't look at him.

"That wasn't what it looked like."

"So you weren't just making out with that . . . that . . . that girl?" She flung an arm in the general direction of where they'd left Snow, her eyes furious, alive with jealousy.

"No. I—wait, what does it matter to you if I was? You're with Joss now, remember?" His voice had risen in anger and resentment. He didn't mean for it to.

Meredith's cheeks flushed—mostly out of anger, but also because Vlad was right. It was no business of hers who Vlad made out with.

Vlad blinked, uncertain what else to say. Part of him wanted to let Meredith run off, to be done with worrying about what she thought, to dance with Snow and feed when he needed and kiss her . . . yes, kiss her. The other part of him wanted—needed—Meredith to know the truth, to know if she loved him no matter what fiendish beast lurked inside of him, to hold her close and transport them back in time, to when things were easier between them. He took a deep breath and spoke before he could stop himself. "I wasn't kissing her. I was feeding from her. I'm . . . I'm a vampire."

At first, Meredith didn't do or say anything at all. He wasn't even certain she'd heard him. Then she looked Vlad in the eye and slapped him hard across the face.

The sting shocked Vlad, and he turned his eyes back to her with a questioning look.

Her own eyes brimmed with tears, as if he'd just insulted her in the worst way, as if he'd invented an outrageous story just to hurt her feelings and demean her intelligence. Her voice wavered as she spoke, but he couldn't tell if it was out of fury or sorrow . . . or maybe a bit of both. "Do me a favor, Vlad. Do us both a favor. Never speak to me again."

Vlad's fingers touched his burning cheek lightly as she turned and found her way into Joss's arms. She didn't believe him. He'd told her the truth, his most guarded secret, and she thought he was lying.

Before he could blink, October was in front of him, looking more than a little irritated. "What are you doing with Meredith? Where's Snow?"

"She's . . ." Vlad lost himself in thought mid-sentence. Meredith didn't believe him. He'd only ever told Henry he was a vampire, only one other person in the world. Snow had learned with a bite; Joss had learned with a fight, and Nelly had known his entire life. But only Henry had been told. And Henry had accepted him without question. Meredith had shunned him, labeling his reality as nothing more than a cruel joke. As if he were no more than an insensitive jerk who'd broken her heart so he could be with Snow. Snow . . . "She's in the hall."

October turned with a huff to go retrieve Snow, but Vlad grabbed her gruffly by the arm. "No. I'll get her."

He crossed the room, still stunned that he'd uttered those fateful words to Meredith and more stunned that she'd reacted the way she did. He found his way to the hall, where Snow was struggling to stand. He helped her up, then acted as a brace for her until her strength returned. When she spoke, her voice sounded broken, distant, sad. "What did you tell her?"

Standing at the end of the hall was Eddie Poe, looking more than a little interested in their conversation. Vlad tensed and wondered aloud, "What does he want?"

"The same thing he wants when he visits The Crypt. Answers. Answers I refuse to give him. Y'know, even if you hadn't ordered me not to talk to him, I wouldn't. That guy is such a weasel."

Vlad almost managed to swallow his esophagus. "He comes to The Crypt? When? For how long now? What does he do?"

Snow held up a hand, stopping his ramble. She waited for Eddie to disappear back into the gym before saying, "I didn't tell you, because I didn't want you stressing out over nothing. Mostly, he just stands in the corner and gawks at me. This last time, he asked me questions about you. It took him a while to work up to the vampire question, but he got there with some determination. But stop worrying about Eddie Poe. I have him under control. Now . . . what did you tell Meredith?"

Barely able to tear his eyes from the door Eddie had walked through, Vlad's words fell into disbelieving whispers. "I told her I'm a vampire."

Snow's eyes widened. "Seriously? What did she think about that?"

He shook his head, trying to erase the memory of Meredith's face when he'd finally told her the truth. She didn't believe him. She thought it was just a ploy to get between her and Joss. "It doesn't matter. None of it matters. All that matters is that I'm sorry I left you to chase after her, Snow. Are you okay?"

"I'm fine. Just a little dizzy." Snow shrugged and smiled up at him, looking more than a little relieved that Meredith had rejected him. "I missed you feeding from me."

Vlad raised an eyebrow. What a weird thing to say. "Really? Cuz it seems like it makes you sick or something."

"Maybe it's having you close that I miss." She ran her finger delicately along the buttons of his vest and met his gaze. "Vlad?"

Was it getting warm in here? Vlad swallowed hard, resisting the urge to undo the top few buttons of his shirt. "Yeah?"

She tilted her head to the side, curiosity filling her lovely eyes. "Do you really like that Meredith girl still?"

He didn't have to think about it, not for a second, and he didn't want to lie. But he knew if he were another boy, a boy like Henry maybe, he wouldn't have answered. He would have bent down and kissed Snow so deeply before dragging her back onto the dance floor with whispered promises and sweet nothings. But he wasn't that kind of boy. He was Vlad. Almost guilty, he said, "Yeah. I do."

"Oh." The hurt was there in her eyes, hurt that shouted loud and clear. Snow wanted to be his everything, no matter the cost.

"It's . . . complicated." Vlad made sure she was steady, then backed away from her. The hall cooled considerably.

"Love usually is." She shrugged again and smiled, all traces of sadness erased. "What's it like to be a vampire?"

"It's . . ." Vlad sighed, shaking his head. "It's complicated too."

"Would you ever . . ." She had her well-groomed eyebrows raised, but then lowered them, shaking her head. "Never mind."

But Vlad couldn't help but wonder if Snow were about to ask him to make her into a vampire as well.

Clearing his throat, Vlad gave the subject a shove in another direction. "Do you wanna dance?"

Snow beamed.

Vlad held out the crook of his arm and led her back into the gym. He hardly thought about Meredith Brookstone the rest of the night.

Not more than five or six thousand times, anyway.

23
V BAR

THE CAB PULLED TO A STOP and Otis slipped the cabbie some money before opening his door. Vlad slid out after him and yawned. The flight to New York City had been short, but uneventful—there had been minor excitement when Otis pointed out the Statue of Liberty as they were landing, but Vlad couldn't see it, so he just nodded noncommittally when Otis asked if he had. From the airport, they drove straight through to Greenwich Village, with promises from Otis that they'd stay in Midtown Manhattan so that Vlad could see Times Square. Vlad was trying to be excited about the trip, but the fact remained that they were here for Otis's pretrial. And according to Vikas, this was Otis's last chance at getting out of the charges filed against him alive.

The cabbie pulled their suitcases from the trunk, wished them a nice day, and before Vlad could open his mouth to say goodbye, he was gone, barreling down the street as if he were in a hurry to get away from his pale, thin, ravenous looking fares. Maybe, Vlad thought, he was.

Otis picked up their suitcases and nodded toward an unassuming café behind Vlad. A small sign hung over the door, painted blue—like the door and window trim—with white letters that read V Bar. Otis leaned closer and said, "Any idea what the *V* might stand for?"

Vlad mulled the possibilities over for just a second. "A vampire bar? Really?"

Otis nodded. "The owner is a good friend of mine. Though not, as it were, a good friend of your father's."

"Why not?"

"I've never been clear on that. But trust me. You didn't want to be in the same room with Tomas and Enrico." Otis stepped forward, leading the way inside the bar.

The moment Vlad stepped over the threshold, he felt at home. V Bar was small, but cozy, with worn wood and small tables. A long bar lined the right side of the room, and a large chalkboard hung over the bar proclaiming the menu to thirsty visitors. To his left was a compilation of interesting artifacts—a statue of an armless woman, an old Ouija board. On the bar sat a picture of Count Chocula. In the corner, a piece of wooden trim was painted to look subtly like blood-tipped fangs.

It was probably the coolest place Vlad had ever been in.

Otis stepped up to the bar and took a seat. After admiring the room a bit more, Vlad sat beside him. A man behind the bar with curly light brown hair and a lean, muscular form smiled at them and gave them a nod, as if to say he'd be with them in a moment. There was quite a selection on the menu, everything from tea to wine, but nothing, Vlad noted, that would satisfy a vampire's palate. He was beginning to wonder if perhaps the *V* in V Bar simply referred to who owned the establishment, not the patrons. He frowned, somewhat disappointed. After such a long trip, he could really use a drink.

"What can I get you gentlemen?" The bartender had warm eyes and a kind smile. The blue of his T-shirt matched the shade of his eyes perfectly. Vlad bet that he was a really nice guy.

Otis smiled back. "The house red, please. For both of us."

The bartender beamed, offering Vlad a sly wink before turning back to Otis. "I thought your guest was part of the club but had to ask to be certain. Are you here on business or pleasure, Mr. Otis?"

"Business, unfortunately."

The bartender nodded, his smile fading some. "I'll make it a double then."

"Would you please let Enrico know that I'm here, and I've brought a guest?"

"Of course." He turned and picked up the phone, speaking quietly into it. Once he hung up, he filled two wineglasses with what looked like red wine and sat them on the bar. With a glance at Vlad, he poured one glass into a plastic cup with a lid and straw. As he slid the cup forward, he said, "For appearances. We wouldn't want to attract any unwanted attention, would we?"

Vlad chuckled and shook his head. The cup was completely see-through, but whatever. He'd just claim it was cranberry juice if anyone asked. He sipped from the straw and recognized the spice immediately. Bloodwine.

Vlad spoke to Otis with his thoughts. *"Is the bartender . . . like us?"*

Otis chuckled. "Why don't you ask him?"

Taking another sip, Vlad looked around to be certain no one would hear. Then he met the eyes of the bartender, who seemed to be awaiting his words. "Excuse me, but are you a vampire too?"

He furrowed his brow, looking quite confused and said, "A vampire? Are you putting me on? They don't exist."

Vlad blinked, lost. He'd been almost certain that the bartender had known exactly what Otis was, what Vlad was. He started to mumble an apology, when Otis and the bartender broke into laughter. The bartender shook his head, his eyes sparkling. "No, little one, I am not. I'm blessed to be one of Enrico's drudges, but I am not a vampire—though I certainly wish to be."

Vlad couldn't help but be a little surprised. Like Tristian, this man looked like a vampire, carried himself like a vampire. Maybe drudges took on those traits after so many years in

Elysia. He couldn't ever imagine Henry doing so, but then, he wasn't sure he moved the way they did, either. "Has Enrico changed many of his drudges?"

"Only one. But there is always hope." He winked again and then stole away down the length of the bar to help another customer.

"Otis Otis." A man's voice behind them, warm and inviting.

Before even turning around, Otis smiled broadly. "Enrico Ciotti."

An Italian man with dark features embraced Otis tightly. "It has been too long, my friend."

"You say that every time I see you, Enrico."

Enrico laughed and released him. "Well then, maybe you should come by more often." He smiled at Vlad and thrust out his hand. "This must be your nephew. I'm pleased to make your acquaintance, Vladimir. Your uncle sings your praises constantly."

Vlad shook his hand, not mentioning that today was the first time Otis had ever mentioned Enrico, and certainly not making mention of his dad. "Nice to meet you."

As Enrico settled onto the stool beside him, Otis said, "I trust you know why I'm here."

He nodded in response. "Ah yes. The pretrial. I was so elated that the Council of Elders chose my fair city for it that I offered up space."

"They turned you down, I trust?"

"On the contrary, they leaped at the offer. Apart from D'Ablo, of course."

"Of course." Otis wet his lips, suddenly looking nervous. Maybe it was just now hitting him that this was his last chance to be proclaimed innocent. "I admit, I'm surprised. I'd thought Central Park or perhaps the library . . ."

"And insult me with their choice?" Enrico shook his head confidently. "Apart from D'Ablo, I am good friends with every member of that council. Refusing my offer would have created a rift—one I'm sure they'd rather avoid, considering my son."

Otis's jaw tightened. "Is he here?"

"He's around, I'm sure. Probably sleeping. We all can't be day owls like yourself, Otis." Laughter bubbled out of Enrico as natural as breath.

"To be fair, the sun has begun to set. It's not as if we came at noon." The tension hadn't left Otis, but he was trying hard to smile and act casual. But Vlad knew otherwise. Something was troubling Otis. Likely the mention of Enrico's son . . . whoever he was. "Still, perhaps it's best that he remains resting while my nephew and I are here. We'll retire to our hotel room in a bit and return for the pretrial at midnight."

Enrico waved a hand through the air, dismissing the notion. "Nonsense. There's no sense avoiding him."

Their conversation continued, but Vlad's attention waned. He felt the strangest compulsion to leave the bar. He shook it off for a good ten minutes, trying to focus on the conversation between Otis and Enrico. Finally, the pull was too strong to ignore, and he slipped from his bar stool and quietly made his way to the door. He paused there, taking the time to look back at Otis, who didn't even glance at him. In fact, no one seemed to notice him at all. The bartender finished wiping off the counter. There was a woman who kept sipping her wine and feverishly scribbling something on the page in front of her. Enrico and Otis kept chatting. All of them seemed blissfully unaware that Vlad had even moved at all. Raising an eyebrow, Vlad stepped out the door and onto the sidewalk.

He turned south, following the pull at his core, and his steps only began to slow when he recognized the man standing at the end of the block. Dark eyes. Pale skin. A thin Cupid's-bow mouth. Copper-colored hair. Vlad would have recognized that face anywhere.

Dorian.

So that's who Otis and Enrico had been talking about. Dorian. And Vlad would have bet anything that Dorian was Enrico's son.

Vlad couldn't help but wonder if Dorian was responsible for the irresistible pull he'd felt at the center of his being, urging him to leave the bar and wander down the street.

Dorian nodded. At first Vlad thought it was in greeting, but then Dorian spoke. "I am responsible for that. I do apologize, but it was really the only way to get you alone without alerting the others."

Vlad remained stiff, the thought of Dorian's cravings for his blood never far from his mind. "And you brought me here why?"

A smile crossed Dorian's lips. "Not for the reason you might expect, though I'm still very open to tasting your blood if you're interested."

Vlad crossed his arms in front of him.

Dorian chuckled. "No? Well then, onto my real motives. Do you have any idea how many vampires are allowed to know the prophecy of the Pravus in its entirety, Vlad?" He paused, but only slightly. "Four. Just four. And I am the last of that four. I am the only vampire in existence that can carry such knowledge. I am the Keeper of the Prophecy."

"The other three are dead?"

"The Foreteller and Transcriber of the Prophecy are both dead. They died to hide this knowledge from Elysia. I keep it so that I may educate vampirekind when the time is right." He wet his lips and stepped forward cautiously, as if knowing how on edge his presence made Vlad feel. He seemed to know just about everything there was to know about Vlad. His eyes met Vlad's and once again, Vlad was struck by how harmless he looked. "I'd like to educate you right now, if you're willing."

Vlad was about to ask about the third person who knew the prophecy, as Dorian had only named two others besides himself, but then in his mind, a film jumped, and he knew that Dorian was sharing a memory with him. The grainy image of two men in a small, dark room came to life, then sharpened. Vlad couldn't shake the feeling that the room seemed somehow familiar, and then it hit him. It was the training room in Siberia. The sounds of their breathing filled Vlad's head, and Vlad knew that he was seeing the memory from Dorian's point of view. Silently, Dorian moved forward and knelt before the men. One knelt beside him and seemed to enter into a

(205)

trance, then started speaking in Elysian code to no one in particular, as if he were reading a book aloud. Dorian's heart drummed in Vlad's ears.

The third man turned around, messing with something on the small table behind him. When he turned back, Vlad could see he was holding a quill in his hand. There was no ink in sight and the metal tip was glowing, like a red-hot coal. Then, in a moment of sheer horror, Vlad saw the man holding the quill lean forward and press the burning pen into Dorian's skin. Dorian cried out but held very still as the man worked over his skin. When the tip would cool, he'd move back to the fireplace and then return to Dorian's skin with a fresh quill, burning words into Dorian's exposed flesh. Vlad couldn't get a good look at what the man was writing, but he was almost positive that it was whatever the chanting man was saying aloud.

Once Dorian healed, the man would begin again, branding and carving words into Dorian again and again. At one point, Dorian tried to break away, unable to face the pain any longer. The man with the pen pulled him back, his face sympathetic, and attached chains to Dorian's wrists to stop him from fleeing. Then he continued to inscribe words on Dorian's skin, over and over again. All Vlad could do was watch in horrified disbelief.

Dorian's thoughts broke in over the memory like the narrator in an old movie. *"They continued for a year, breaking only to feed, though I was not allowed to partake. By the time we were done, I had not only put the prophecy of the Pravus to memory, but ingrained it on my soul."*

The film jumped forward then. Exhausted and aged by his ordeal, Dorian lay on the floor of the training room, spent. The chanting man had stopped chanting and the man with the pen had ceased as well. A fourth man, one Vlad knew well, entered the room and set Dorian free. Vlad watched as Vikas killed the Foreteller and the Transcriber, though neither fought it. It was as if they'd expected it, as if they all knew they had a role to play and were willing to play it. Dorian crawled forward, lapping at the blood from their fatal wounds.

"Ever since I emerged from that room I have craved nothing but vampire blood, and as I am the Keeper of the Prophecy, as it is stored within my veins, all of Elysia bow to my whims. Perhaps they figure it is a small price compared to the torment that I endured. I don't know."

The image froze on Dorian's hand lovingly caressing the dead face of the Inscriber, and just like that, Vlad was no longer watching Dorian's memory.

Dorian said, "So to answer your question of where the prophecy is, the answer stands before you. Simply put, it is within me."

Vlad took a deep breath and blew it out, trying to erase those images from his mind. "I don't suppose you could jot it down for me."

A smile touched Dorian's lips. "No. I'm afraid I can't. Nor

can I tell you the prophecy verbatim. I have discussed portions of it with various vampires over time and books have been written on the subject based on those conversations, but none but I know the prophecy in its entirety. However, I can answer direct questions. And I will . . . in time."

Dorian turned around and started walking away. Over his shoulder, he called out, "Your uncle will notice your departure in a moment. I suggest you hurry back."

"Wait. First tell me something. Something not about the prophecy. Something about you." Dorian paused and Vlad ran to catch up with him. Once he reached his side, he asked, "Where do you get your powers from?"

Once again, Dorian smiled. "Ask your uncle."

"Is that one of your secrets, Dorian?"

"I have only one secret, and that is not it. Perhaps one day I will share my secret with you, but that day isn't today." Dorian started walking again, and this time, Vlad didn't follow.

He hurried back to V Bar and, just as he'd entered the door, Otis straightened and looked around. His expression darkened when he saw Vlad returning. While Vlad found his seat once again, Enrico excused himself to go help the bartender. Otis eyed Vlad for a moment before he spoke. "Enrico has invited us along for dinner. I'm assuming you missed that part of the conversation."

Vlad swallowed hard, feeling very much like he was in trouble, but not knowing why. "I did. Good, though. I'm starved."

Otis emptied his glass and sat it on the bar. "He's asked us to join him in hunting humans for sport."

At Vlad's gawk, he said, "You don't have to take part, but I'm not about to leave you alone in a hotel room in New York City."

24
THE HUNT

O TIS WHISPERED, as if he didn't want the other vampires to hear, which struck Vlad as enormously stupid, what with them having telepathy and all, but hey . . . whatever floated Otis's boat. They had just exited the subway and were now walking along the sidewalk, making their way north, toward Times Square and beyond it, Central Park. "Are you ready for this, Vladimir? The hunt is exhilarating, but not something I'm sure you'd agree with."

Actually, Vlad found himself more intrigued by the idea than he'd ever admit. "I don't want to be rude or anything. It'll be okay."

"After your reaction to the very idea of hunting in Siberia a few years ago, I thought the notion might sicken you." Otis cocked an eyebrow at him, as if defying him to deny it, or perhaps coaxing him to admit he was curious. "But if you're all right with it . . ."

Vlad chewed his bottom lip thoughtfully. "How is it done? I mean . . . we won't hurt anyone, will we?"

"We?" Otis slowed his steps, as if in disbelief. "You plan to hunt?"

"No. I just . . . no." He swallowed hard, resolving that he wouldn't be partaking in any fresh human blood tonight. Not even a drop. No matter how much it appealed to him.

Licking his lips, as if parched by the subject, Otis said, "Every vampire hunts differently. I always aim for the sick or homeless, those who don't have a chance of surviving much longer anyway. Enrico prefers tourists."

"But don't they have families to go home to?"

"Think of it this way, Vlad. Do the chickens and cows that humans devour have families who will miss them? Perhaps. But whether or not they do is of no consequence on the hunt."

Vlad furrowed his brow, more than a little disturbed. "You can't kill them, Otis. You just can't."

After a thoughtful pause, Otis called up to Enrico. "Let's try to let them live tonight."

Enrico's laughter drifted back to them. "Let them live? That *would* be a cruel fate."

Vlad shot a glance at Otis. "What does he mean by that?"

"He means that killing them would be fast. Letting them live will require a satisfying chase. And I can't guarantee that the thirst won't cloud our reasoning a bit. We may kill them

(211)

anyway." Otis paused midstep, as if he were having second thoughts about bringing Vlad along. "Are you sure you're up to this? You look a little green. Maybe I should take you back to the hotel."

Vlad shrugged. He didn't want Otis to miss out on the fun. Even if he was having a hard time with the idea of attacking innocent people. "It would be easier if I knew they were willing victims."

"Victims are never willing, Vlad. That's why they're called victims and not volunteers." Otis sighed. "You don't have to participate. Neither do I if it makes the evening more . . . palatable for you."

Enrico's voice found them again with a tone of celebration. "Ah . . . as usual, our hunting ground is full. Herd your choices to the park, gentlemen, and let the games begin."

Times Square was far cooler than any of the times he'd seen it on TV. Bright lights were everywhere. The smells of food filled the air. And the people . . . so many people.

Otis spoke in a hurried tone, as if he'd all but forgotten his suggestion that maybe they should sit this hunt out. "The key to a good hunt is to choose a human who fits your mood. If you're looking for a struggle, if you truly want a fight that will fulfill your animalistic urges, choose a strong human, preferably a runner. If you want a fast meal, the elderly are a good choice."

Vlad flinched. "The elderly?"

"You're feeling conflicted. That's normal." Then Otis hurried ahead into the crowd.

Vlad shook his head and followed, albeit reluctantly. "Nothing about this is normal, Otis."

When he caught up with his uncle, Otis started rambling, and Vlad could tell the scent of blood had him now. Otis looked captivated by the crowd. "Let me put it into perspective for you. Being raised among humans, you have adapted many of their so-called morals. You've been raised to believe that you shouldn't bring harm on humankind, that humans are not food, that you should do everything in your power to protect your fellow man. I was raised that way too, and for twenty years after I turned, I struggled with guilt at the things I was doing. The urges inside me were too powerful to ignore, but eventually, I realized that I was only hurting myself by ignoring them. I was no longer human, so I needed to learn a new way of living, a new way of looking at the world. You, Vladimir, may be half human, but every bit of you that I have seen is a vampire. And this is the vampire way."

Vlad shrugged, unwilling to listen to his uncle when he was chattering on like some starved lunatic. "I guess . . ."

Otis gestured to the crowd with a nod. "All that blood, just waiting to be devoured. You may never hunt, but at least let me show you how to do it right. Look around, smell the blood pumping through their veins. Find the one whose blood really calls to you."

"I . . . I can't, Otis. I think, I mean, you're not acting like yourself."

"Okay. That's okay." But it wasn't okay. Not that Otis could reason that at the moment. "Look over there. The man in the

blue business suit? His blood smells like a mixture of black-
berries and pomegranates to me. So, now that I've found my
meal, I'll plant thoughts in his head to direct him up the street
to the park."

Vlad shook his head in disgust. He didn't dare mention
that the man was neither sick, nor elderly. "Not so much a
hunt than it is herding people like cattle, huh?"

"The hunt really begins when we hit the park."

Once the man had stepped from the cold, hard streets of
Midtown Manhattan, into the lush green of Central Park, he
slowed his steps, turning some in mild confusion, as if he
were waking from a dream. Vlad glanced at Otis and said, "I
thought group hunting was illegal in cities."

"While I'm thrilled you've been reading the *Compendium*,
you may have missed the short paragraph about the only un-
governed city. As you might guess, it makes New York a popular area for vampires to visit."

The man stepped forward, moving deeper into the woods.
Vlad could feel the tension rise up in Otis and, with it, his
hunger. Otis's face had paled; his fangs had elongated. He
looked positively fierce in the light of the street lamps. Vlad
stuttered, actually frightened by the changes he saw in his
uncle. "S-so as long as you hunt here, you w-won't get in trouble?"

"That's right." Otis barely glanced at him, like it was virtually impossible to tear his gaze from his prey. His pupils were
pinpoints. His voice was accompanied by a guttural growl.
"Let the games begin."

Otis bolted across the few yards between where Vlad stood and where Otis's intended victim was wandering in a daze. In an instant, the man seemed to gather his senses and realize that someone . . . some*thing* was coming up behind him fast. He turned, eyes terrified and round, mouth opening wide to scream. Otis jumped up, pouncing on the man in a catlike move. Saliva dripped from his fangs, and he growled, "Run. Or you will die."

The man shoved Otis off of him—or thought he did; Vlad knew that Otis had let him go—and ran deeper into the park, much to Otis's visible pleasure. He sat there, crouched, giving the man time to flee, and when Vlad approached him, he looked up with a strange light in his eye. "It seems cruel, I know. But his adrenaline will ease the pain of death some, so it's better that he's afraid."

A hard, hot, hollow spot formed at Vlad's center. "You are seriously freaking me out, Otis."

"I can't stop now. He'd run for help, expose us all. Besides," Otis grinned, his sharp fangs bared. "It makes the blood even sweeter."

It was very apparent that Otis—the real Otis, the one who taught mythology at Bathory High and nuzzled Nelly's neck when he thought Vlad wasn't looking—wasn't here anymore. This man, this vampire, wasn't the Otis that Vlad knew. He was a hunter through and through, a creature that thirsted for blood and would do anything within his power to get it. The sight of him scared Vlad like nothing ever had before.

After another moment passed, the vampire Otis took off at

a sprint, delaying the chase purposefully. Vlad followed at a distance, watching out for Otis in a way that made him feel very much like the responsible one of the two. He'd smelled the guy's blood, so rich and warm and tangy with fear, but couldn't understand why the hunt hadn't taken control of him the way it had his uncle. Maybe it was because Vlad had never hunted before. Maybe it was because he was part human. Whatever it was, he was glad. Otis seemed hypnotized, bewitched by the power of an ancient, carnal need, and Vlad wanted no part of it . . . no matter how much his gums throbbed and his stomach growled.

As he followed Otis, ignoring the terrified screams of the man he was chasing, Vlad passed Enrico feeding on a platinum blonde in the bushes. He looked drunk, like Otis, and the human part of Vlad wanted very much to run like hell.

When he caught up to Otis, he had the man cornered by a large tree. Otis was growling. Then, in a flash, as if he'd reached the pinnacle of his thrill, Otis leaped on the man. He tilted his head back, his long fangs glistening, ready to tear open the man's throat and swallow mouthfuls of his blood.

A monster. Otis was a monster. Maybe Joss and the Slayer Society weren't so wrong after all. Maybe vampires really were horrible beings, bent on human pain and destruction. Maybe their use of stakes wasn't entirely misguided.

Despite his horror, Vlad found himself moving closer to Otis's victim. The scent of the man's blood was almost too much to bear. He wanted it. Desperately.

But more than that, he wanted his uncle back.

(216)

"Otis! NO!"

Otis seemed to have just noticed him for the first time. Blinking, he looked up from his impending meal.

Vlad shook his head sternly. "I'm not going to let you do this, Otis. It's wrong. Look at him: he's terrified!"

The vampire Otis glanced briefly down at the man, as if the very idea that humans could feel terror had never occurred to him.

"You call this hunting. You chase innocent people through the woods, terrify them, then kill them. That's not hunting, Otis. It's not sport. It's murder and you know it. If this is the vampire way, then I'm really glad my dad took me away from Elysia. It's . . . it's horrible. And you're horrible for doing it."

That scary light left Otis's eyes at last, and he looked sober again and filled with shame.

But Vlad didn't hang around long enough to be sure. He took off running, the wind whipping through his hair, moving with vampire speed until he was back at the hotel. He stepped into their room and closed the door, lying on the bed for what seemed like an eternity.

Otis would feed. Of that he was certain.

Disgust filled him, and guilt too. He'd never spoken to his uncle that way before. But then, it wasn't his uncle he'd been speaking to. It had been the vampire Otis, someone he didn't even know.

After a long time, the door opened and Otis stepped inside. His eyes were red, his expression drawn. He didn't meet Vlad's gaze, but sat on the foot of the bed, his shoulders slumped. He was quiet for a long time. Then, as if unable to stand the silence anymore, he spoke. "It hurts that you see me as a monster, Vladimir."

"I never said that Otis. I never said you were a monster."

He'd thought it. Oh yes, he'd thought it. But he would never admit that to his uncle, never reveal that for a moment, he understood Joss's motives.

"You don't have to say it. And . . . you're right, to an extent." Otis sighed, burying his head in his hands. "It's so difficult to resist gorging myself on their blood. Every day in Bathory, I somehow manage, always teetering on the verge of a thirst-fueled madness. I don't know how you do it. I don't know how you manage to refrain from slaughtering the entire town. You're immensely strong. Far stronger than me."

Vlad raised an eyebrow. He'd never thought of himself as particularly strong before. "What about Nelly? You two cuddle all the time, but you don't seem to be chomping down on her. You're strong too, Otis."

Otis shook his head. "That's different. I don't think of her in that way. But everyone else . . . especially the humans I don't know by name . . . it's immensely difficult to resist."

Vlad swallowed hard. He couldn't imagine what it was like to be a vampire used to taking meals by force and then going stone sober. It had to be an awful habit to break. "Did you kill that man, Otis?"

He looked up then and closed his eyes. Vlad couldn't be sure if his expression was one of relief or regret. "No. I did not. I wiped the experience from his memory and returned him to Times Square. Then I went for a long walk before returning here to beg your forgiveness."

Vlad sat up, reached forward, and squeezed Otis's shoulder. Otis placed his hand over Vlad's and met his eyes.

"You don't need to, Otis. There's nothing to forgive."

25
THE PRETRIAL

AFTER A SHORT SUBWAY RIDE, Otis and Vlad headed back to V Bar. The city had come alive in the night-time hours, something that was the absolute opposite of life in small town Bathory. Even V Bar was overflowing with customers, so it took Otis a minute to garner the attention of the bartender. Once he did, the bartender led them through the cellar door in the sidewalk to the storage area beneath. He closed the metal doors over them, and Otis moved to the small glyph behind a table and brushed it with his trembling fingers.

This was it. The moment that determined whether Otis would live or die.

"Otis?" Vlad's voice shook slightly. "I'm scared."

A section of wall opened to the right. Otis met Vlad's eyes and sighed. "Me too, Vlad. Me too."

After Otis entered the room, a familiar person stepped from the shadows. Dorian whispered, "It is important that you don't speak at this hearing, Vlad, unless you are called on. Also, telepathy is not allowed. Do you understand?"

Vlad nodded and Dorian placed a hand on Vlad's elbow to guide him inside. Beside the door was a second glyph. Ignoring all the fear that Dorian had inflicted on him, Vlad tapped Dorian's hand and nodded to the marking. "What's that?"

"That's insurance that my influence cannot enter this room. It's a new addition to pretrials. Apparently my gifts at bringing about true justice are not appreciated. As Em, the president of this council, despises me . . ."

Vlad's entire body went cold. "All it takes is a glyph to stop you?"

The corner of Dorian's mouth rose in a smirk. He whispered, "No, but I like to let Em think it will. Besides . . . Em is probably the only vampire in this world capable of killing me. I had hoped that she would be absent, as she normally is for such proceedings, and I would be able to influence the others, but alas . . ." He sighed and Vlad could see that he was troubled. "Suffice it to say that Otis is on his own, my young friend. His future lies in Em's hands."

With a deep breath, Vlad stepped through the door with Dorian at his side. He was oddly comforted by Dorian's presence.

The room was surprisingly posh for such a small, hidden

space beneath the streets of Greenwich Village. A long, mahogany table commanded the front of the room, home to nine vampires. Vikas sat to the far right, D'Ablo to the far left, and at the center sat a girl who looked no more than sixteen or seventeen years old. She was dressed in black skinny jeans and a band T-shirt, her hair cut in such a way that her burgundy-colored bangs curtained her left eye. Her Converse-clad feet were tapping the concrete floor beneath the table, as if she was having a difficult time holding still. Otis stood before the table and several vampires sat in chairs behind him, waiting for the proceedings to begin. Dorian led Vlad to an empty chair and then took one himself, only a few chairs away.

Every vampire in the room had their eyes locked on Dorian, their expressions a mingling of disgust, fear, and immense respect. The vampires to either side of him stood and moved to the back of the room. The look in Dorian's eyes said he was used to this response, used to being the most feared, loathed, and respected vampire in all of Elysia. Almost immediately, Vlad felt immensely sorry for him. Dorian might be used to getting what he wanted, but there was a reason his social skills were lacking—no one wanted to be social with him. Dorian glanced at Vlad, his eyes betraying a sadness. Without telepathy, it seemed Dorian knew that Vlad had witnessed his pain. He looked grateful.

The girl at the center began. "Otis Otis, you face a variety of charges, and as this is your pretrial, not yet your trial, we shall approach this with a more casual effort and assume that you know of the charges of which I speak?"

Otis's voice was sure and strong, but hushed. "I do."

"And do you have any evidence-supported reason that these matters should not go to trial?"

Otis's Adam's apple bobbed as he swallowed hard. "I do not have such evidence, but I do have suspicions of treachery."

"Treachery?" She rolled it over on her tongue, as if unfamiliar with the word. "How so?"

"Em . . . I . . . I would rather we speak in private, as my theories involve a certain member of this council." His eyes darted to D'Ablo, who merely scowled in return.

"I see." She wet her lips, as if debating his request, then said, "Speak here. This council holds no secrets from one another."

A small bead of sweat ran down Otis's forehead. "I believe that D'Ablo holds personal prejudice against me. Me . . . and my nephew. I can better explain this in private. Please . . ."

The room grew very silent. Finally, Em stood. "If the council will pardon us . . ."

She left her place at the table and she and Otis moved outside, into the storage area, for several minutes. When they returned, she acted as if nothing had happened and took her place once more. "As there is no evidence to support not going to trial—"

"Em, please." Otis's eyes were shimmering, pleading with her.

"—your trial date has been set for May eleventh at nine P.M., at this location. This session is adjourned."

"Em." A tear rolled down his cheek, his tone bordering on desperation. Apparently, he'd been counting on their private conversation clearing him of wrongdoing.

She crossed her ankles and frowned, her voice firm. "This session is adjourned, Otis."

Her eyes locked pointedly on Vlad for a moment, but he couldn't read her expression.

Slowly, the vampires filed out, first the audience, and then the council, at last Dorian, until the only ones left in the room were Otis and Vlad. Vlad approached his uncle slowly and placed a caring palm on his shoulder. Otis reached up and cupped his hand. Neither spoke for a long time.

Vlad tried to think of something comforting to say. He settled on, "She can't be the last word in whether you live or die, Otis."

Otis took a shuddered breath and released another tear. "Em is the oldest vampire in existence, Vladimir. If I cannot convince her of D'Ablo's treachery, then I have no hope."

He turned and walked out of the room, resolving himself to die at the word of a teenage vampire.

26
Not-So-Happy New Year

NELLY SLIPPED A SILVER CUFF BRACELET onto her left wrist and checked her hair in the mirror for the five millionth time. She looked beautiful in her black satin cocktail dress with rhinestones dotting the bodice. She had on heels, something that Vlad couldn't recall ever having seen her wear before. Plus, underneath the nervous exterior, she was positively glowing over her and Otis's New Year plans . . . which both thrilled Vlad to no end and grossed him out at the same time. Despite the "ew" factor of his aunt and uncle dating, Vlad was pretty happy for the two of them.

"My earrings!" Nelly gasped, disappearing upstairs for a moment. When she came back down, black and silver teardrops hung from her ears.

When the doorbell rang, Vlad first watched Nelly turn back to the mirror, her fingers trembling, and then went to open the door. He had no idea why Otis still knocked or rang the bell. It wasn't like he didn't practically live there or anything. But Nelly was nervous and Otis probably was too, being that this was the first date they'd gone on where both referred to the event as a date, so Vlad wasn't about to make waves. He opened the door and smiled at Otis, who was looking dapper in a three-piece charcoal gray suit. Vlad kept his voice low. "She's in the living room, checking for gray hairs."

Otis chuckled and when Nelly stepped out to see him, their eyes twinkled. An electricity filled the air between them, one that made Vlad enormously uncomfortable. A brief flash of something—the fear of losing her, maybe—crossed Otis's eyes. Then Otis stepped closer to Nelly without a word and kissed her full on the mouth. Vlad coughed into his fist, trying not to make a retching sound, and the lovers parted, cheeks flushed. Otis said, "I'm so blessed to have such beauty in my life, Nelly."

If she hadn't been wearing an expensive dress, Vlad was pretty sure Nelly would have melted into a pile of goo right there. "So," he said, in an effort to remind them that they weren't alone just yet, "where is this shindig, anyway?"

"It's in the ballroom at the Karloff Hotel in Stokerton, and I'll have her home by three A.M."

"Three? I dunno . . ." Vlad smirked, taking on a parental tone. "Promise to behave yourselves?"

Otis grinned. "Not at all."

Nelly blinked as if remembering that she had a ward and he'd probably require something like sustenance and company eventually. "What time will Henry be here? The pizza's getting cold."

Glancing at the clock, Vlad said, "About a half hour from now. I'm going to warm up some blood after he gets here."

Then, Otis's face suddenly dropped and all traces of joy were erased in an instant. Before Vlad could ask what was wrong, he heard Vikas's voice in his thoughts. *"Come, Mahlyenki Dyavol, something terrible has happened. I need you and your uncle both. Get here as soon as you are able. It's urgent."*

His voice sounded shaken and gruff in Vlad's mind, as if his thoughts had been full of sorrow. Vlad looked at Otis, who was placing a trembling kiss on Nelly's hand. "We have to go. Vikas needs us. And I'm afraid I don't know how long we'll be."

Nelly looked heartbroken, but understanding. She nodded.

Otis led Vlad to the door, looking more troubled with every step he took. "Nelly . . ." he said as he opened the door, turning back to her with an anxious step.

She looked up, blinking disappointed tears away, but didn't speak.

"I love you." Otis's tone was brimming with meaning.

Vlad paused midstep and looked over at his aunt. A small smile found her lips. "I love you too, Otis."

Vlad was pretty sure that was the first time that either of them had admitted it. It was sweet and wonderful, and Vlad could barely contain his hopes that this would mean they really would be a family one day . . . if they weren't already.

They exchanged quiet smiles for a long time, until Vlad tugged Otis's sleeve, reminding him of Vikas's silent call. Once he and Otis were in the car, Vlad turned to his uncle. "Vikas sounded scared."

"More than that, he sounded as if he were in anguish. Buckle up. I'm going to drive fast."

Otis backed out of the driveway faster than he ever had and before Vlad knew it, they were speeding through Bathory, barely stopping at stop signs. Not for the first time, Vlad wished they could use their vampire speed out in the open. Finally, Otis parked at the curb and they exited the car. Vlad followed his uncle's lead around the house to the backyard, where they found Vikas digging near the rosebushes.

He was standing at the bottom of a very deep, very wide hole, slamming a shovel into the frozen earth with a *chink* and tossing piles of dirt next to the hole. Occasionally, a brown, roseless thorn would catch his skin and tear it open, but his wounds healed immediately and he didn't seem to notice the thorns at all. Nor did he seem to notice Vlad or Otis, who were standing by the hole, looking very confused. Otis crouched down and placed a caring hand on Vikas's shoulder. Vikas threw it off and muttered, "Help me."

Otis furrowed his brow. "Vikas, what's happened?"

"Help me!" As he yelled, he threw an extra shovel to Otis, who caught it just before it would have hit him. Without another word, Otis removed his jacket, handed it to Vlad, and dropped into the hole, then began digging.

Vlad watched them dig for an hour, all the while wondering what they were digging for. Then the realization hit him and he spoke, his words quiet in the too-quiet night. "It's a grave."

Otis shot Vlad a look, then seemed to realize he was right. They both looked at Vikas, who'd finished digging at last and wiped the sweat from his brow with his sleeve. His haunted eyes moved to a lump in the shadows near the house. The lump was hastily wrapped in heavy canvas, but Vlad spied a lock of hair sticking out at one end. With a gasp, his hand found his mouth. He would've recognized that hair anywhere. "Oh my god . . . Tristian."

When Vlad flicked his gaze back to Vikas, he saw Vikas's shoulders slump and his moist eyes drop to the hole he and Otis were standing in. "He left several hours ago to retrieve household supplies from the store. When he didn't come back right away, I contacted him telepathically. His response was weak, muffled, his thoughts clouded. Then everything went black, and the pain . . . the pain . . ."

Vlad furrowed his brow. He knew that pain. He'd been in Jasik's mind when his life had ended. The experience had scarred him. And Jasik was virtually a stranger to him; he couldn't imagine what it would be like to have been inside his drudge's mind, Henry's mind, when he died. Losing a drudge was bad enough, but witnessing it helplessly from inside his skull . . . what an unimaginable nightmare.

Otis climbed from Tristian's grave and reached his hand down to help Vikas out as well. It was only then that Vlad realized there was anything odd about this scene at all. He frowned. "Why a grave, Vikas? Why not a pyre?"

Vikas spoke through tears. "Tristian was a good drudge, Mahlyenki Dyavol, but he was human. We cannot honor him the way that we honor vampirekind."

Together, the three of them laid Tristian to rest in the earth. Vlad thought about asking if they should call the police, but he was pretty sure that would bring about an amount of trouble that they just didn't need right now. Besides, they already knew who did it, even though they couldn't really prove it. The Slayer Society. Maybe one slayer in particular.

Actually, there was no "maybe" about it. Joss had murdered Tristian. That much was clear by the open wound on Tristian's chest. But what Vlad wanted to know was *why*?

Once the earth was restored, Vikas said, "We should act immediately."

Otis's tone was clipped, angry. Rightfully so. "He's out walking alone. There's no time like the present."

Vlad shook his head, trying to maintain reason. He'd already seen one dead boy tonight. He didn't want to see two. Besides, even though he hated Joss for taking Tristian's life, he also understood Joss's anger toward vampirekind. Vampires hadn't exactly been nurturing toward Vlad—he could only imagine how they treated slayers. So there was a reason that Joss did the awful things that he did. Unforgivable, yes, but not completely without reason. "Wait. You don't know for sure that Joss did this. What if it was someone else? I mean, it could've been some psycho."

But even Vlad didn't believe the words that were rolling off his tongue.

They both looked at him, incredulous, and then Vikas spoke, his voice grave, bitter. "I found Tristian with a stake buried in his chest. And I know of no other slayer in Bathory tonight."

Vlad shot his uncle a look. "You can't go after him, Otis. You can't kill Joss."

Vikas exploded. "I can and I will! He murdered my Tristian. He stole my drudge away from me. Innocent, sweet Tristian. And you would have me sit idly by while he toast to his kill? This is madness!"

Otis released a tense breath. "Calm, Vikas. I'm sure my nephew has his reasons. What would you have us do, Vladimir?"

"Let me handle it."

Vikas said something else loudly in Russian. Vlad didn't know the language, but he knew when someone was swearing at him.

Otis, who spoke Russian fluently, held up a hand to calm Vikas's ranting. "What do you mean, handle it? This isn't a situation that calls for a light touch, Vladimir. It calls for blood."

Vikas growled behind him. "Much blood!"

"You'll have blood, Otis, but let me handle it." His eyes moved to Tristian's grave and back to Otis. "Please."

Otis didn't speak. Or rather, he didn't speak out loud. It became very obvious that he and Vikas were discussing something telepathically. After a long while, Vikas swore again in Russian and made his way into the house. Otis offered Vlad a single nod and then followed Vikas inside.

Vlad left immediately. He searched the town, every street, every inch, until finally, at 2 A.M., only the cemetery remained. He crossed under the archway that marked the entrance and moved between the stones, and there, standing near Vlad's parents' tombstone, stood Joss. The look on his face was one of respect. He was gazing at the stone, looking unaware of Vlad's presence, but something about the feeling in the air told Vlad that Joss was very much aware that he was near. Vlad approached him cautiously and stood beside him, looking down at the stone.

Joss spoke calmly, as if they were continuing a conversation they'd begun earlier that day. "Your parents, did they know?"

Vlad swept his eyes over his mother's name. His heart skipped a beat. "About me being a vampire? Well . . . yeah. My dad was a vampire."

"You mean your creator."

"No. I mean my dad. He and my mom made me the same way your parents made you."

"Gross."

"Yeah." He was hoping that Joss was referring to the fact

that parents doing anything at all required to make babies was gross, and not the fact that his dad was doing just that with a human, but he suspected it was the latter. They stood there silent for a long time, until Vlad finally said, "What are you doing at my parents' grave?"

Joss's voice was calm. Too calm. For some reason, it reminded Vlad of Dorian. "I was apologizing to your mother . . . before I kill you."

Vlad barely had time to notice Joss flip open his jacket and withdraw his wooden stake from a leather holster on his belt. But once the stake was in Joss's hand, Vlad noticed—oh man, did he notice—and moved across the cemetery with vampire speed. Joss blinked, and then realized that Vlad was standing ten headstones away. A smirk touched his lips. He looked both challenged and irritated. "You've learned a new trick."

Vlad brushed his hair from his eyes. "That's just a taste. I'm not the same vampire I was when you backstabbed me freshman year."

The corner of Joss's mouth twitched subtly. "Good. Because I'm not the same slayer I was. This time, you won't get back up."

Joss flew at Vlad faster than he ever had before, but it still wasn't fast enough. Vlad moved with vampiric speed, barely breaking a sweat, dodging Joss's attack. He played keep-away for a while, darting back and forth across the graveyard, until an image solidified in his mind, one he couldn't shake: the image of Tristian, lying dead.

Joss had killed Tristian. Without reason. Without sense. All because he though Tristian might be a vampire, like Vlad. He'd killed him, and now was hoping that Vlad's death would soon follow.

Enraged, Vlad grabbed Joss by the shirt. Joss swung forward, catching the corner of Vlad's mouth with his fist. Vlad threw him across the cemetery. Joss hit a large tombstone and crumpled to the ground. Blood seeped from his mouth, and his arm was bending at a weird angle.

As Vlad bent over Joss and retrieved the cell phone from his inside jacket pocket, he whispered, "I know how you think of yourself as an extinguisher of evil and all, but just so you know, Tristian was human. So that makes you a murderer."

He dialed 911 and when the operator answered Vlad wiped the blood from his lip and said, "My friend's been beaten up pretty badly. He needs an ambulance. We're at Long Road Cemetery in Bathory."

Joss rolled onto his back with a moan. Vlad knelt down, the phone still to his ear, and said, "It's okay, Joss. Help is on the way."

Joss was lying in the hospital bed, his left arm hooked up to an IV, his right arm in a cast. Other than the broken arm and some bruised ribs, he was fine, but the staff insisted on keeping him overnight for observation. Vlad sat in a chair beside the bed, waiting for Joss to say something, to say anything, really. Joss hadn't spoken to him since they left the cemetery.

Finally, breaking the silence, Joss croaked, "I didn't kill Tris-

tian, Vlad. I mean, he looked just like a vampire, and I probably would have eventually—but only for good reasons, only
to help people. But I didn't. I swear."

One look at Joss, at the tears welling in his eyes and spill-
ing over onto his cheeks, and he knew that there was no need
for him to say anything at all to hurt Joss. He was beating
himself up enough already, over an act he'd never committed.
But if Joss didn't kill Tristian—and really, why deny it now, after being beaten so badly? Vlad had no reason to doubt his
claim—then who did? But then, it was likely a lie. One that
would ensure he'd live through the night. Vlad swallowed
hard, trying to calm the bitter anger that threatened to well
up inside of him. "Otis and Vikas wanted to come after you,
but I stopped them."

"I guess I'd have more than just a broken arm if you
hadn't."

"You'd be dead." Their eyes met and both nodded in agreement.

Joss swallowed hard, his voice raspy, as if he were either
very thirsty or on the verge of tears. "Why did you stop them?
Why are you here?"

"Believe it or not, despite everything you've done, despite
everything that's happened, I still think of you as a friend, Joss.
Besides, I wanted to do something you wouldn't do when you
put me in the hospital." Vlad chewed his bottom lip for a moment, remembering his hospital stay, and how much it had
hurt that Joss refused to even acknowledge he felt even the

tiniest bit bad for almost taking Vlad's life. It was awful, probably even worse than the physical pain he'd endured. "I wanted to apologize."

A look of immense shame crossed Joss's face.

"I'm sorry I broke your arm, Joss. I'm sorry I put you in the hospital."

Joss swallowed hard, trying to get his emotions under control. "I guess you could've done worse."

"Yeah. I could've." Vlad was surprised how confident his words sounded, but it was true. He was far more powerful than Joss now, and if he really wanted to, he could kill him in an instant. "You swear on your sister's soul you didn't kill Tristian?"

Joss's eyes never left Vlad's. "I swear it."

Vlad grew quiet, thinking for a while. If it hadn't been Joss, who else could it be? Eddie Poe? Doubtful. Eddie was far weaker than Tristian. Another slayer? Possibly. But who? Not Joss, that much was certain.

"And my dad's journal. Did you take it?"

Joss's eyes grew wide. "No. No, I didn't. I don't know anything about that."

With a deep breath, he met Joss's eyes and hoped for the impossible. "Joss, let's end this. Whatever this is between us, let's just stop. You don't try to kill me anymore and I won't be forced to defend myself. Let's just get things back to the way they used to be."

"I can't."

"Joss—"

"No, you don't understand. I can't. If I don't fulfill my duties, I'll be excommunicated from the Slayer Society, and they'll cleanse Bathory of every living being in sight just to be sure they got all of the vampires." He shook his head, his voice softening. "Besides, I made a promise to Cecile. It was my fault she died. I was too scared to stop a vampire then. I'm not too scared now. I have to keep going, Vlad."

For a long time, neither spoke. Vlad thought about what Joss had said, about the Slayer Society killing every living being in Bathory just to make certain they'd rid the town of every vampire. He'd heard the love in Joss's voice when he spoke of his sister. They must have been very close. Then Vlad sighed, resolving himself to whatever fate had in mind.

"Okay, Joss. Whatever has to happen, will happen." He reached into his pocket and withdrew Joss's slayer coin. Then he turned it over in the light and placed it neatly on Joss's hospital bed, like some sort of peace offering.

Joss closed his hand over the coin and met Vlad's gaze, an understanding passing silently between them.

27

SCORE ONE FOR EDDIE POE

V LAD SLID OUT OF HENRY'S CAR and closed the door. Henry had barely cut the engine when a group of girls met him by the driver's side. Knowing it would take Henry several minutes to peel himself away, Vlad shook his head and headed across the parking lot, then up the front steps of Bathory High through a sea of students. The first day back after winter break was always hectic, but today was stressful too, knowing what awaited him in first period.

As he passed the small groups, several heads turned his way, but Vlad thought nothing of it. His mind was really focused on just one thing: the huge exam awaiting him in trigonometry. If he failed it, there was a good chance he might flunk the entire semester. If he aced it, which was just about as close to fiction as an idea could get, he'd likely pass. So today was really a life or death kind of situation for Vlad. He had to do well on that test . . . or Nelly was going to kill him.

He pulled open the front door and when he stepped inside, he couldn't help but notice that everyone seemed to be holding a school newspaper. And looking at him. It was like a flashback in time to his freshman year, when Eddie had published that blurry picture of him floating down from the belfry.

Eddie. Eddie knew about the belfry.

His thoughts turning back to the present, Vlad met the eyes of several of his peers, and finally, his curiosity driven to the brink, Vlad pushed gently into one mind after another. A jumbled stream of words filled his thoughts, pummeling him like physical blows. "—*monster.*" "*I had no idea . . .*" "—*a killer in our town?*" "*What a freak!*" "*That picture of him biting that girl . . .*" "*Vlad is a vampire?*"

With each word, Vlad's eyes widened. He looked at the papers in their hands and swallowed hard.

Oh no. Not this. Anything but this.

At the end of the hall stood a very smug-looking Eddie Poe. It was all Vlad could do to restrain himself from racing down the hallway and breaking Eddie's nose.

Otis stepped out of his classroom and snatched one of the papers from Kelly Anbrock's hand. His eyes scanned the page and then, horrified, he looked up and met Vlad's gaze. Vlad didn't need to read his thoughts to know what was happening. Eddie had outed him as a vampire in the school newspaper. And by the look in Otis's eyes, he'd used Vlad's name this time. Otis's Adam's apple bobbed as he swallowed and he thought just two words to Vlad: *"They know."*

Vlad tightened his grip on the handle on his backpack and threw a glance around the hall at every single accusing gaze. His breathing picked up, his eyes began to water, and just as Otis had said, *"Don't,"* Vlad turned and bolted back out the front door.

He raced down the front steps and the sidewalk away from the school. He thought he heard Henry call after him, but couldn't be sure, couldn't care. Didn't care. Once he was clear of the school, he picked up the pace, moving as fast as a vampire can move, whipping between houses, around trees, until he was safe in his bedroom at last. There he paced back and forth, not knowing what to do. His secret was out. Those who wouldn't believe Eddie surely wouldn't doubt Joss. And Joss had made it abundantly clear last week that their friendship could not be mended.

It was over. They'd won.

The only thing Vlad could think to do was get as far away from Bathory as he possibly could.

He unzipped his backpack, dumping the contents on his bed. Then, with a determined pace, he grabbed several items of clothing from his dresser and closet, as well as the $54.38 from his secret box. It wouldn't get him far, but it was a start.

Zipping the bag closed, Vlad considered writing a note for Nelly, but nothing he could think to write would ever make her understand. He threw his backpack over his shoulder and headed for the door.

A small breeze brushed his face and then Otis appeared, looking worried, but not winded in the slightest. "You shouldn't use your vampiric speed out in the open like that, Vladimir. It could cause some raised eyebrows."

"You said it yourself, Otis. They already know." He set his jaw and fought back tears. "I'm done hiding."

Otis folded his arms in front of him. "But not done running, it seems. Where are you going?"

"Away from here."

"What about Nelly?"

"She'll be fine. You'll take care of her."

"And Henry? What do you suppose it would do to a drudge to be abandoned by his master?"

That gave Vlad pause, but only briefly. "I'll release him before I go."

"And me, Vladimir? Do you really think I'll be okay without my nephew around?" Hurt lurked in Otis's eyes, blended neatly with concern. "Because if that's what you're thinking, I can assure you that you're wrong."

"They know about me, Otis! What do you expect me to do?"

Otis quieted his voice, forcing his tone into something resembling calm, but it was a falsehood, betrayed by the look in his eye. "I expect you to be a man and face your problems head-on. Running away is never the answer."

Vlad's face grew hotter and in his imagination a couple hundred school papers changed hands, chased by a murmur of gossip. They knew. They all knew. What else was there to do but get away? He regarded his uncle with a glare. "What if it is? What if the only way I'll ever be happy or safe or okay again is if I run away from Bathory and make a new life for myself somewhere else? What if I can't bear to see the way people will look at me now? What if I can't stand to hear them whispering about me?"

"How selfish of you, Vladimir. You'd abandon the woman who's been a mother to you these last seven years, who helped bring you into the world, and made certain you were well-nourished since your very first intake of breath. You'd tear away a part of your best friend's soul. You'd rip yourself from my life, taking with you any real meaning that I have found in all of Elysia. You would do all of that because you're afraid of the unknown?" Otis set his jaw and shook his head curtly. "Very selfish, indeed."

Selfish or not, Vlad was absolutely finished with this conversation. "Are you done? I have to call a cab."

Otis paused for a moment, but then moved out of Vlad's way without saying a word.

Vlad hurried down the steps, then turned and made his way into the kitchen where he picked up the phone. As he dialed the number of the cab company, he looked about the room. Memories filled him. Memories of countless breakfasts with Henry after he stayed the night. Memories of holiday meals and baking cookies with Nelly. Memories of his first dinner with Otis and threatening him with a flash of fangs. This kitchen was important to him, the way that Nelly was important to him. He pictured her finding out from Otis that he'd run away, sobbing into a kitchen towel at the long plank table. She looked hollow, sad, more lost than he ever cared to see her look. Vlad's heart cracked, a small, thin, crooked line, and good sense somehow managed to find its way in. He returned the phone to its cradle and dropped his bag to the floor. His back to the wall, he slid to the floor, tears escaping his frustrated eyes. With shuddering sobs, Vlad broke down and cried into his hands.

"Vladimir." Otis's voice, much softer this time, as if he didn't want to interrupt.

Vlad looked up, not bothering to wipe away the tears that refused to stop ebbing from his eyes. He was lost. He couldn't stay here in Bathory, but he couldn't run away. He was trapped between what he loved and what he hated, with no way out.

Otis crouched down beside him and handed him a handkerchief, understanding in his eyes.

Vlad sniffled. "You would've let me go."

"I did let you go." Otis looked around the kitchen, then back to Vlad. "You didn't get very far."

Vlad wiped at his eyes with the handkerchief and took a

moment to steady his breathing. "What am I going to do, Otis? They all know about me. Because of Eddie, they all know."

"I think you underestimate the ignorance of humankind. This will blow over, Vlad. Give it time."

"No. It won't. It will change everything." Vlad released a shuddering sigh. "One thing's for sure."

Otis looked at him, his eyes full of curiosity. "What's that?"

"I am never going back to Bathory High."

28
THE EMPTINESS

V LAD STARED UP AT HIS BEDROOM CEILING, memo-
rizing the small, crooked crack in the plaster just over his
bed, where he laid. He was trying very hard not to think about
what happened at school, and failing miserably. It was over.
His promise to his dad that he wouldn't reveal his secret had
been broken. Everyone at school knew what he was. And
soon, Elysia would descend on him for breaking the law in a
major way. It was so screwed up that all Vlad could do was
lie on his bed, stare at the ceiling, and wait for his world to
crumble into tiny little pieces.

There was a soft knock on the door. When Vlad didn't answer, Otis opened the door anyway and stepped inside, closing it quietly behind him. He stood there, watching Vlad with-

out speaking for several minutes. When Vlad refused to break the silence first, Otis said, "Vladimir, it's been two days. Nelly says you've hardly eaten and barely left your room. She's worried about you."

Vlad stared straight ahead, drawing a line with his eyes along the crack in the ceiling. Otis wasn't telling him anything that he hadn't already known.

After a pause, Otis ran a frustrated hand through his hair and sighed. "Come back to school, Vlad. Please."

Vlad swallowed hard, a small tear escaping his eye. It rolled down the side of his head and settled on his earlobe. Wetting his dry, cracked lips, he opened his parched mouth and said, "There's nothing left for me there."

Otis watched him for a moment, then opened the door again. He hesitated in the doorway for a moment, frustration ebbing from him. At last, he turned back to Vlad. "I'm there."

Without another word, Otis stepped out into the hall and closed the door behind him.

Vlad lay still for a while, but finally sat up, forcing his attention away from his flawed ceiling. He was hungry. And he couldn't help but wonder if anything good was on TV.

29
AGAINST HIS WILL

WELL YOU CAN'T STAY HOME FOREVER!" Nelly's voice had risen in both tone and pitch to the point that Vlad was almost certain she was on the cusp of shouting—something Nelly never did. He was still staring at her with a confounded expression on his face when she pushed his backpack into his arms and pointed at the front door. "March, Mister. Straight to school. And don't let me catch you skipping. You are done running from your problems and missing out on your education."

Vlad blinked. She sounded serious. Was she being serious? It had been three days since everyone at Bathory High had learned his secret. She couldn't possibly expect him to go back to the stares and giggles, back to being the walking freak show.

Nelly stomped over to the front door and opened it. "Go on."

He blinked again. Oh crap, she really was serious! "Nelly, I—"

Then she did something that no words could defend against. She gave him that look. That mom look. The one that said if Vlad didn't get his butt out the front door and fast, she was going to bury him in the backyard and plant daisies over his remains.

With a heavy sigh, he slid the strap of his backpack over one shoulder and stepped out onto the porch. Nelly promptly shut the door hard behind him. Not quite slamming it, but threatening to. Then she locked it. He was going to school, whether he liked it or not.

He watched the door for a moment in disbelief, contemplating what she might do if he snuck in the back door, and then turned and moved down the steps. He'd just stepped onto the walk when he spied a familiar figure standing outside the gate. Joss was wearing a sheepish grin. His arm was still in a cast. "Hey, Vlad."

"Hey . . . Joss."

"Henry's got a dentist appointment. I thought we'd walk to school together."

Vlad parted his lips and made a sound that sounded like, "Ooookay."

They crossed the street together and made their way down the sidewalk, toward the school. Vlad had opted for the longer route to school for two reasons: 1) He really wanted to delay going back to school, and 2) He was curious like crazy why Joss was acting completely normal. After several long, silent steps, Vlad cleared his throat and said, "So, what's this about, anyway?"

"What do you mean?"

"What do I . . ." Vlad ran a frustrated hand through his hair. "A week and a half ago, you were trying to drive a stake through my chest, and now we're walking to school together as though nothing ever happened."

Joss grew quiet, but Vlad could tell he was thinking of a way to phrase whatever it was he was thinking. Finally, taking a deep breath, as if this weren't very easy for him either, he said, "The way I see it, day and night are very different things . . . just like us. So the way I figure it, maybe we should take a break from trying to kill each another. During the day, we'll be friends . . . y'know? If you want, I mean."

"And at night?"

"Foes. For the reasons we discussed in the hospital."

They walked along in silence as Vlad mulled over the idea. In truth, he really liked it, but he wasn't sure if he could trust Joss. Not after everything that had taken place between them. He shook his head, berating himself for making himself vulnerable to the sadistic whims of a slayer, and said, "Okay. But you've got to leave Otis and Vikas out of this. And no confrontations in Nelly's house. I don't want her involved."

"Okay. But you can't hide inside Nelly's house every night either."

"Deal." They approached the front of the school and Vlad slowed his steps. "Hey Joss . . . has anyone said anything about Eddie's article lately?"

Joss smiled. Vlad couldn't tell what his smile meant. "Everyone's said something, Vlad."

"Like what?"

But Joss was already up the steps and opening the front door.

Vlad took a brave breath and huffed up the stairs. Once he was inside, it seemed like business as usual. Students were hurrying from their lockers to first hour. Teachers were trying to keep the peace. The jocks were being jock-y and the cheerleaders were swooning at their jock-yness. The art kids were sharing their sketchbooks with one another. It was a scene like any other morning at Bathory High. Vlad was in shock. He'd fully expected torches and pitchforks.

A large wall of flesh slammed into Vlad's side, knocking him off-kilter. Tom Gaiber snorted, "Watch where you're going, goth boy."

Bill Jensen snorted too. Vlad was beginning to think he was surrounded by horses. Two large, annoying horses with bad body odor and low IQs. "You're a vampire, right? Show us your fangs, vampire boy."

Vlad's defenses raised, but he said nothing. Sometimes silence was your best defense. Tom guffawed. "Yeah, you're as much of a vampire as I am a werewolf. And I'm not one."

Resisting rolling his eyes was giving Vlad a migraine, so he closed them for a moment instead. "Are you done yet? I have to get to class."

Tom snorted. "Class? You've got none of that, loser."

Thankfully, Mr. Hunjo appeared and shooed them both off with a warning glance before they decided to beat some class into Vlad.

Vlad shot an expectant look at Joss, who smiled as he shuffled the stack of books in his hands. "Where's Eddie?"

Joss shrugged. "He was expelled for writing a bogus article about a fellow student—something Principal Snelgrove views as a form of bullying."

And just like that, Vlad's tension melted away. It was over. In a good way.

As Vlad and Joss walked into Otis's classroom, Otis shot him a look that said he doubted his nephew's sanity. *"Is this your way of handling it? A broken arm and a mended friendship? I knew you went after him, but I assumed it was to stop his heart from beating."*

Vlad cut Otis off with a crunch. It was none of his business anyway. Besides, he wanted blood, he got it. He never said anything about death.

Otis looked at Joss and managed a somewhat pleasant tone. "Joss, it's good to see you back. I was worried something happened to you."

Joss wasn't smiling. "Something did, but I survived."

"Well, it's good to have you back. I trust you and your friend are ready for a pop quiz."

Vlad shot Otis a look before letting his eyes wander over to Meredith's desk. Sadly, he found it empty.

As if reading his thoughts, Joss leaned forward and said, "She's out with mono. Won't be back until after spring break."

Vlad nodded his thanks and then turned his attention back to the pop quiz that had just been put on his desk. The air between him and Joss was strange, awkward. Because even though they'd agreed not to kill each other during daylight hours, there was always that other thing.

There was always the fact that both of them loved Meredith Brookstone.

30
THE PRAVUS

VIKAS RAN AT VLAD with the stake held high, but he didn't just run, he shifted in that superquick way that only vampires could move. For the evening, they'd moved their training session to an old abandoned barn at the edge of town. Vikas had said they'd require more space than the basement could supply. He never mentioned that he wouldn't be holding back at all and, if Vlad didn't defend, could seriously endanger his life.

In a flash, Vlad dodged his blow and spun around, ready for another attack.

"Good, Mahlyenki Dyavol. Excellent." But no sooner had the compliment left his lips than Vikas had leaped through the air and landed on top of Vlad, who hit the ground hard, knocking the wind momentarily from his lungs. Vikas raised the stake once more, a hopeful glimmer in his eye. He would not hold back, just as a slayer wouldn't hold back. He would not give up, just as a slayer wouldn't give up. He would never stop.

Vlad managed to slide his knee up between them and kicked Vikas backward. His chest felt light, so much lighter than it ever had. Vlad felt a strange energy pulse through him. He gave into its will, leaped to his feet, and snatched the stake from Vikas's hand almost without effort. Vikas came after him, but Vlad was light . . . so light and full of energy. He ran as hard and fast as he could to the other end of the barn and, to his amazement, he kept going, running halfway up the barn wall, its old boards creaking under his feet. He flipped over then, planting his feet against a large beam, bouncing his way back and forth between the wall and the beam until he was on the ground again and advancing on Vikas. With a grin, he hit Vikas full force. Vikas fell to the ground and Vlad brought the stake down, stopping before he broke the skin. Weirdly both energized and exhausted, Vlad wiped the sweat from his brow and helped Vikas to his feet. "How was that, old man?"

Vikas looked visibly shaken. He exchanged shocked glances with Otis, who stood at the barn door and both shook their heads.

Vlad blinked, wondering if he'd done something wrong. "What? What is it?"

Otis stepped closer, slowly, carefully. After a moment,

Vikas squeezed Vlad's shoulder. "We have never seen a vampire move in the way that you just moved."

Vlad looked back and forth between them, confused. "But how can that be?"

Otis shook his head. "We don't know."

Vlad turned the corner, exhausted from training and wanting nothing more than to go home and fall into his bed. He was so tired that it barely registered that Dorian was waiting for him just around the bend. Gasping, he grabbed his chest, feeling his heart hammer against his ribs in surprise. "Jeez, Dorian! You almost scared me to death!"

"This fear is new to you? I was under the impression you're always frightened of me. Less so lately, but frightened, still." He smiled his charming smile and, once Vlad's heart rate had settled, continued. "I've been trying to come up with an answer to our plight, my young friend. I wanted to discuss it with you."

"We have a plight?" Vlad searched his exhausted mind for a bit, then nodded. "Oh, you mean that whole you wanting to drink my blood and me being totally against it thing."

"That would be the one, yes." Dorian closed his eyes for a moment and inhaled, as if tasting the scent of blood in the air of Vlad's hometown. When he opened them again, he said, "Would you like to hear the solution I've come up with?"

Vlad chewed his bottom lip thoughtfully before answering with a nod.

"What if I allow you to control my actions? You can make

me bite you as gently as possible, drink as little as you deem fit, and stop me when you'd prefer."

"No offense, Dorian, but that idea sucks."

Dorian sighed. "You're right. And to be frank, the only reason that I haven't forced you to my whims is that I have a sort of respect for you, Vlad . . . that and I am duty-bound. But even my appetite is not why I have come here tonight. You have questions for me. So . . . what would you ask of me?"

Vlad didn't even want to know how Dorian knew that he'd been mulling over some prophecy-based questions just hours before. But he was curious what Dorian meant by being duty-bound. "What do you do all day, Dorian? Just wait around for some sense that I might have questions for you?"

"Sometimes. I also travel the world. I'm rather fond of airplanes."

"Don't you spend time with family? Friends?"

"I visit my father, when he hasn't much company, but as for friends . . . well, I don't have any to speak of. Apart from a few bribery attempts from various vampires over the years—D'Ablo being one of them—I haven't spent extended time with our kind. They . . . dislike me." He shrugged then, and changed the subject. "About your questions . . ."

Vlad chewed his bottom lip for a moment. It had never occurred to him how lonely Dorian might be. Or maybe he wasn't lonely. Maybe he was just bored a lot. He thought for a moment before speaking. "Is the Pravus evil?"

Dorian cocked an eyebrow. "What a strange query, my young friend."

Vlad shrugged. Strange or not, he needed to know if he was going to somehow morph into this evil being, mad with power. "Well, people say that the Pravus will rule over all vampirekind and enslave the human race, so . . ."

"What people say this?"

"I don't know. Vampire people. Vikas, for one." Vlad was feeling oddly frustrated and he wasn't sure why, exactly. Maybe it was because he hadn't expected criticism or query in response to his simple question. "Is he wrong?"

Dorian raised a sharp eyebrow. "That's difficult to say. Can you be more direct in your questioning?"

Jeez. It was like talking to a Magic 8 Ball. With a sigh, Vlad pinched the bridge of his nose and asked, "Will the Pravus rule over vampirekind and enslave the human race?"

"He will do one out of necessity. The other will be done in charity."

"Which one will he . . . I do out of necessity?"

"The Pravus will rule over vampirekind."

Vlad's heart thumped twice, hard. "And if I don't want to?"

Dorian shook his head. "You're asking my advice now, advice that I cannot give."

After mulling this over for a bit, Vlad wondered aloud, "How can I enslave the human race out of charity?"

Dorian narrowed his eyes, his attention waning. "Would you be opposed to slitting open a vein and filling a cup? It would be cold, but I think it might satiate my need."

"No, Dorian." He wouldn't let Dorian feed . . . and he would continue to keep their interactions to himself. He wasn't sure why, exactly, but Vlad wanted to handle this on his own. Besides, Otis and Vikas had enough on their plates.

"You can't blame a vampire for trying." His sly smile slipped into a more serious purse as he shook his head. "I must leave. The urge to feed from you is becoming too intense. It's almost unbearable now."

Vlad nodded at this, still questioning Dorian's motives. "Does this mean you're not going to attack me anymore?"

Dorian flashed him a smile as he turned to leave. "For now, my young friend. Sleep well."

31
MIDNIGHT
MASQUERADE

VLAD FINISHED JOTTING DOWN THE DETAILS of his day and closed his journal with a snap. It was getting full. Soon there would be no more room to write at all.

But there was no time for musing about how full his journal had gotten. Vlad had an appointment. A very important appointment. One he'd kept almost every night and certainly every weekend night for the past four months. In fact, the past few months had been oddly full of bliss—no sign of D'Ablo, no interference by Dorian, not even so much as a sniffle from Eddie. Vlad's life felt, for lack of a better word, normal.

He dropped his journal on the chair and made his way to the arched windows, then stepped from the belfry and floated gently down to the ground. He had made it a block from school when a wooden stake whizzed by his head and stuck fast in a tree trunk.

The corner of his mouth rose in a smirk before he turned around. That one was close. But he knew Joss wouldn't get it much closer. Ever since the hospital, their fights were the equivalent of sparring and showing off.

Vlad turned, searching the darkness for Joss. When he found him—merely a shadow within the shadows—he darted forward with vampire speed, clotheslining the slayer. Joss made an *oof* sound and fell to the ground.

It was like a play, a theatrical representation of what vampires and slayers were meant to do. The players moved back and forth across the stage, knowing that when the sun rose, when the curtain came down, life would resume and the play would be all but forgotten.

As a courtesy, neither of the players mentioned Meredith.

A bead of sweat dripped into Vlad's left eye, but he brushed it away with the back of his hand and high kicked Joss in the center of his chest. Joss did a windmill kick, knocking Vlad's feet out from under him. But neither stayed on the ground for very long.

Vlad took to the trees, hopping almost silently from treetop to treetop in a circle around Joss, who stood at the ready, scanning the darkness for any clue of where he'd gone. In a breath, Vlad dropped from a branch, ripped the stake from the tree's trunk and slashed forward, stopping with the sharp, silver point pressing into Joss's back.

The sun peeked over the horizon. Joss turned with a grin,

taking his stake and slipping it into the leather holster on his belt. Normalcy returned to the stage. "Morning, Vlad."

Vlad could barely contain a chuckle. "Morning, Joss. How was your night?"

"Oh, not bad. Had to fend off this vicious bloodsucker, but that's about it." He shrugged casually, a twinkle in his eye. It was so good to see the old Joss again, the one from before Joss had learned Vlad's secret. But really, their friendship was even better now. No more hiding things, no more lies. Joss knew Vlad was a vampire, and though he wasn't okay with it, he was okay with Vlad.

Vlad smirked. "Bloodsucker, eh?"

Joss straightened his shoulders in an effort to make himself look bigger, tougher. The scary thing is, it worked. Nobody would've pegged Joss as a muscular kinda guy, but in his position, he had to be. "More like a mosquito, really. Bothersome, but no real threat to me."

He rolled his eyes in response. "You had it easy. Some guy kept trying to poke me with a toothpick."

They locked eyes and laughed out loud. Then Joss slugged him gently in the shoulder and said, "You comin' over for breakfast?"

"Actually, I have to pack."

They both knew what he was packing for. They both knew Otis's trial was tonight, but neither wanted to talk about it. Joss had pretty much decided that he loathed every fiber of Otis's being, and Vlad just wanted to forget the trial was coming up at all.

A look of sympathy came over Joss's face. "Oh. Well . . . see ya."

Vlad walked home alone, and quietly stole upstairs to his bedroom. A heavy feeling filled his chest. He was escorting Otis to his death today, and no one—not Nelly, not Henry, not anyone but the vampires involved—knew that it was coming.

Through his open bedroom door, he heard Nelly and Otis talking at the bottom of the stairs. Nelly's voice sounded clueless and concerned. "Promise you'll take care of him and hurry back soon."

Otis didn't speak for several seconds, then finally lied as well as he was able. "We'll be back before you can miss us."

As he listened to Otis ascend the stairs, a horrifying thought occupied his mind.

He was about to lose a father for the second time.

32

THE TRYING OF OTIS OTIS

I MUST ADMIT, I DO FEEL A BIT BETTER about your letting Joss survive after yesterday's test." Otis's tone matched the bemused smirk he wore. He was in an awfully good mood, considering they were in the midst of packing for a trip that likely would end in his demise.

"What's with all these quizzes, tests, and extra assignments lately, anyway? Am I being punished for letting Joss live?" Vlad tossed some socks into his duffel bag and shot Otis a mock-angry look. "Oh, I see. That's your plan, isn't it? Do me in with a bunch of quizzes. Bore me to death."

"If I wanted to do you in, Vladimir, I can think of a few other ways."

"Don't I have enough people after me, Otis? Joss, Prinicipal Snelgrove . . ."

"Don't forget D'Ablo."

"There's somebody I could live without." Vlad furrowed his brow. "Speaking of which, he's been decidedly absent for a while now. Quiet, compared to how he usually is. I don't trust it."

Otis folded a T-shirt and placed it in Vlad's duffel bag. "Think he's working on some sordid plan to do you in?"

"Count on it. I'm that guy's favorite hobby."

"Maybe he's changed."

They exchanged looks and burst out laughing.

Vlad shook his head. "The question isn't *if* he's planning anything . . . it's *what*."

A smile danced on Otis's lips. "You're very wise for being only sixteen years of age."

Vlad met his smile with one of his own. "I learned from the best. This really old guy I know, goes by the name Otis. You might know him."

Otis rolled his eyes. "I'm hardly old."

"Oh, really? What year were you born?"

"Age is more than just a number, Vladimir."

Vlad grew quiet for a moment, thinking about the immense age difference between Otis and Nelly. He wondered if he would just go on aging or if at some point in his life, time would freeze for him as well. "Have you told Nelly? Y'know, that you might not be coming back?"

"No. There's no need to upset her right now. She'll learn of my death soon enough." His words seemed so final, like there wasn't even a remote chance that he'd survive his trial. He withdrew a parchment envelope from his inside jacket pocket and handed it to Vlad. "If you would. It's for Nelly. To explain why you've returned home without me."

"But, Otis . . ."

"Please, Vladimir." Otis's somber gaze showed that he meant business. It also meant that he didn't want to entertain any far-fetched notions of him possibly surviving his trial proceedings. "For me."

Vlad gripped the envelope in his hand and offered his uncle a small nod. Just moments ago they were laughing, and now, a solemn feeling hung in the air. He would be escorting Otis to his funeral in just a few hours.

"Who wants cookies? I just pulled some out of the oven, and I thought you boys might . . ." Nelly's voice was almost singsongy as she entered the room. Her face dropped as she looked at each of them. "What's wrong? You both look upset."

Vlad and Otis exchanged looks and at once, Otis said, "Not a thing, darling. Vlad's just feeling rather sullen about going on another trip without you. I must admit, I share his troubles. Is that chocolate chip I smell?"

Nelly's smile returned and she held up the plate of freshly baked goods. Otis plucked one from the plate and took a bite. "Mmmm. Warm chocolate chip cookies. Not even AB negative can compare."

Nelly practically floated down the stairs and, just before he turned to follow, Otis flashed Vlad a look that said everything, without speaking or using telepathy. *Don't ruin this day for her. Give her one last moment with me to hold onto. Please.*

Before zipping up the duffel bag, Vlad slipped Otis's letter inside and hoped beyond hope that Nelly would never have to see it. He carried the bag downstairs and dropped it next to the front door before retiring to the kitchen for a few cookies of his own. Once he was there, he put on a pleasant smile and endured chatter about the vacation Otis and Nelly had been thinking about. He pretended that Otis was really coming back from New York and that when he did, he was going to propose to Nelly and they were going to live happily as a family. He pretended that everything was just fine, and that he and Otis had years left together, and after he pretended for a while, he began to believe it.

That is, until he saw the sad glimmer in Otis's eyes when Nelly wasn't looking.

Then he knew the truth. That Otis really was going to his death. That they would never be a family and that he would be the one to tell Nelly of Otis's passing. His heart felt lifeless and heavy, hollow and cold. There was nothing to look forward to now. Otis Otis, the strange teacher in a purple top hat who'd stepped into his life as a threat and was now his uncle, his mentor, his friend, was about to leave him forever. And there was nothing anybody could do about it.

"*Vladimir.*"

Vlad looked up from his tormented, distracted thoughts to

Otis, who smiled and squeezed his shoulder. *"I'll miss you too."*

A half hour later, after they'd eaten all the cookies they could eat, Otis kissed Nelly goodbye while Vlad loaded his bag into the car. As if in a hurry to get his demise over with, Otis all but ran down the front steps and slid into the driver's seat. He barely spoke all the way to Stokerton International Airport. He didn't utter a word during the entire flight. He grunted V Bar's address to the cabbie once they left baggage claim at LaGuardia, but all the way there, he did not speak. He did, however, grow paler and paler the closer they got to his trial.

"Vladimir," he finally managed to say once they'd exited the cab in front of V Bar. "Avenge my death, would you?"

Vlad was still blinking at Otis's casual tone when Otis stepped into the bar. He'd said it like it was an afterthought. Pick up some milk on your way home, don't forget to pay the electric bill, and oh, be a dear and avenge my death for me, would you? But then, he couldn't imagine what must have been going through his uncle's mind at the moment. Vlad shook his head and followed Otis inside.

Enrico greeted them both with handshakes. He offered them drinks, but neither Vlad nor Otis was feeling particularly hungry. After a small amount of chatter, Enrico said, "It's about that time, my friend."

He led them outside and down through the cellar door on the sidewalk, into the cellar. Once Enrico touched the glyph that opened the hidden room, Vlad noticed that something was different. The large table was covered with a black cloth. Several large candleholders stood in the corners of the room, casting a soft glow over the gathered group. It looked as if they were attending a funeral. In a way, Vlad thought with a gulp, they were.

The chairs that had been placed at the back of the room had been removed. Apparently, there would be no audience to Otis's trial.

Even Dorian, who'd seemed unusually kind at the pretrial, was decidedly absent from these proceedings.

Once they were shut inside the room, the small girl named Em spoke. "The council calls Otis Otis before us. You have been accused of killing a fellow vampire, your father, Ignatius; of disfiguring a council president; of revealing your true nature to two humans—one Nelly, last name unknown, and one Henry McMillan; and of aiding and abetting the known fugitive Tomas Tod. How do you plead?"

Otis's Adam's apple bobbed as he swallowed hard. "Innocent of all charges, good council."

There was a murmur among the council and a distinct feeling of unease in the air. Even Vlad raised an eyebrow at his uncle's words. Otis was definitely innocent of blasting D'Ablo's hand off (that was Vlad's fault) and of aiding and abetting Vlad's dad (who was no longer with the living, but some people apparently cannot take a hint), but letting Nelly and Henry in on the secret that he was a vampire? Oh yeah. Way guilty.

Still, Vlad admired his uncle's guts. It had to take a lot of them to face the Council of Elders, let alone lie to them.

Em raised her eyebrows a bit and then said, "As head of this council, I am dismissing the charge against you of taking a fellow vampire's life. Ignatius had a bounty on his head, placed there by this council, and as such, you are due the reward monies from collecting on that bounty."

Otis looked surprised and at the same time, mildly relieved. "I'd like the monies placed in a trust for my nephew's college fund, if the council would see to it."

With nods from several members, Em said, "Your request is granted. Five hundred thousand dollars will be placed in trust for your nephew's college fund."

D'Ablo stood, eliciting disapproving glances from almost every member of the council. "On the charge of disfiguring a council president, I call a witness. Vladimir Tod, take the stand please."

Vlad shot a glance at Otis, whose mouth pursed some, but he didn't make eye contact. Then Vlad crossed the room and took a seat on the chair to the left of the council. Once he was seated, D'Ablo unwrapped the stump that used to be his hand and held it up for all to see. From the looks of it, it had healed up perfectly; there was no trace of a scar. There was also no trace of a hand, which was D'Ablo's primary concern, Vlad would have bet. "I give you exhibit A."

The room was quiet. Too quiet, considering that no one was supposed to know about D'Ablo's missing hand. Vlad felt his insides sour. Something wasn't right here. Why wasn't anyone crying out for D'Ablo to be removed as council president? Why, all of a sudden, was D'Ablo's disfigurement no big deal?

The room was so quiet for so long that Vlad was beginning to wonder if D'Ablo was ever going to ask him a question. Then, as if suddenly pleased with himself, D'Ablo flashed a small smile at Otis and turned to Vlad. "You were there the night my hand was permanently removed from my arm, yes?"

"Yes."

"And precisely how was my hand destroyed?"

"By the . . ." Vlad paused for a moment, trying to see exactly where D'Ablo was going with this. He couldn't pin the loss of his hand on Otis, and he certainly couldn't count on Vlad to pin it on Otis either. "By the Lucis."

"And who was it that used the Lucis against me that night, obliterating my hand and leaving me disfigured?"

To be honest, that was Vlad. But Vlad wasn't sure where D'Ablo was going with his line of questioning. He glanced at Otis, hesitating with the answer stuck in his throat.

D'Ablo took a step closer and hissed, "Stop protecting him, Vlad. Your uncle broke into the Stokerton council building and viciously attacked me with the most dangerous weapon known to vampirekind, didn't he? If allowed to live, Otis will try to finish the job, won't he?"

He couldn't take it anymore. There was no way he was going to let this pompous windbag make his uncle take the fall. Vlad stood. "No! It wasn't Otis and you know it. It was me, okay? I ruined your hand. But you—"

D'Ablo grinned broadly, turning back to the council. "I move to clear Otis Otis of the second charge."

Otis released an uneasy sigh.

Vikas said, "Motion granted. On the third charge of revealing your true nature to two humans, I present myself as a witness and attest that I have spent much time with Otis and the two aforementioned humans. They believe that Otis is very much human. I would wager my seat on this council on it. I move to clear Otis Otis of the third charge."

He was lying. Everyone knew he was lying. But still Em said, "Motion granted. On the charge of aiding and abetting Tomas Tod . . ."

"A ridiculous charge, good council." Enrico's voice piped up from somewhere behind Vlad.

"Enrico, it is only out of our deep respect and admiration for you that this council allows your presence at these hearings. Speak out of turn once more and you may have charges levied against you for interference." Em's eyebrows were brought together in irritation. She meant business. She looked at the papers on the table in front of her and said, "Now, on the charge of aiding and abetting Tomas Tod . . . I am under the impression that Mr. Tod is alive and well and fleeing his own charges. Is this true?"

Otis wet his lips and said, "As I explained to the Stokerton council four years ago, Tomas Tod perished in a fire at his home in Bathory."

A low murmur flowed through the council. Clearly, something was up.

After muttering quietly to Vikas and listening to his response, Em nodded. She turned to D'Ablo with a sneer. "D'Ablo, why hasn't this council heard news of this report prior to today? If the accused has presented your council with such a theory, it is to be investigated thoroughly before charges can be brought upon him."

Vikas suppressed a smirk. "If it pleases the rest of the council—"

"I believe Otis has had quite enough help from you, Vikas," Em snapped.

Vikas held up his hands in a relenting gesture. "I was merely going to suggest that you ask Vladimir about his father. He stands as witness to Tomas's demise."

When Em met Vlad's eyes, he was struck by the age and wisdom that lurked within hers. He cleared his throat. "I found my father and mother burned to death in their bed, where I'd left them alive that morning. It's true. My dad is . . . he's no longer with us."

"I see." Em turned to her fellow council members. They spoke for a long time in whispers and murmurs. At one point, D'Ablo's whispered voice rose above the others, but Vlad still couldn't make out what they were saying.

"Otis Otis." Otis looked up, his eyes sunk in, his lips trembling ever so subtly. He didn't seem to be breathing. Horrible, seemingly unending tension hung in the air as everyone waited for Em to speak again. This was it. This was the moment that would steal Otis away from Vlad. Vlad's heart had ceased beating as he waited for the guillotine blade to fall, severing him from his uncle forever. The corners of Em's mouth rose slightly. "You are hereby cleared of all charges. May the blessings of Elysia follow you now and always."

Otis inhaled at last, tears shimmering in his eyes. Vlad all but flew across the room to hug him. Otis was going to be just fine.

"The council calls Vladimir Tod before us."

Vlad's heart shot into his throat.

Otis looked up from their embrace. "What?"

Vikas snapped his eyes to Em. "What?"

But the smirk on D'Ablo's face said it all.

33

PROBABLY THE WORST
TEN MINUTES EVER

GLANCING BETWEEN OTIS AND VIKAS, Vlad slowly stepped forward and met the eyes of Em, the only other teenage vampire he'd ever encountered. Except she was old. Way old. The oldest vampire in existence. Without batting an eye, Em spoke, all business. "Vladimir, you have been accused of disfiguring a council president, of revealing your true nature to three humans—one Nelly, last name unknown, one Henry McMillan, and one Joss McMillan—of leading the vampire Jasik to his death via mind control, and entering into a romantic relationship with a human—one Meredith Brookstone. As your father is deceased, you will also stand trial for your father's crime of the same nature—a romance with one Mellina Tod. How do you plead?"

Vlad blinked, unable to comprehend what she was saying, what was happening. Was she even speaking English? "I . . . what? Henry is my drudge and Joss is a slayer. How they count as part of—"

"Based on your own admission here today, you are found guilty of the charge of disfiguring a council president. On the charge of revealing your true nature to three humans—"

"I stand witness to the fact that both the boy named Henry and the boy named Joss know Vlad's true nature. If Jasik were here, he would attest to that as well. And let me assure you that I can stand as witness to the third charge also." D'Ablo's shoulders were back, a sneer on his face.

Vlad's stomach shrank. Oh no. No, no, no. D'Ablo had set him up. Otis's whole trial was just some sadistic way to get to Vlad. And if that were true . . . Vikas being poisoned, his dad's journal, Tristian's death . . . it must all have been D'Ablo's do-ing, or someone working for D'Ablo all along. He shot a glance at his nemesis, knowing that D'Ablo was somehow responsi-ble for all of it, all of Vlad's pain and anguish. Why was he even a bit surprised?

Em raised a sharp eyebrow. "And this . . . Nelly?"

D'Ablo dropped his gaze from hers, but only briefly. "I have no knowledge of her beliefs concerning Vladimir Tod."

"Noted." Em turned back to Vlad, who was inwardly plot-ting D'Ablo's painful demise. "This council finds you guilty of revealing your true nature to two humans and of causing the death of the vampire Jasik."

The few gathered started whispering among themselves.

Vlad didn't have to strain to hear what they were saying. They spoke of his impending death. Vlad shuddered.

Otis cried out, "This is madness! He's just a boy!"

Enrico moved forward and placed a calm hand on Otis's shoulder.

Vlad met Em's sea green eyes and held her gaze for a moment before speaking. "Excuse me, but I never got a pretrial. According to the *Compendium of Conscientia*, all accused vampires must undergo a pretrial."

Em set her jaw, as if bothered slightly by the knowledge that he'd read the book. "That law governs vampires. And you are half-human."

"By that logic, any sentence you give won't matter." He shook his head. This was going nowhere fast. And it didn't matter what Vlad said, didn't matter what arguments he brought forth, Em wouldn't hear him. She'd already made up her mind about that.

The corners of Em's mouth rose in a small smile. "I assure you, it will."

"So you can pick and choose when to acknowledge I'm a vampire and when to acknowledge I'm less than that? That's not fair." His voice was rising in upset, but he didn't care. His thoughts raced back to the gathering of vampires this past fall. There had been speculation about Em—that she might be one of D'Ablo's followers. If that was true . . .

"Young one, life isn't fair." She picked up a pen and scribbled something on the papers in front of her, dismissing him.

D'Ablo was practically glowing.

Vlad hissed, "What is D'Ablo giving you to make this okay in the eyes of vampiric law, Em? Or rather . . . what is he holding over your head?"

Em snapped her eyes up. They gleamed with anger and a hint of insult. "On the charge of entering into a romance with a human . . ."

Vlad felt Em slip into his mind and shuffle through his memories. It was against the rules of the courtroom, but Em was beyond the law, beyond any law. And she would stop at nothing to satisfy the wishes of her cult leader. Rules, laws were in place for a reason, but apparently all bets were now off. Images of Meredith passed through Vlad's thoughts against his will. Their first kiss. Their first dance. Walking her home. Their breakup.

Ignoring Vikas's pleas, Em consulted the rest of the council quietly before speaking again. "Vladimir Tod, you are guilty on all counts but one, and so you are sentenced to death. As this council is mercifully understanding that you are yet a child, we grant you one week to get your affairs in order. This council is adjourned."

Vlad snapped his eyes to D'Ablo. "It was never Joss. It was you. Vikas, the journal, Tristian. Even Otis's trial wasn't your goal—but you knew it would get me here. Why?"

D'Ablo waited until the room was nearly empty before he responded with a smirk. "Again with your presumptions, Master Pravus."

"Why?" Vlad set his jaw, almost growling the word.

D'Ablo paused for the span of two heartbeats. "To put it

simply, you destroyed my dagger and I knew that if you managed to escape the rest of the ritual, I would need a fail-safe at
the ready. If I can't have your status, Master Pravus . . . no one
can."

He walked out of the room and Vlad wished for the first
time that he could turn back the clock and fire the Lucis
straight at D'Ablo's heart.

34
GOING HOME

VLAD SLUMPED IN HIS SEAT on the plane, leaning his forehead against the plastic wall by the tiny window to his right, staring at the clouds outside. He'd never noticed how fluffy clouds were or how sometimes, when you were soaring miles above them, they looked exactly like a soft blanket of snow. He'd also never noticed how beautiful snow was. Or even . . . Snow. He could picture her now, her pale skin, her black hair, her painted lips. So loyal, so trusting. In perfect contrast to Meredith.

Meredith . . . who wore pink and always had a slight tan.

Meredith . . . who wanted nothing to do with him.

And Snow.

Beside him, Otis shifted so that he was facing Vlad, as if

that would make carrying on a conversation easier. But Vlad didn't want to talk. He didn't feel like talking. All he wanted to do was think about how pretty the world really was and how much he was going to miss being a part of it.

"Vladimir, please try not to worry. Vikas has assured me that he will do everything in his power to prevent your sentence from being carried out, and Dorian has even volunteered to step in and make the council truly listen to your appeal. You're going to be fine."

What Otis seemed to be forgetting was that if D'Ablo was smart enough to arrange Vlad's trial in secrecy, he was probably smart enough to know that Dorian would volunteer to help Vlad out of his sentencing.

Vlad watched out the window, looking for even a small break in the clouds.

There was none.

Otis must have taken the hint, because he didn't speak for the rest of the plane ride. Two hours later, the plane landed on the runway at Stokerton International Airport. Together, they wandered over to baggage claim to collect their bags. They chatted but didn't say anything of consequence. Vlad had sunk too deep into his gloom to carry on any conversation with substance. As they moved through the security gate, Vlad lugging his heavy duffel along behind him, Otis paused midstep.

Vlad followed suit, raising an eyebrow at his uncle, whose face had gone completely white. "Otis? You okay?"

"Yes. I'm . . . I'm fine. Take my bag, will you?"

But Vlad didn't have a chance to answer. Otis dropped his bag on the floor and hurried through security, where Nelly was waiting. She moved to hug him, but he dropped immediately to his knees. He looked like a man in dire need, pleading before the only person in the world who could help him. Nelly's eyes moved to Vlad and then back to Otis on the floor in front of her.

Vlad dragged the bags closer. He'd never seen his uncle look so scared.

"Damn the laws, Nelly, and damn the legal system too. I love you. I can't stop loving you just for fear of being put to death by a corrupt government. I need you." His eyes shined with tears, as if he was terrified of her response. From his inside jacket pocket, he withdrew a black velvet box. "Will you be my wife?"

Nelly's eyes shined too, but hers were shining with joy. She bent down, hugging him tightly. She didn't have to say yes. And Vlad could tell by the way Otis swept her up in his arms and kissed her that they'd be married soon.

He only hoped it would be before his sentence was carried out.

And that . . . was highly unlikely.

35

A Slayer's Lament

J OSS PLUCKED THE PARCHMENT from the table in frustration, rereading what he had already read five times, each time hoping the words would be different. At the top of the letter was the seal of the Slayer Society: S.S. At the bottom was their creed: FOR THE GOOD OF MANKIND.

His eyes moved over the page slowly, searching for even a hint that the letter wasn't authentic. But it was.

Joss,

It has come to our attention that you have not yet fulfilled your recently assigned duties. While we appreciate the detailed reconnaissance that you have faithfully provided us with, the vampire that you have been sent to dispatch remains alive, and according to our sources, there are at least two other known vampires residing there in Bathory. We are deeply disappointed in your lack of progress and have convened in your absence to discuss a new plan of action. As you insist against our gathered intelligence that the vampire you have been sent to kill has eluded you, and due to your past confusion with referring to the vampire known as Vladimir Tod as your "friend," we have determined that if you do not fulfill your obligation to mankind and this Society by dispatching these horrendous creatures by the end of the school year, the town of Bathory will be cleansed. The choice is yours, slayer.

The letter was unsigned, but Joss didn't need signatures to know who had sent it. The Slayer Society was coming. And like the village of Jeremiah's Lot in Vermont, the ship *Mary Celeste*—both places where many people had seemingly disappeared overnight—and many others both before and since, the Society was planning to extinguish the entire town of Bathory, just to make certain they rid it of every vampire in it.

Aunt Matilda, Uncle Mike, Mom, Dad, Henry, Vlad, Meredith. Everyone. All dead.

And there was nothing Joss could do to stop it . . . short of killing the vampires himself.

36

THE GREATEST GIFT

SMALL DROPS OF RAIN WERE FALLING in the alley behind
The Crypt, tapping Vlad gently on the shoulder, as if urging him to move things along, get this over with as quickly
and as painlessly as possible. Behind his back, Vlad held a
long-stem blood-red rose. He squeezed the stem in his palm
out of anxiousness, its thorns digging into his flesh, piercing
the skin. The door opened and, finally, Snow joined him.

She looked pretty as ever, with her dark eyes and curious
smile. Tilting her head up, she smiled as raindrops danced on
her skin. "I love the rain. Especially when it's warm like this.
Don't you?"

In truth, Vlad hadn't really thought much about the rain.
He couldn't even think about it much now, even as it dripped

(284)

onto his shoulders and pasted his long black bangs against his pale forehead. All he could really think about was the decision he'd made on the plane, what he came here to do, and how very much he felt for Snow. He loved her. Against his will, he loved her. Even though he still loved Meredith too.

Wetting his lips, he said, "Did you miss me while I was away?"

She smiled brightly, the light of her obvious happiness shining in her eyes. "Of course I did. I'm really glad you're back. After what you said the last time we talked, I wasn't sure you'd be coming back at all. What about you, did you miss me at all?"

Vlad didn't answer her question. Instead, he said, "I have a gift for you, Snow. Close your eyes."

Her cheeks were slick with rain; her black eyeliner smudged some under her eyes, making her look raccoonlike. She moved closer and Vlad felt the warmth of her skin from even a foot away. She closed her eyes, her lips curled up in a trusting smile. He remembered what it had been like to kiss Snow, to have her lips pressed against his, to feel warm and happy and confused and frightened. The memory was what he focused on as he pulled the rose from behind his back. Ever so gently, he pushed the petals to her nose. She inhaled and opened her eyes, taking the bud in her hand. "Oh, Vlad, that's so sweet! It's beautiful!"

Vlad shook his head slowly, his fangs slipping from his gums. "That's not the gift, Snow. This is."

He grabbed her by the shoulders forcibly . . . unlike he'd

ever grabbed her before. He pulled her close, determined. Determined not to go back on his decision, determined to do the right thing, no matter the cost. She gasped but didn't fight him, and Vlad closed his mouth over her neck, popping his fangs through her smooth, pale flesh to the rushing river of crimson within. He forced himself not to drink, but oh, how he wanted to, how he yearned to swallow every drop of her blood. With tears escaping his eyes, he fed his intent into the wound, releasing Snow as his drudge.

When he finished, he pulled away and she slumped against him, weakly clutching the rose in her hand, the same as she did whenever he fed from her. Maybe it was the bite that made her weak. Or maybe it was him. Vlad helped her gently to the ground and placed a small, adoring kiss on her forehead. He whispered, "Goodbye, Snow. You deserve to have someone who loves you, who really loves you . . . not a monster like me."

Then he straightened, wiping her blood from the corner of his mouth, and walked out of the alley—and away from Snow—forever.

37
SAYING GOODBYE

"HOW LONG WILL YOU BE GONE?" Vlad climbed higher, just one more branch, and settled onto the old oak in his backyard, dangling his tiny, eight-year-old feet, trying hard not to look down. He couldn't go as high as Henry, no matter what Henry said. It was too scary.

Henry sat in the crook much higher than Vlad, looking out over the yard without fear. He shrugged. "I dunno. My mom says we'll be visiting for a while."

Vlad's mother made her way to the back door of the house with an armload of groceries. She was dressed in a pretty yellow sundress and brown leather sandals, her dark hair in a loose, beribboned ponytail. Her steps slowed as she turned her eyes to the boys. "Be careful out there, you two."

Vlad's father seemed to appear out of nowhere to take a bag from her hands. His dark eyes twinkled with kindness. He smiled reassuringly. "Mellina, darling, they're fine."

His mom frowned, bit her bottom lip gently, her eyes full of concern. "I don't like when he climbs that tree. He could fall, Tomas."

Tomas brushed his lips against her cheek and nodded, turning back to Vlad and Henry as Melina made her way into the house. "Be careful, boys. And Vlad . . ."

He put a finger to his lips, reminding Vlad to keep his secret. But he didn't need to remind Vlad about that. Vlad knew it was important not to say anything to anyone about being a vampire. Well, half-vampire, anyway. Not even Henry. Not even though he really, really, really, really, really wanted to. It was important. His dad had said so.

"My cousin Joss has a cool tree fort. We should build one in this tree."

Vlad shrugged, wishing they could just get out of the tree already. He only ever climbed it because Henry wanted to. "But I don't know how to build stuff, Henry."

"So we'll make it up. It'll be fun." Henry hooked his legs on the branch and flipped over gingerly, until he was hanging upside-down, grinning at Vlad. Then Henry's grin slipped. He fell to the ground several feet below with a thump, crying out as his body made impact.

Vlad shimmied down the tree as fast as he could. "Henry! Are you okay?"

Henry sat up, clutching his wounded knee. He looked very much like he was going to start crying any second. A small, thin line of blood oozed from the scrape on his knee.

Vlad's tiny fangs shot from his gums.

Henry's eyes went wide, his injury all but forgotten. "What are those?"

Vlad's small shoulders sank. He'd let his dad down. "They're my fangs."

"Vlad, are you a vampire or something?" Henry's eyes were big, and Vlad was certain he saw fear in them. Not as much fear as when Henry had been falling from the tree, but close.

He took a deep breath, glancing at the house. Then he sat down in front of Henry and said, "Yeah, Henry. I'm a vampire. But it's a secret. A very, very, very big secret and you can't tell anyone ever."

Henry sat very still for a moment, and then cocked his head, admiring Vlad's fangs. "Do you drink blood and stuff?"

"Yeah."

"Does it hurt when they go in the skin?"

"Not really. I bit my finger before, and it didn't really feel like anything."

"Bite me."

"What?"

"Bite me! It'll be like we're blood brothers or something."

Vlad thought for a moment. He'd never bit a person before, aside from himself. He was curious, even though his dad said that good vampires only drank donated blood, the kind that

Aunt Nelly brought to his house in bags. But it wasn't like Henry was any old person. He was Henry. "Promise not to tell anyone?"

Henry nodded and held out his hand. Vlad licked his lips, leaned forward, and—

"Ow!" Henry pulled back his finger before Vlad could take a bite. Their eyes met and they both laughed, then Henry held out his hand again, for real this time.

Vlad bit into his finger. The tips of his fangs popped through the skin easily, and warm, yummy blood covered his tongue. It sent a tingly shiver all through his body. He swallowed and sat back, wondering if Henry would be mad.

Henry examined his finger closely, then looked at Vlad. "Cool."

Vlad beamed, relieved. "I can kinda float a little too. Wanna see?"

Henry laughed. "You suck, Vlad."

Vlad furrowed his brow. "What's that mean?"

Henry shrugged and poked at the disappearing hole in his fingertip. "I dunno. My brother, Greg, said it, so it must be cool."

Vlad shook the memory from his thoughts, trying not to focus on the fact that he was going to say goodbye to Henry today. He walked to school in a haze. Ever since his trial, everything he did was in a crazy fog that refused to lift from his weary shoulders. Nothing mattered anymore, not Henry's jokes, not Otis's reassurances, not even Nelly's baked goods. Vlad was going to die.

Unless he did something really drastic.

That was the plan. Take drastic action. Say goodbye to everyone and everything he'd ever known, without cluing them in that he was doing just that. Run like hell until he could think of a better course of action. Survive.

Joss had been missing from Vlad's midnight wanderings last night, something that greatly troubled him. Even Eddie seemed to be keeping his distance. Maybe they could tell on some level that he was doomed. Maybe they could smell death on him. Whatever it was, Vlad was alone. Even when he was hanging out with the goths on the steps of Bathory High last night, he was alone. And saying goodbye.

In broad daylight, Vlad floated up to the belfry. He couldn't face school today, no matter what Nelly or Otis might say about him skipping. His education at the moment was on hold until he figured out a way to escape the vengeful justice of Elysia.

As he stepped through the arch, he turned in an afterthought to be sure no one saw him. Eddie Poe was standing on the ground, mouth agape. But it didn't matter. Nothing did. He offered Eddie a two-finger salute and stepped inside his sanctuary.

Just a few hours. That's all Vlad needed. Just a few more hours to mourn his impending death, and this afternoon he'd start saying goodbye to everyone and everything he loved.

Like Meredith. Like Henry. Like Joss. Like Otis. Like Nelly.
Everything.
Everything.

After watching the sun move from morning to afternoon, Vlad
stood at the sound of the final bell and stepped from the bal-
cony, descending to a chorus of clicks from Eddie's camera.
He didn't care anymore. Let Eddie have his fun.

The moment his feet touched the ground, he stepped forward, walking out to the parking lot, to Henry's car. Concen-
trating on his drudge, he whispered aloud, "Hurry, Henry."

Not ten seconds later, Henry burst out of the front door of
the school and booked it to where Vlad stood. "Are you okay?
I got the weirdest feeling something was up. It's the last day
of school. Where have you been all day?"

Vlad forced a smile, trying hard to act like it was business
as usual. "I'm fine, just decided to start summer break early."

Henry watched him for a moment, as if he couldn't trust
what Vlad was saying, but had no idea why.

Vlad slid into the passenger seat and once Henry gunned
the engine to life, he said, "Did you know that I hang out in
the old belfry all the time?"

Henry settled back in his seat, letting the car idle for a bit,
the look on his face one of immense surprise. "Really? I had
no idea. What's it like up there?"

"It's nice. Sort of my secret place. Somewhere I can go
when I really want to be alone."

"So why are you telling me now?"

Vlad wet his lips. He was giving Henry one of his most prized possessions, willing it to him. He only hoped Henry would go there someday, break the boards that covered the door and go inside. "Because you should check it out if you get the chance. I think you'd like it there."

"Henry!" They both looked up to see Meredith jogging across the parking lot, waving.

Henry snapped his eyes to Vlad. "Should I floor it?"

"No, it's okay." It was more than okay, actually. It was perfect. Two birds, one stone.

She reached the driver's side breathless and held out Henry's iPod to him. "You dropped this when you ran out. Everything okay?"

Henry took it, shrugging. "Yeah. Just happy to officially be a senior."

There was a moment when she seemed to be debating something. Then she met Vlad's eyes. Hers were full of a questioning, of hesitancy, of loss. "Hi, Vlad."

Vlad smiled as warmly as he was able to. "Hey, Meredith. You look very pretty today."

A gentle smile touched her lips. "Thank you."

And he wasn't lying. She looked lovely with her tan skin and her pink shorts, pink tennis shoes, and pink T-shirt. In a strange way, he felt like he was talking to someone he had once known, but didn't anymore.

A whiff of the sweet nectar that lurked in her veins teased Vlad's senses, but he remained still and strong. "I don't think I ever told you how much you mean to me. I mean, I know you're going out with Joss now and that's great. He's a good guy. I just wanted to make sure you knew."

Henry's jaw hit the floor. He looked at Meredith and shook his head, laughing the way people surely laughed whenever a crazy person was near. Panicked. Almost frightened. "He's . . . been taking cold medicine. It makes him ramble on about some crazy stuff."

"Actually, I'm quite lucid, Henry." He looked from his friend back to Meredith. "I mean it. I'll never forget you."

An echoed blend of sadness and concern crossed her brown eyes. "Why does that sound like goodbye?"

Vlad merely shrugged.

Once Meredith had joined Joss on the sidewalk, Henry turned back to Vlad, flabbergasted. "*What* was *that*?"

Vlad shook his head, his response at the ready. "Nothing. Just making sure she knows how I feel."

As Henry put the car in gear, he shook his head too. "Man, you are acting really weird today, Vlad. You sure you're not sucking down cold medicine?"

Vlad stared out the window as the car pulled from the parking lot. "Nope. Not me. I'm actually feeling more rational than I ever have."

Henry turned the radio up and drove him home.

It was the best, most subtle goodbye he could give his friend.

But he didn't have the guts to release his drudge.

38
An Unexpected Ending

VLAD LOOKED OUT OVER THE SCHOOL GROUNDS at Freedom Fest from atop the hill behind the school, at the hot-air balloon rides being offered, at the carnival games, at the many, many booths of deep-fried everything and cotton candy, at the crowd of people all wearing smiles on their faces, and sighed. Beside him, Otis sighed too, but more out of contentment. "Otis?"

"Yes, Vlad?"

"I think it's time we cleaned out my parents' old bedroom."

Vlad could feel Otis looking at him from the corner of his eye. After a long silence, Otis replied, "If you feel you're ready . . ."

He thought about the room, still charred, still home to whatever was left of his parents' memory. He thought about all the tears he had shed and how much he wanted to remember the good things rather than the bad. With a hard swallow, Vlad said, "I do. And I want to do it tonight."

He had to do it tonight, after all. He was leaving tomorrow night, just after midnight.

"Can I ask what brought about this decision?"

"The need for change. I've held on to a lot of things from my past." Down the hill, walking hand in hand were Meredith and Joss, smiles lighting up their faces, looking very much in love. Vlad dropped his gaze to the ground between his feet. "I think it's time I start letting go, don't you?"

When Vlad glanced at Otis, he too was watching the happy couple. After a moment, he met Vlad's eyes. "I think that's a very healthy attitude. Just make sure you only let go and don't forget the past entirely."

Meredith and Joss disappeared into the crowd. Vlad watched the glowing balloons for a while before breaking the comfortable silence between him and his uncle. "Otis?"

"Yes, Vlad?"

Vlad wet his lips. Tonight was a night for change. A night for honesty. A night for closure. "You know I was feeding on Snow . . . don't you?"

"Yes, Vlad."

"But you didn't say anything, didn't tell me you told me so, didn't point out all of my lies."

Otis paused briefly, as if weighing whether or not Vlad really wanted him to answer. "No . . . I didn't."

"Why?"

"Because if all I had to do to see you eating right was listen to a few fibs about it, then so be it." He shrugged, and it occurred to Vlad that he'd kept his secret needlessly. Otis would have understood. Otis quieted his voice some, speaking gently, as if sensing the subject was a sensitive one. It was. "Of course, you weren't always feeding on her. There was a time midwinter that you looked completely ravenous. Was it a crisis of conscience?"

Vlad scanned the crowd, looking for any sign of Henry or October, but the faces all blended together. "Yeah . . . kinda. Snow was starting to develop feelings for me."

Otis clucked his tongue. "That's why I never feed on drudges. It's too easy for them to mistake the closeness of feeding sessions for romance."

An image of Snow's face flickered through his imagination, and Vlad felt something hard and hollow at the center of his being. He recognized it instantly as longing, but couldn't really explain where it had come from. He missed Snow. More than he would admit. Absently, he said to Otis, "You must have had thousands of drudges by now."

"Why would you get that impression?" Otis shook his head. "I have none, actually. Never have. I'm not comfortable with the attachment, and I've heard the temptation to create many is overwhelming. It's against the law to have more than two, you know, and like the rest of Elysia, if I don't kill them, I release them immediately."

Vlad gaped openly at his uncle. "Is that such a common practice? To release them so soon?"

Otis looked more than a little confused. "Of course it is. I assumed you'd read that in the *Compendium of Conscientia*."

The book. Oh crap. Vlad knew he'd forgotten something. He'd spent all of last night searching but couldn't seem to find the book anywhere. He'd hoped to take it with him, but apparently that wasn't an option. "About that . . . I kinda lost it."

Otis's eyes widened. He didn't appear the least bit happy. "Lost it?"

Vlad cringed. "Yeah. Sorry."

To Otis's credit, he didn't yell. But he did get quiet for a really, really long time. After a while, he released what seemed like a very tense breath. "I'd bet that your good friend Joss knows where the book is. You understand, of course, how crucial it is that we retrieve the *Compendium*, yes?"

"Of course." Vlad did understand, though it had never occurred to him that Joss might have taken the book, which made him feel more than a little stupid. It could have been part of Joss's reconnaissance, after all. Maybe he could just ask Joss for the book, before Otis had a reason to attack him. If Joss had it, he'd hand it over. Unless . . . unless D'Ablo took it, for some reason. Anxious to drag Otis away from that line of thinking, Vlad said, "Will you keep feeding on humans after you and Nelly are married?"

It was an innocent question, but something about the look in Otis's eyes said that the answer would be anything but innocent. "I'd give up anything to be with your aunt. Even if it meant starvation."

Vlad inhaled and against his will he took in the scent of human blood from the gathered crowd, a delectable potpourri that Vlad found almost irresistible. Strangely, he didn't feel guilty for feeling that way. It seemed right, somehow. It seemed . . . normal. "Can I tell you something, Otis?"

"I would hope that you'd feel comfortable enough to come to me with anything."

He inhaled the scent again, enjoying it. "I don't really feel human anymore. These days, I feel much more like a vampire."

"Is that such a bad thing?" Otis raised an eyebrow, a smirk planted firmly on his lips. "You are a vampire, Vlad. There's no shame in it."

Vlad nodded down the hill toward the crowd. He spotted Henry near the cotton candy machine, his bottom lip covered in fluffy pink. "What do you see when you look at them, Otis? Do you see people, or do you see warm meals?"

Otis laughed warmly. "That depends on how hungry I am."

And there it was. The guilt. Vlad moved his eyes from Henry to a girl he'd once sat behind in algebra to Eddie Poe to Mr. Hunjo. People he knew. People. He swallowed hard and asked, "And if you're hungry when you look at Nelly? What will you see when you look at her?"

The expression on Otis's face became haunted.

Vlad shook his head, berating himself for tolerating the monster within him, even for a moment. "There is shame in it, Otis. It's just not a shame anyone talks about."

As Vlad turned to walk away, Otis called after him. "I'll never hurt her, Vlad. I swear that to you."

Only it wasn't just Nelly that Vlad was worried about. It was everyone. Every human he had ever known. But Otis had no way of knowing that. He peered over his shoulder briefly as he made his way to the sidewalk and spoke to his uncle with his thoughts. "*I know you won't, Otis. But I'm not as strong as you are.*"

Bathory was quiet as Vlad moved down the sidewalk in the direction of Nelly's house. She wouldn't be there, as she was working another late shift at the hospital, a fact that made his journey even quieter, even longer.

Darkness surrounded Vlad and with it, a silence that he took great comfort in. For the first time in a long time, Vlad felt at peace. It was time to clean out his parents' bedroom, and then . . . it was time to leave Bathory forever.

Out of the darkness came a sound. It was soft and breathy, a whisper that had only barely escaped the speaker's lips before it raced to Vlad's ear. "For you, Cecile."

Vlad turned quickly, remembering those words from the night Joss staked him. Terror enveloped his entire being as he scanned the dark. Joss was nowhere to be found.

Then another sound. A low whistling. Vlad stepped back quickly, ready to run, fearing the worst. To his left, someone said, "No!" Their tone was a mixture of surprise and fear. Then, before he could blink, a dark figure stepped just in front of him. The figure staggered back, turning toward him, and Vlad recognized him instantly.

"Dorian?"

Dorian's lips turned up in a semi-smile before he collapsed into Vlad's arms. Vlad managed to catch him, but half fell, easing Dorian onto the ground. Vlad's eyebrows were drawn together in concern and confusion. He was about to ask what was wrong, when he noticed the stake—Joss's stake, Vlad would have recognized it anywhere—sticking out of Dorian's chest.

Dorian had saved him. What's more, he'd saved him from someone that Vlad had begun to trust once again. Quickly— quicker than Vlad thought was possible—blood seeped from Dorian's back onto the ground, soaking Vlad's jeans. A lump formed in Vlad's throat and tears welled in his eyes. Dorian— the only vampire in existence who knew the truth of the Pravus prophecy—was going to die in his arms. He swallowed hard. "Why are you here?"

Dorian coughed, blood spattering his lips. "I came . . . to tell you my secret."

In the distance, Vlad heard movement. Feet moving over grass. He searched the darkness but couldn't see Joss anywhere. If he didn't get him and Dorian to safety soon, they'd be in real trouble. But there was no way Dorian was going to be able to move like this. He met Dorian's eyes. "This stake has to come out, Dorian."

Dorian closed his eyes briefly. "No."

Vlad thought about the night he'd been staked and how Otis and Vikas had saved him. He gripped the stake and pulled hard.

Dorian screamed, but once it was out, he looked much more comfortable. Vlad flung the stake behind him and put his wrist to his mouth. He was about to bite the skin open and feed Dorian, when Dorian grabbed his arm and spoke sternly. "No, Vlad. No. I'm . . . dying. Drink from me. Quickly. Drink deep."

Vlad furrowed his brow, darting his eyes about their dark surroundings for any sign of the slayer. "Why?"

"Because of my secret. I told you that four vampires can know the prophecy, but I only told you about the Foreteller, the Transcriber, and the Keeper. Do you recall?"

Vlad did. It had been that day in New York, the day before Otis's pretrial. That night Otis had changed. Or maybe he hadn't. Maybe Vlad was only seeing the real him for the first time. He shook his head, clearing his mind, and listened.

"There is one more. You, Vladimir. You are the Subject of the Prophecy. Therefore, it is yours to carry. As the Pravus, if you drink my blood, you will begin to understand all that was foretold about you. I couldn't tell you before, because you weren't ready. But you are now. I can feel it. You're ready to know the truth. The truth of everything." Dorian gasped, then settled again and spoke with urgency. "The knowledge will come slowly. Drink, and you will know much of it, but over time the parts you do not understand will become clear. It is a lot of knowledge. It will take time to become known to you."

"No. Dorian, I—"

A twig broke behind him. Just yards away.

Dorian grabbed him by the shirt collar and pulled him close, so close that Vlad could feel his heartbeat weakening. His eyes were narrowed, his words forceful, desperate. "Drink, before I die. This is the duty which I spoke of—my duty—to pass this knowledge on to the Pravus. Now drink. Quickly."

After a pause, one filled with thoughts of how Dorian's blood had infected Otis, Vlad nodded slowly and leaned forward, biting into Dorian's neck. He swallowed mouthfuls of blood and with each, he felt a strange surge of power. He pulled away, unwilling to take Dorian's life. Dorian stared up at him, an odd smile on his lips. "How strange. It's true about your eyes . . . that was the one thing I doubted."

Dorian stretched out a hand, his skin paling drastically, and brushed the tips of his fingers against Vlad's Mark. In an instant that took Vlad's breath away, Dorian's eyes flashed iridescent blue. Vlad gasped. Dorian smiled. "Foolish of me to doubt, or perhaps arrogant. The other two, the Transcriber and the Foreteller, their eyes were the same as ours, but orange and red. We were chosen, the four of us, by something much larger than any of us, for a purpose that must be served at any cost."

"But why? Why do our eyes do that? Why were we chosen?"

A knowing smile, full of wisdom that Vlad couldn't comprehend, knowledge of the ages. "You'll know that soon enough."

Vlad spoke, his voice gruff, the weight of the world on his shoulders as Dorian's life slipped helplessly through his fingers. "Why now? Why didn't you come to me when I was ten or thirteen? Why did you wait?"

"You were a boy before, but with this—" He sucked in his breath, the pain on his face intense and real. "—all of this, you've become a man. You've finally become the vampire I see in my visions. The timing of our introduction was never up to me."

Fresh blood, warm and heavy, drizzled from Dorian's back. Vlad tensed, realizing that he could see the end. His voice grew hoarse. "I wish we'd met sooner. There's so much I need to ask you, so much I don't know."

A look of fear washed over Dorian, and astonishment at feeling that fear, as if he'd never been afraid before. "Our time together draws short."

Vlad clutched Dorian to him. He heard the slayer closing in but couldn't bring himself to face him just yet. He whispered, "Don't die, Dorian. Don't die."

It was odd, but he'd come to feel a strange sort of connection to Dorian, a connection that felt even stronger now. Dorian was a lost soul; so was Vlad. Freaks, in every sense of the word. And now Dorian was dying.

Something strange and terrifying raced through Vlad's veins. He got the oddest impression that the same brilliant madness was rushing through Dorian. A moment later it felt as if his insides were on fire, as if the prophecy itself was being burned into his very soul. In his mind's eye, he saw a vision—it was the only word he could think of to describe it. It was like a movie image, but more, as if he were standing on set while they filmed. He saw himself standing on the steps of Bathory High, his arms raised. The ground was littered with bodies. Dead bodies. People Vlad knew. People he'd known his entire life, right alongside those he'd only met in recent years. Blood and carnage surrounded him, and his only reaction was immense control over the situation. His face lit up with power. Vampires and humans were everywhere, on the steps, in the parking lot, in the street, engaged in combat and defense. Vlad watched in horror as his eyes flashed that iridescent purple, much more brilliant than ever before. Everyone froze at his command.

He was controlling them. He was ruling their every move. He was the Pravus, reigning over vampirekind and enslaving the human race. Vlad's thoughts shrank back, terrified of the thing he'd become, or would become.

Then the vision was over. End scene.

Vlad gasped, his heart sinking. It was true. The prophecy was true. And it was going to happen right here in Bathory. There was nothing Vlad could do to stop it, nothing at all.

Dorian gasped for air, the blood from his wound slowing at last. "I have foreseen the comings of kings and the crumbling of empires. But I never saw . . . this."

Then Dorian went still.

Vlad watched him, waiting for him to move, but he didn't.

He felt Dorian's weight grow heavy, felt the life ebb from him as his flesh settled into a dead state. And rather than feel sorrow, rather than feel a sense of mourning, Vlad felt an enormous amount of anger and fury and want of justice welling up from inside of him.

A whisper behind him. "For you, Cecile. And for me."

With an infuriated roar, Vlad slipped from under Dorian and turned with vampiric speed, landing on his feet just inches from a very surprised Joss, who held the stake in his hand. It was still covered in Dorian's blood.

Vlad grabbed Joss by the shirt, picking him up in the air, and threw him against a tree several yards away.

On the ground lay Joss's messenger bag. Sticking out of the open flap was Vlad's father's journal.

Before Joss could recover, Vlad moved as fast as he was able to stand in front of his once friend, his ultimate betrayer, the lying fiend, throwing punch after punch after punch until Joss's face was bleeding, his body trembling in pain.

But still the slayer gripped the stake.

Vlad ripped the wooden instrument from Joss's hand and pulled back his arm, ready to end this, ready to stop Joss forever, ready to send a message to any slayer who dared enter Bathory with blood on his mind. It would be easy. And the price would be worth it. He gripped the stake tightly in his hand and pulled back farther, aiming for Joss's heart.

And then . . . he heard a familiar voice. A voice he would have known anywhere. "Stop, Vlad. Let him live."

Suddenly, Vlad couldn't breathe. It was as if all the air that surrounded him refused to enter his lungs. His mouth fell open in utter shock. His fingers trembled. He released Joss, who slid down the trunk of the tree, and turned to face the speaker. He grasped at words, but at first nothing came. Then he met the eyes of the intruder and all he could think was a single word—a word that would change his life forever, a word that shook as it left his lips and shattered everything that he ever thought he knew about his life.

"Dad?"

An Evening with Vlad

(An exclusive conversation between
VLADIMIR TOD and HEATHER BREWER)

The night was warm but pleasant, and my adrenaline was still buzzing. I had just exited the library, happy and content as I always am after a successful event, when I heard the sound. It was familiar to me, but at the same time strange. The rustle of someone shifting their feet—almost impatiently—as if waiting. Waiting for me.

Pushing the unlock button on my key ring, I smiled and examined the shadows around the building. He was here. He had to be.

After a moment—a long moment in which I'd begun to doubt my sanity—a boy stepped from the darkness, his eyes guarded. I had to remind myself that he wasn't a boy, not just a boy, not just *any* boy.

He was dressed in black on black on black, and if I hadn't expected his arrival, I might not have seen him in the darkness. After glancing around, as if assuring himself that we were alone, he approached me, a small smile on his lips, his fangs only slightly visible.

Opening the back door of my car, I dropped my books inside, then turned back to him. "Vlad. I was wondering when I'd see you again."

He shrugged with one shoulder, so casual and once again at ease. "I wanted to thank you."

"For what?" I raised an eyebrow. The one thing I was certain Vlad didn't owe me was gratitude.

He leaned against my car, smiling almost sheepishly. "You listened. Really listened. I told you my story—what happened all the way from my eighth-grade year through my junior year—and you wrote it down, just like I told you. That deserves a thank you, I think."

The corners of my mouth tugged up in a smile. "It's the least I could do. Besides, Vlad, it's not like I'm not enjoying hearing your story. And if you're here, telling me your tale, that means everything turned out okay, right? That means I can sleep a little better knowing that no matter what, you're alright."

Something in his eyes broke then and he drew inside of himself, suddenly distant, suddenly quiet, folding his arms in front of him, as if a cool breeze had whipped through the parking lot. It hadn't.

Clearing my throat, uncomfortable with the strange silence between us, I said, "By the way, I ran into Joss the other day. He wants to share his story too."

Vlad looked troubled. It was all I could do not to apologize, even though I had nothing to apologize for. It wasn't the idea that I was betraying him by telling Joss's story that had upset him—I could see that much in his eyes. It was something else, something dark and brooding within him. A secret, perhaps. One he'd not yet shared with me. "Who says everything turned out okay, Heather? You believe in vampires. What makes you think you don't believe in ghosts? You could be talking to one right now and not even realize it."

My trembling hand found my mouth. No. He couldn't be serious. Everything would be fine by the end of his senior year . . . wouldn't it? It had to be. He couldn't be dead. Could he?

Without another word, without another clue about exactly what had happened in the twelfth grade, he turned and started walking back to the shadows, as if distance from me would give him distance from whatever nightmare was plaguing his thoughts.

I called after him, my voice shaking, "What about the final book, Vlad? When are we going to discuss what happened your senior year?"

After several steps, he turned back briefly, his hands in his pockets, that same troubled look in his eyes. "Don't worry. I know where to find you when I'm ready to talk. But Heather . . ."

His eyes flashed brightly, that strange iridescent purple. Before I realized it, a gasp escaped me.

Then his eyes darkened, brooding and troubled once again. His voice was gravelly as he spoke, his words sending a shiver down my spine.

". . . I'm not sure that even you're ready for what happened next."

—————— ACKNOWLEDGMENTS ——————

Many thanks to my keen and amazing editor, Maureen Sullivan, for her incredible input and divine patience; and to my brilliant and incredible agent, Michael Bourret, who always has excellent advice and never fails to talk me down off the ledge. Huge thanks to Team Vlad at Penguin Young Readers: Don Weisberg, Lauri Hornik, Felicia Frazier, Andrea Mai, Scottie Bowditch, Erin Dempsey, Jennifer Haller, Maureen Sullivan, Andrew Harwell, Shanta Newlin, Christian Fuenf-hausen, Emily Romero, Courtney Wood, and Allison Verost—you are the makers of dreams and I owe you big time.

I'd also like to thank my sister, Dawn Vanniman, for supporting me at every turn, no matter what. And MTB, for keeping me (relatively) sane.

This list wouldn't be complete if I forgot to thank my three favorite people on the planet. Paul, Jacob, and Alexandria—you are my everything. Without you, none of this would be possible. Thank you.